MW01531913

...WHAT

DOESN'T

KILL YOU

...WHAT

DOESN'T

KILL YOU

CARROLL SILVERA

TATE PUBLISHING
AND ENTERPRISES, LLC

...what doesn't kill you
Copyright © 2015 by Carroll Silvera. All rights reserved.

No part of this publication may be reproduced, stored in a retrieval system or transmitted in any way by any means, electronic, mechanical, photocopy, recording or otherwise without the prior permission of the author except as provided by USA copyright law.

This novel is a work of fiction. Names, descriptions, entities, and incidents included in the story are products of the author's imagination. Any resemblance to actual persons, events, and entities is entirely coincidental.

The opinions expressed by the author are not necessarily those of Tate Publishing, LLC.

Published by Tate Publishing & Enterprises, LLC
127 E. Trade Center Terrace | Mustang, Oklahoma 73064 USA
1.888.361.9473 | www.tatepublishing.com

Tate Publishing is committed to excellence in the publishing industry. The company reflects the philosophy established by the founders, based on Psalm 68:11,

"The Lord gave the word and great was the company of those who published it."

Book design copyright © 2015 by Tate Publishing, LLC. All rights reserved.
Cover design by Samson Lim
Interior design by Manolito Bastasa

Published in the United States of America

ISBN: 978-1-63418-332-1
1. Family & Relationships / Abuse / Domestic Partner Abuse
2. Fiction / Contemporary Women
15.01.30

With all the love in my heart,
for my Daughters.

Acknowledgments

· · · · · · · · · · · · · · · · · · · ·

To my daughter who, throughout her life, has always encouraged and supported me and, more importantly, loved me always. To my parents, you have taught me so much in life.

To my readers, Sally Silvera, Carol Bradley, and Darlene Watts: my appreciation is beyond words. To Shiela Mariz, who edited this book. To Gavin de Becker, for his wonderful book *The Gift of Fear*, thank you.

To all the characters within these pages, you have profoundly enriched my life.

And last but not least, to Gregory, who instills within me the need to let "my fingers fly across the keyboard."

Thank you.

Chapter 1

The dining room is small but very cozy and well-appointed. The table, set with china and crystal. Sterling silver sparkles in the candlelight.

Norma is rawboned, her skin seemingly stretched taut over large, sharp, thick bones. Her face deeply lined for her years. The skin, blue-veined and wrinkled.

Her husband was a large, heavyset, jovial man, who seems to tread lightly in her presence. The dining room is dominated by the size and stature of these two people. How nice of her to invite us to dinner, I think.

With nerves close to exploding, I cast a glance to the far end of the table where Tony sits, with an old tattered flannel shirt on, cuffs frayed at the edges, the collar ragged around his neck.

I can't see them, but I know his Levi's are filthy dirty, with blood stains spattered across the legs. He had worn them hunting the night before.

I can also picture the slippers that cover his feet. Once soft deerskin, lined with sheepskin, now there are splattered with coffee, and soiled from wearing them outside, with the soles turned over. The neck of his once-white undershirt is yellowed and frayed and shows through his open collar. He must have looked hard to find that one.

This is my punishment for making him come tonight, as this strikingly handsome husband of mine has many beautifully tailored clothes, with the ability to look and behave quite debonair indeed.

"I ain't goin', they're a bunch of phony sons a bitches, and I ain't goin'."

"Please," I plead. "It is important that we do this. It is nice that they have invited us to come, and I think you'll like them. They are nice, intelligent people."

"Bunch of phonies is what they are. All uppity with their high-mindedness."

"Please, just this once. If you don't like it, we won't do it again."

"Yeah, yeah, once I go, you'll have me doin' this all the time. I tell ya, they're a bunch of highfalutin fakes," he says, mimicking the mannerisms of having a tea cup, with his thick meaty little finger sticking out.

"Oh, Antonio Nicolas, come on. I like her. And she works for me. Come on. I'll go to the bar with you and to your friends' parties."

"Yeah, but they are real people."

Well, here we are, just look how he is dressed. I thought it best to just go along with it. He won't do this again, I thought. He'll be far more embarrassed than me.

But so far, it hasn't seemed to faze him. As a matter of fact, I think he is enjoying their shock.

Both Norma and Gordon have been most gracious, complimenting me on my black wool suit and the beautiful lace collar I got in Ireland.

The salad has been removed from the table as beautiful thick steaks arrive at our plates.

I look up to see his face as if to say, See, this isn't so bad. The food is wonderful, and they have been more than nice.

The shock of what I see is nearly more than I can bear. I want to cry; I am so embarrassed. This is just too much. He is holding his hunting knife, using it to cut his steak, the sheath lying on the white damask tablecloth.

We did not repeat that again; in fact, we rarely went anyplace together. We didn't seem to be fighting or arguing, only to have found things uncomfortable in each of our by-now very separate worlds. I often found it necessary to travel; he preferred to stay at home.

For fear of losing my license to operate the skilled nursing facilities, I rarely, if ever, attended the parties his friends had, as drugs and liquor were in abundance.

Chapter 2

· · · · · · · · · · · · · · · · · · · ·

The room feels foreign to me. The brown and orange of the shag carpet, the table that sits in the semicircle of the brown sectional sofa, the rock fireplace jutting out from the wall. All, foreign and cold. I can't believe this is happening. I sit next to Tony on this worn sofa, and Jillian sits across from us.

"No! It's you," Jillian says, her voice an accusation in the otherwise silent, tension-filled room. I am so upset I can't hear what is being said. I don't know when it started. Everything seemed so normal. And now...

"I am leaving, and you can't make me stay." Her voice was a cold, determined soliloquy in my mind. Lord, how did this happen?

I can hear the crackle of the fire as it pops and spits from the fireplace. I can hear the drops of winter rain as they fall through the lattice of the patio cover, see the long thick green of the orchid leaves as they act as a shuttle for the water that drips from their leaves, but I can't make out my daughter's voice. Nor, can I hear what my husband is saying.

My heart aches as the tears roll down my cheeks. "Jillian, everyone has rules. It's important to have boundaries." My voice soft, a plea for understanding, for acceptance.

"I understand that, Mother, but *he* is unreasonable. While he drinks and sits on the couch, you go to work every day and wait on him every night."

"But, Jillian, you can't leave home. Where will you go? You are still so young."

"You did it. I can too. And I won't live like this. I won't, and I don't think you should either," she replied, surprisingly calm and rational, as she sits, crumbling my lofty dreams for her.

"Please, please, Jillian, don't do this. I can't bear for you to say these things."

"Oh, Mother, stop." Repugnance laces each syllable.

"What about your school? You have to finish school. Please, we can work this out."

"No, Mother, we can't work this out. It's him, and he isn't going change," she says with a quick nod in Tony's direction, her long slender fingers splayed on her thighs, nearly gripping her pants.

"Let her go if she wants to."

"Tony, please don't say that. How can you say that?"

"She'll find out it's no piece of cake out there. And if she can't do what she's told, then she has to go."

"No, Tony, no. I don't even know what this is about."

She is up and walking away. I get up from the couch, but Tony's hand reaches up, pulling me to sit down. "Let her go."

"No," I nearly shout at him. I follow her to her vacant bedroom.

The room stands bare and barren. She sold her bedroom furniture last week to buy the neighbors' old bedroom set. Hers, "too little girlish." She did it with my permission, but Tony had a fit.

"Now we gotta buy the kid a new bed, or didn't you notice that old shit didn't come with a bed?"

"That's all right. We can get a new bed. We bought Samantha a new bed when she was younger than this," I tried to reason with him. But he hadn't worked in months, and the fact that I made so much money is only one more sore spot.

"Jillian, please don't go." I reach out to touch her, to try and dissuade her from this most foolish action. But she pulls her arm from me.

"Mother, stop. I am going, and I am leaving tonight."

"But why, I don't understand. Do you have any money? Where are you going to stay? Please, Jillian."

"Stop it, Mother. You're just making it worse."

"How much worse can it get?"

I watch as she shoves clothing into a small bag. No makeup, she doesn't use it. Only pants and shirts and tennis shoes and hiking boots.

"Jillian…"

"Stop, Mother. You can't stop me, you don't understand."

What in the world happened between the two of them.

The door closes behind her, and I lean against it, my heart breaking. As the hot tears slide down my cheeks, I slide down the door and curl in a fetal position on the cold of the ceramic tile floor.

Tony pulls on my arm, telling me to stand up. He says there is not a thing to do; she was gone.

The living room is strewn with the unpacked decorations of Christmas, I see as I gather myself together and go to the bathroom to wash my face. How did this happen, Lord? How did this unspeakable thing happen?

I hear the bathroom door open, and Samantha softly say, "Mother, she will be all right. She is just mad, and she is tough, Mother."

The tears come fresh as I hold Samantha close to me. "She is not that tough. It's hard out there all by yourself."

"She'll be all right, Mother. She will."

During the next week, she called me at work twice, and the following week, she came asking for money. Having anticipated that, I had already decided not to give her any, but in the end, I gave her twenty dollars.

"Won't you tell me where you are? Are you really all right? Will you come for Christmas? Are you going to school?"

She sits across from my desk as if she were an employee, someone whom I had just met. The hysteria so close to my heart, I feel weak from fighting it back. And all I can do is interrogate her. That is not my intent. But I need to know these things. This is my daughter sitting across from me. I won't let her ruin her life. I will not.

Thy will be done, not mine. I know, Lord, I know. But...ah, but there are no buts.

She rises from her seat; I can't let her go. "Jillian, do you want to come to dinner? Can I get you some lunch?"

"No, no, Mother, I gotta get goin'."

"Oh, Jillian, please. I'm so worried about you. It's Christmas, Jillian. Could you come over this weekend and bake cookies with us?"

"Maybe...I'll call you. I'm okay, Mother. Really." She stands and opens the door to my office and is gone. I watch as she gets into her car and leaves the parking lot of the hospital.

The house is silent, as I return from work in the evening. Samantha is attending the local college during the day and works at a department store in the evenings. Tony is at the restaurant, working or drinking. Who knows? Only the yip of tiny dogs greet me as I enter the house. A house that seems so unlike my *home* in every sense of the word.

I don't even know what to do. I pace the floor, turn on the Christmas lights, change my clothes, fix me something to eat.

This too shall pass.

The phone rings, and I answer, sure that the hospital is calling.

"Mother, it's Jillian. Is it okay if I come Saturday to make cookies with you, and can I bring Susanne?"

"That would be wonderful, Jillian. I don't know who Susanne is."

"She's a new friend of mine, she's nice."

"Well then, of course, bring her."

"Okay, I'll see you Saturday." The line is dead. Hope springs eternal as my heart lightens at the prospect of her coming home again. Everything will be all right, I am certain.

Saturday comes, and with it I am up early and cooking. Excitement fills my heart and home.

Tony refuses to stay. "She'll just piss me off. I'm not stickin' around while you coddle her."

Samantha and I make tuna salad for lunch and the little cheese rolls Jillian likes, and I make care packages for her to take with her, just in case she insists on leaving again. We make cookie dough and get everything ready.

I hear the beautiful Westminster chimes of the clock in the living room as they chime three o'clock. I should have asked her when she was coming. Where is she? The fear escalates to frightening levels as Samantha comforts and cajoles. "Let's just make cookies, Mother. You can't wait on her forever."

Oh Lord, I silently implore. Please keep my child safe.

The thought no sooner completed, and Jillian and her friend walk through the door, "Jillian, I am so glad you are here." As I embrace her, she stumbles, reaches for the wall to steady herself as her friend giggles.

"Got anything to eat?" she says as she stumbles on the tile of the foyer to the carpeted floor of the family room. Yet again stumbling.

"Jillian, are you drunk?" I ask, dumbfounded. Remembering the occasion when she invited her fourteen-year-old friends to imbibe of all the alcohol in the bar and I had to rush a teenage girl to the emergency room where she was diagnosed with severe alcohol poisoning and the near lawsuit that came of that.

"No, we don't drink anymore." Both girls giggle again.

What do I say to that?

"Mother, this is Susanne. Susanne, this is my mother and my sister, Samantha."

I extend my hand to the tall, lean black girl who stands before me. "I am glad to meet you, Susanne. Where did you and Jillian meet? Do you go to her high school?"

"Naw, I quit school. She lives with my brother and his friend."

I reach for one of the piano stools that skirt the bar, at the edge of the once-happy heart of our home. The kitchen seems slightly unfamiliar as I look around at everything. What is there, some five-year rule; that says everything has to go bad? My breathing is so shallow, I feel I might pass out. Control Cara, control. For the first time since this little episode has begun, I am mad. I am very mad.

"Lunch is in the refrigerator, help yourselves," I say as I rise from the stool, not certain as to what will happen next. I am more than a little relieved Tony is not here. Samantha is standing in the dining room, motioning for me to come there.

"I'll be right back, girls. Go ahead and eat," I say as I make the circular trek through the family room, foyer, living room, to the dining room, rather than crossing the kitchen, having them know we are coconspirators.

"She is high, Mother," Samantha whispers.

"What do you mean she is high?" I whisper back at her.

"High, you know, marijuana high. Mother, both of them are."

"Really, are you sure?"

"Oh Mother, look at them. What are you going to do?"

"I don't know, but I'll do something."

For the next three hours, they ate and baked cookies, frosted them, and ate some more, acting more normal as the afternoon wore on. The smell of cookies, the sound of Christmas music filtered from the stereo, and the laughter of children filled the house, and for a brief moment in time, I could pretend all was well in my world.

However, the truth was apparent—from the small innuendos she would occasionally drop to the laughter or secret looks that passed between them—that all was not well in the world my child had chosen. The 'men' in their lives were in their twenties, and did not work. But they made lots of money, and drove nice cars. Drugs. The thought, a paralytic one. Still, I calmly went through the motions of frosting cookies, and making plans for Christmas dinner, which is only a week away.

The clock chimes three, only now it is three in the morning, as I stand amid the silence of my youngest daughter's empty bedroom. The rest of the house is sleeping soundlessly in the wee hours of the morning. Sleep eludes me as fear runs rampant through my heart and mind. The green book is clutched close to my chest. Should it be the Bible?

Lord, have you forsaken me? As I bargain with the Lord for my daughter's soul and her human life. willing to give up everything, *everything*, but my oldest child. Lord, do you hear me? Everything.

She is not yours. These are the only words I hear Him say to me in the stillness of my heart. *She never was.*

The tears fill my eyes as I think of the times I have come so close to losing her over the years; the truth stands clear and bright. She is not mine. She belongs to Him. He has only entrusted her to me to keep her safe and to guide her. Not for me, but for Him.

Resolve fills my very being

I step softly across the white carpeted floor to the side of Samantha's bed and stoop to kiss her on the forehead as she lies in deep slumber. As I do, I try desperately to etch the fragrance of her in my mind—a precautionary act should she, too, decide to leave me.

Then, I walk down the hallway to where my sleeping husband lies and crawl into the bed, feeling the warmth and strength of his back and smelling his manly fragrance. Will the Lord take this man from me in exchange for my child? I know one cannot bargain with the Lord. But my fear is real, as is my resolve.

"Tony," I whisper to him. "Tony…"

"What, are you all right?" His voice was husky from sleep.

"Yes, I'm all right. Tomorrow, will you call Tom Rigghetti and have them go get Jillian?"

"What? What are you talking about?" Rolling over, he gathers me in his arms. "Leave it alone, Cara. There is nothing you can do."

"No, there is something I can do, but I need your help. Tell me you will help me. Please."

"Shush," he whispers in my ear. "I'll do whatever you want me to. Now go to sleep."

"Thank you, thank you." The tears slide once more to pool in the small recesses of my ears, knowing that his acquiescence is of self-survival as the last weeks of my being so distraught have proven unbearable to him.

"Shush," I hear him whisper again. "Go to sleep." As he pulls me close to his big warm body.

Chapter 3

"Well, ordinarily we wouldn't do this, you know. There's not much to do about runaways, but well, Tony here and I go way back. So sure, Cara, we'll do it. Only I don't know how you expect to get her if you don't even know where she is." He sits on the sofa, leaning forward, hands laced between his knees. His partner stands at the doorway of the family room.

My relief is nearly audible as I hear his words.

"I know, I know, Tom, but the ol' lady thinks she can, and well…I've seen her do stuff like this before. So…you know how it is. Mama's not happy…I told her the kid is just a bad seed."

I hate him today. He has told me that at least twice. And I don't ever want to hear it again. Samantha stands in the kitchen, and as I look up, I see her roll her eyes in resignation and disgust.

"Tony, stop that," I say with a vehemence he, for certain, will recognize. Today, Lord, you can have him.

All day long, I have been praying for guidance and for direction as to where she is and how to find her, also where I will work and how we will eat when He takes our home and our income. But it is clear that this is my job. To see to it that this child knows I will sacrifice everything, even her love for me, for her.

Tony and I are in the Jaguar, and the two police cars are behind us, lights flashing and sirens blaring, we pull up to the large apartment complex. There sits her car. You were right Lord, thank you.

I get out of the car, and Tony says, "Now what?"

"I don't know. Just come with me."

"Do you know which apartment she is in?"

"No, but the Lord is in charge here, so we just go."

He throws the cigarette butt in the parking lot, and making a small snorting noise, he says, "Sure you're not speaking with the devil?"

"I wouldn't speak to the devil, and the Lord knows that."

I walk along the dimly lit path, when the light from the first floor apartment suddenly shows through draperies pulled back. The face of a large black man peers from the draperies.

"This is it," I say, acting only on impulse now, feeling disconnected from my physical body.

The policeman and Tony stand behind me as I knock on the door of the apartment. The door opens, and I look past to see Jillian sitting on the sofa, knitting. I could not believe my eyes—the room is small and brightly lit. Another smaller, heavier black man sits opposite her in a chair, his legs slung over the arm of a chair, a book in his hand.

"Can I help ya?" the man standing in the doorway says.

"Yes, you can," I say as I push my way through the doorway. "I came to get my daughter. Jillian, get your things."

"Mother, you can't do this." She stands, looking like a shocked little girl. Her knitting drops to the floor.

"Oh, but I can and I will, Jillian Tesstorrio. You get your things, and you come with me now."

"Look here, ma'am, she don't want to go with y'all."

I place my left arm across the midsection of this very large man and say, "I really don't care what she wants to do. She is coming home with us now. And you are never to see her again or bother her. Do you understand?"

"Look, ma'am, you can't do this," he says, as he pushes back at me.

"Oh, you just watch me." I move quickly into the house. "Come, Jillian get your stuff. Where is your room?"

The black man comes right behind me. His hand is on my shoulder now, gripping it tightly.

"Let go of me now. There are two police cars and a very big father standing right there. Do you see them? She is sixteen years old. How much time do you think that will get you? And drugs, shall we look for drugs?" I look at the police and at Tony. "Jillian, now." I move rapidly in the direction of the bedroom she alludes to. She stands, shocked, as if a deer caught in the headlights. "Mother, I am staying here."

"No, my darling daughter, you are not. You are coming home with me and your father. You are going to finish school, and you are going to do as you are told, and when I think you are stable enough and mature enough to go out into the world, you can. Until then you will stay with me and do what I say. Do you understand me? Move, now."

I follow her into the room, a room she obviously has occupied alone, we'll deal with that later, I think to myself. She starts throwing things into her suitcase.

"Come Jillian we are going now."

"But I don't have all my things."

"Then you will leave them here," I hear myself say. "Come. Get your coat. Tell the nice men good-bye."

In the doorway stands Tony and the policeman. The inhabitants of the apartment are standing stock-still in the room. For an instant, I wonder what will happen next as I seem to be on autopilot. Then once more I give in to *His* direction.

"Give me your car keys." She is docile as she drops them in to my outstretched palm. In that one instant, I knew I had done what she had wished me to do.

"Go with your father right now. I will deal with you when I get home."

Tom advances in front of Tony, saying with great authority, "You better come with us, young lady. We will take you home. And you fellas here better leave the jail bait alone, or we got other things to get you on," as he lifted the lid of a small box that was sitting on the small table.

I watch as they shove her head down gently and place her safely in the back of the police car. The sirens sound on both cars as they pull away from the parking lot.

"Do you want me to drive Jillian's car?" Tony says.

"No, take the Jaguar, and I'll drive her car."

I get into her car. Fortunately, it starts immediately.

With only a brief ten minutes having past, I am so calm, so systematic in what I am doing that I am unable to identify with this personality. Hands on the steering wheel, I with great deliberation, I remove the rings from each of my fingers and the bracelets and watch from my wrists. And I place them neatly in the zippered pocket of my purse.

I arrive at the house in time to see the garage door as it slides to close on the Jaguar. I pull the little car up next to the curb in front of the house, get out, and go around to the hood of the car. Opening it, I reach in and take the rotor out.

Closing the hood, I haul all of her things out of the car and lock it up. Still calm. Still controlled by whom or what. I can only hope it to be God or angels.

Stepping into the family room, I am aware that it is dark, with the faint light from the living room as well as the light in the foyer the only illumination. Tony sits in his spot on the sofa, the glow from a cigarette apparent.

Jillian stands in front of the windows. She has taken her jacket off and is standing defiantly, foot stuck out, and arms folded across her chest. The bravado has returned.

Instantly I knew why I had taken off my jewelry. I was going to do something I would have never believed possible. And I wasn't going to feel bad about it.

But first I needed to take off this coat. The jacket was navy blue suede and heavy, constricting.

"You can't make me stay, you know."

I hear her voice as I place the coat on the chair, amongst all of Tony's shirts.

"Oh…I think you will do as you are told, my dear. Merry Christmas, Jillian." And with that, I doubled up my fist and slugged her. A good right uppercut to the jaw. Her hand flew as suddenly to the side of her face. Her body flies back from the impact of my fist as I hit her again. "Do you understand? You will not, I repeat, you will not ruin your life. I love you more than I have ever loved anything in this world, and if you learn to hate me, so be it. You will not ruin the life God gave you. You will do as you are told until I say you can make you own decisions. Do you understand? How dare you do this to my child. How dare you!"

I need no answer, and I wait for none as I hit her again. She falls down and lies on the floor, covering her face with both hands, whimpering, cowering before me. I am ready to kick her. Tony is upon me in a second. "Cara, Cara, stop. Stop. Stop it now."

I pull my arm from his viselike grip and go to the living room. And from under the Christmas tree, I take a large package.

Going back, I find she is still lying on the floor. "Get up now and open this."

"No, I don't want to open a Christmas present." Her voice was soft and whimpering.

"Open it now," I say as I throw the package at her, the weight of it knocking her off balance yet again.

"No, Mother, please."

"Open it now," I say through gritted teeth.

As she is tearing the paper from the erstwhile sleeping bag, the tears plummet down her face, and still I feel only resolve.

"Since you sold your bed and have nowhere else to sleep, this is your bed for the next few weeks."

She sits cross-legged on the floor, tears streaming down her face. Her face hidden in the shadows of the room. I hear the refrigerator door open and the pop of a beer can, then the running of water. The sound of ice and a towel. Tony appears as if by magic, and offering Jillian a glass of water, he says, "Here, kid, put this on your eye. It'll help," as he hands her a tightly wrapped towel of ice.

"Let me tell you what you are going to do so there is no mistaking it, all right?" I say, my voice a monotone, cold.

She continues to look at the floor.

"Answer me!" I shout at her. She starts and looks at me.

"What, what do you want me to say?"

"Say...'I am listening, Mother.'"

"I am listening, Mother."

"Fine. You will get up with me every morning at five. We will run on the beach for thirty minutes. We will come home. I will fix you breakfast. You will go to school. You will go to St. James, and you will not ditch. You will get decent grades, you will graduate. You will only play with me, you will not see any of your other friends until I say it is all right. There will be no television, no entertainment of any sort until I say. Your car is off-limits. I will drive you to school and pick you up. Do you understand?"

"Yes," she murmurs.

"I can't hear you, Jillian."

"I said yes, Mother."

"That's better. Have you eaten?"

"Yes."

"Fine, go in and take a shower and get into bed. Do not for an instant think of leaving this house, or you will be sleeping with us. Do you understand?"

"Yes," she said, sobbing loudly and uncontrollably now.

She leaves the room, a room still filled with violence and anger. Then my sobs come uncontrollably, and the trembling in my body will not subside.

"Oh God, what have I done?" I sob into Tony's chest, his arms wrapped securely around my heaving body.

"The only thing I think you could," he whispers into my face.

"Is she all right?" I ask, afraid of the answer.

"Oh, she'll be fine. You really got a good upper cut there, Red." Laughing quietly, he pats me and held me until I, too, felt the fight slowly die in me. "How ya gonna do that, get up, take her to school, and work?"

"I don't know, but I will do it."

The sunrise of the early winter morning is glorious as we stand on the golden wet sand of this magnificent beach. I feel the crash of waves as they thunder against the shoreline with the mighty strength of Poseidon, their white, foamy froth kissing our faces with the salt of the ocean spray.

"Now what?" she says to me, resolute in her continuous look of disgust during any of our limited sentences. Her face is bruised; her eye black. It shames me to look at what I have done to her. But the fact remains she is here with me and not high and living with black men half again her age.

"We run. We'll go to that cove and back," I say with some determination as it looks nearly a mile away. Can I do that?

"Why?" she says, shivering in her parka, her long, brown, well-muscled legs covered with goose bumps.

"Because it will be good for us physically and get rid of some of the anger."

"I hate you, you know." She is looking at the sand as she said it, drawing lines in the wet sand with her tennis shoe. She raises her face to look at me, and a lone tear falls from her eye.

"I know you do, Jillian, but I love you more than you will ever know, and this is the only way I know to help you. I would die to help you." Wanting desperately to hold this lost child of mine in my arms, to take away the pain of growing up, to erase the years of hurt and pain that had come to all of us.

"I'll never treat my kids like this. I am going to be a mother like Ellie."

"Good, I hope you can be. I was never given that option. So do you want to race or just run?"

———

Tennis was a treacherous feat for me to try to match myself with her. Her strength at plummeting the ball across the net with such accuracy and anger was such that making contact with the ball would jar my shoulder painfully. But persevere I did. The *game* was for her life, and if I had to go home and cry, that is what I would do.

———

The weeks flew by. And my resolve stayed firm. We rose at five in the morning. We ran on the beach, ate breakfast, and I took her to St. James to school.

There was some problem getting her enrolled in a prestigious school with her grades, but money does work miracles, and she likes it. I pick her up at three every day, and we go home to do our chores, play tennis every other afternoon and to sit on the couch.

Today she said, "How long are we going to have to just sit here staring at each other?"

"Until we learn to like and respect each other, Jillian."

Chapter 4

. . . .

The sun glistens on the ripples of the water as the lake water laps against the shore. The boat sits to the left, moored to the shore.

The lake is something that we have enjoyed for the last seven years. The small condo, room for only four, is filled to the maximum with sometimes fifteen people, with the girls alternately bringing their friends.

Tony and his friends hold a monopoly on the habitation of most weekends. The girls are like fish. They both swim so strong and gracefully. Tony drives the boat in a long-sleeved woolen shirt in the dead of the one-hundred-degree weather. The sweat pours down his face as with the heel of his hand he pushes it up into his black sweat-soaked hair. No amount of cajoling can get him to wear less clothing or a swimsuit while we sit ready to ski in bikinis.

The girls are both athletic, but Samantha is for some reason unable to water ski. We have a standard joke that we just drag her around the lake. They are both strong, perfectly formed individuals. They play tennis, snow ski, and any other sport that demands strength and endurance.

As I look up, I see Jillian rise out of the water. The sun glints behind her, an illusion of some mythical goddess has risen from the waters, gilded and bejeweled. Her hair, blonde and wet, clings to her shoulders. Her beautiful body is tanned to a golden bronze, and her strong, beautifully-shaped legs are long and lean as the stride lengthens to climb the small incline. Each bead of water, like golden beads of a costume that covers her body. Her ample bosom, small waist, the full womanly hips, all enhanced by the starkness of the white crocheted bathing suit. She shakes her head, and the beads of water cascade as if in slow motion from the startling whiteness of her hair, her dark eyebrows, and eyelashes locked in the grip of wetness. She is lovely, kind, and generous.

Poignant memories flood my mind and heart as I look at this stunning creature, and I am filled with love and gratitude. Raising her has been like raising a small lion cub. She is curious and fearless. We have battled more often than not, as she has tested both Tony's and my patience to the extreme.

From the time she was but ten years old, she had skipped school. Her explanation was, "They were doing stupid things."

I would sew into the night, making her beautiful clothing to wear to school, only to see a young girl riding a bicycle, looking remarkably like my daughter, in jeans and an old T-shirt. Waiting at home, at an unexpected time, to find in fact it was my daughter, her nice clothing piled neatly in a stack at the side of the garage.

At six years of age, she was left in the backyard unattended while I vacuumed or attended to other domestic duties, only to discover her missing afterward. "How did you get out, Jillian?" I asked when she had returned.

"I climbed the fence," she glibly said. The fence was six foot tall, with no apparent foot holds.

At thirteen, she climbed out the window of her bedroom, sneaking away to a party she had been told she could not attend.

She thought nothing of bringing four or five of her friends into my bathroom and using all my things.

"She took the car without asking and smoked in the teachers' parking lot." Did she think she wouldn't get caught? I don't think she thought there was anything wrong with it. Rules are for everyone else.

She always dragged friends, puppies, and strange people into our home. School was a social event only.

Then of course, there is the time she left home.

So I enrolled her in a Catholic school. She loved it, and it seemed to be the answer to all our problems. She blossomed. She graduated from St. James last week with honors. I thought even Tony was going to cry. I did.

She now has enrolled at the local college and is working part-time at two other jobs.

Her graduation present is a cruise to St. Thomas and all the islands there for fourteen days. It sounds like an old-person thing to me, but that is what she wanted, and she wants me to go with her. I couldn't believe my ears when she said that. I had offered to pay for a friend, but she said, "No, Mother, I really would like to go with you. You went with Samantha to Hawaii for her graduation present. Please come with me."

Thank you, Lord, she must not hate me any longer.

Actually, the years since my *brutal love* have seemed to heal us all. And I am so proud of her.

"Mother…Mother." I am jolted out of my reverie by the sound of my daughter's voice. "Are you all right, Mother?"

"Sure, I was just thinking how beautiful you look all brown and dripping with water."

"Oh yeah, right. I'm fat. Daddy said if you would drive the boat, we could go back out and ski. Will you please?"

"Lord, Jillian, it must be a hundred degrees out. Let's wait a while. And you are not fat. Quit saying that."

She has a penchant for butter, milk, eggs, and bread, as do I, but we (meaning, the girls and I) eat no meat and consume enormous amounts of vegetables.

"Okay, but come on, Mother, it's not as hot in the water."

"Oh, I guess, but just for a little while, and then we can go again later this afternoon."

Chapter 5

We all sit talking, drinking coffee, and eating cookies. Jenny and Paul have brought their friends over to visit. Gabriela is clamoring all over Tony—funny such a gruff man can be such a magnet to small children, and, I might add, other women. She is two, and Paul's first child. But they have two children our children's ages, by Jenny's previous marriage.

Gabriela is fat, soft, and has Tony at her mercy.

We have never met their friends before. George and Arlene are their names, approximately our ages. They seem very pleasant and have not been married very long. After having been here perhaps an hour, Arlene tells us that her son was recently killed. My heart just breaks for her as she tells us of the anguish she has suffered. Then to both Tony's and my astonishment, she tells us that George, her new husband, who is sitting right there, killed her son. With a gun, he shot her son.

I hear myself say, "Oh my gosh!" My hands become wet with sweat, and the nausea is overpowering. "Excuse me, I'll be right back." I go to the bathroom and try to compose myself, breathing deeply. I sit on the toilet and place my head between my knees. I just can't shake this horrendous feeling that she has brought into our home.

There is a knock at the bathroom door, and Jenny comes in. "Cara, are you all right? You look like you have seen a ghost."

"Yeah, I'm fine. You know me, a sponge. I just seem to feel everything that poor woman feels. How can she live with a man who killed her son?"

"Well, he didn't do it on purpose," says my dear ever-pragmatic Jenny.

"I know, but…"

She hands me a cold washcloth as I try to pull myself together and return to our guests. By now the conversation having gone elsewhere.

"Show Arlene the pictures of your and Jillian's cruise," Jenny says.

I haul the pictures out, Tony rolling his eyes in disapproval of my flaunting an indulgence of the girls.

He is right, I have taken them everywhere with me—on any business trip I have had to make, on very nice vacations. But he won't go, and they are very excited to do so. They are very good company. If I felt they were too young to be alone in a big city such as San Francisco or New York, I took a girlfriend of mine to watch them while I was in meetings.

"You're gonna make 'em phony, stuck-up assholes, pompous asses like all those people you have here to dinner."

"Oh, Tony, they are nice people. The girls and I have been to their homes, and they don't live any differently than we do. They have been very good to us. They're not phonies. I love the symphony and the opera. It touches me so deeply sometimes it brings me to tears."

Last month, I had a dinner party for a small group of business associates. Tony not only would not eat at the table with us, but he lay on the family room floor in his undershirt and stocking feet in front of the television. Brat!

"Do you really want to see them?" I ask everyone, looking at Tony in defiance.

"Yes, we do," they all chimed in, my composure having returned to normal. The feeling of overwhelming grief having finally left.

But I was gentle and kind to this woman, whose suffering I felt so profoundly.

"So you had a good time?" my brother chides me after all my enthusiastic explanations of each and every photo.

"Well, I think Jillian had the time of her life. She really had a good time from the very beginning of the cruise. It took me ten of the fourteen days to relax and just enjoy it. Yes, it was fantastic. The only way it could have been better is if Tony would have gone and had a good time with us."

We all laugh as Tony says, "Don't hold your breath, Red. It ain't never happenin'."

Chapter 6

I feel as if a warm blanket of softness has settled around me. We lay spooned in that familiar posture of sleep that long-married couples develop. The safety that separates you from the harshness and cruelties of everyday living. His thick, muscular arm wrapped tightly around my naked body. His strong, gentle hands tucked under my ribcage, pulling me softly to the smoothness of his body. I can feel his breath on the back of my neck as it rhythmically rises and falls. Smell the warm, sleeping maleness of him. His shoulders rising above mine, making me feel protected, safe in his arms. Lord, how I love this man.

I hear the gentle rap at the french doors of the bedroom. The room is shrouded in the softness of early morning light. The soft warm hues of the blue of our sex lovingly cascading over the walls, the ivory furnishings dappled in the morning light.

I hear the water as it tumbles over the fountain of rocks and into the small koi pond across the small expanse of covered patio. The fragrance of wisteria gently drifting into the room.

I rise slowly, glancing at the clock on the bedside table; it's two o'clock in the morning. She's forgotten her key again.

"Shh," I say to this sleeping man. "It's Jillian. go back to sleep."

He tugs me closer, kisses the back of my neck, and sleepily turns over.

I sit up and swing my feet to the floor, feeling the thick blue carpet beneath my feet, reaching for the long white silk robe.

The moonlight trails through the small pretty window above the bed as I, barefooted, make my way across the floor to the door, pulling my robe around me. I open the door.

"I'm sorry," she says as she steps into the bedroom. "I forgot my key."

The moonlight is resting on her naturally pale blonde head, and it shimmers like the palest of silk. It's cut short with just a little natural wave, framing a face of natural beauty. Her skin is soft and flawless, a golden brown that God grants only those of goddesses.

She's not as tall as I am, which always shocks me, because she was my biggest baby.

She tips her head up to look at me, and I see her beautiful deep blue eyes. Round, not almond-shaped as mine are, but big blue eyes, eyes that are so expressive, so intensely blue, framed by dark, perfectly arching brows, and thick, dark lashes. No makeup, as she can't be bothered.

I kiss the top of her head and lay my hand on the back of her shoulder as I pull the door closed.

"It's all right," I whisper. "Are you all right?"

She looks up at me. "Yeah, I think so."

"What do you mean?" I whisper back.

She is crossing the room as she turns to me. "I have bells in my ears."

"You mean your ears are ringing?"

"No, Mother, I have bells in my ears. They are like church bells ringing."

"Does it hurt?" I ask.

"No," she says. "It's just bells, bells that are ringing."

"Have you taken a lot of aspirin?"

"No."

"Jillian, have you been taking any drugs?" I ask my eighteen-year-old daughter. I hesitate to bring up the past. But fear floods my very being and grips my heart.

"No," she adamantly states. "Honest, Mother."

I look into the eyes of my precious child, her face a vision of beauty in the moonlight. There's a softness, a vulnerability about her that is reminiscent of me. She is so open to life. So alive in her approach to everything about life. Believing innately that life is safe, that everyone is as good as she is. We have fought so hard to come this far. I believe her.

"All right," I tell her. "But if they're not gone soon, we'll call the doctor. Can you get some rest now?"

"Yeah," she says. "I'm going to bed now." She makes her way to her room.

"I love you, sleep well," I whisper to her back as I crawl back into the safety of my sleeping husband's arms.

"Is she all right?" he whispers in the huskiness of a sleep-filled voice.

"She has bells in her ears, church bells that are ringing," I say, as I snuggle up closer.

"The bells of Christ," he offers.

I don't know what those are. I think to myself, I'll ask him in the morning.

I awaken to Jillian crawling in bed with me. "Mother," she says, "I don't want to do anything today." as she snuggles her body up to mine.

"Uhm," I whisper, "do you feel better?" I hug her close to me. "You have to get up, you'll be late. Are your ears still ringing?" I ask.

"Yes, but I'm okay."

"Get up," I say. "Come on, we have to get up." Being slow to awaken on any given day, this day is no exception. and I, yawning, turn to find Tony gone. "Has Daddy gone already?"

"Yeah, he left about fifteen minutes ago."

"Come on, kiddo, get up. Up, up, up."

"Okay, okay," she says laughing. "But you have to help me put all that clown makeup on."

"I have to go down and help Daddy, but I'll help you for a minute. Maybe you could come down before you go. There is going to be all the little leagues down for pizza, and they would love to see you all dressed up."

"I'll stop on my way to the party."

She has been working for the City Recreation Department, teaching children during the weekends, waitressing at Denny's at night, and going to college during the day. A heavy load. But she says she likes it, and I did it, so I think it's fine. But Tony thinks it's way too much.

As I walk through the back door of the restaurant, I am assaulted by the reek of yeast. Who would ever know that beer could smell so bad? "Bleach, bleach," I tell him constantly.

There are the restrooms that need cleaning, and beer taps to clean. The cleaning people who come at night just don't do an adequate job.

The music from the juke box drifts through to the hallway, Elton John's "Yellow Brick Road"... There are boxes stacked high along the walls with cases of new glasses, tomato sauce, pickles, and potato chips. Storage has been a constant problem. I work some sixty hours a week at the hospital, and really he could probably get along without me on the weekends, but Jillian and I have been coming down and helping him if he has a large group of people coming in on Saturday or Sunday.

Tomorrow I am going to go help Samantha at her new place. We are going to put fabric on the walls of one of her bedrooms. She has a nice little house; I think she is happy. She really never wanted to grow up. Having been the culprit in what she has seen as adulthood, I can readily understand that. Turning eighteen to her was likened to someone turning sixty. We all just laughed, with the exception of Samantha. After spending her nineteenth year nursing her parents, she more than likely decided it would be easier to live alone. I think her boyfriend of the last four years stays there sometimes, but mum's the word. So Sunday, Tony will have Jillian to help him. She said the other day that "the family that works together, stays together," and then laughed as Mass has become something we only do on a Saturday evenings in jeans.

A dreadful thing for a drinking man to own; a restaurant with a bar. He drinks all day long, sipping at it perhaps, but drinking nonetheless. It is hard and constant work. Tony, not being the most ambitious of men, has difficulty with the constant pressures. However, after his accident, he is unable to do manual labor, so after all the money was spent on the gunsmith school in Colorado, he does that only for friends, so it is not very lucrative.

We bought this bar and restaurant as this is what he chose to do.

The interior of the restaurant is dark and bar-like where I stand, on this side of the restaurant. Knotty pine paneling on the walls, captain's chairs placed neatly around the small round tables. Three pool tables sit to my right, three televisions blaring the end of the baseball games. To my left is a long old bar with barstools covered in nasty orange vinyl, dotted with gold-colored studs. The back bar is a profusion of glassware, pizza ovens, refrigerators, and a large Wolf range and grill. And booze. Through the front windows, one can see the busy little street of the Old Towne.

My husband cooks and pours drinks all day long, a far stretch for a man that can't wash his own dishes or cook his own meals in our home.

A large archway connects a dining room of enormous proportions; on most Saturday afternoons, it is filled to capacity with baseball teams, football teams, basketball players, and their families and coaches as Tony gives them a discount to bring the business here. A very good idea.

Wearing moccasins and jeans and a tailored white shirt, I have come prepared to cook, clean, and waitress.

"Hi, Red, how ya doin'?" Tony comes toward me, his leg dragging slowly across the floor with his feet clad in soft deerskin slippers. He holds a cane in one hand. With his tongue, he tucks the ever-present toothpick up alongside his gum line so his kiss doesn't poke me. How he does that I will never know. But he has always had a toothpick in his mouth.

"I'm good. How are you? Jillian said you left early this morning."

"Yeah, had a delivery. Where is the little loon? She still have bells in her ears?"

"Oh, she has that party today for the city recreation department. I helped her paint her face like a clown, and we piled balloons and cake into her Volkswagen this morning. She said she would maybe stop to see the kids on her way to work. I forgot to ask her about the bells."

"Good, they'll like that. It's a bunch of ten-year-olds today. Thirty-six, they said. How's Sam?"

"Good, I talked to her on the phone before I left. So what do you want me to do?"

Our conversation is one of everyday life, a life so full of work and busyness; we catch up like old friends here at his work, with me trying hard not to interfere in the workings of his business and him trying hard to ignore my interference.

"Just chop vegetables, I guess, and fill the cheese bins. I figure most of the kids will want pizza, but a few hamburger patties need to be ready too."

"Okay. So do you have help coming in?"

"Yeah, Judy is coming any minute now," he says above the din of noise as he fills salt shakers and napkin holders.

"Are you coming home for dinner tonight?" I ask as I tie the apron around my waist and retrieve the enormous butcher knife from the magnetic strip next to the sink.

The door opens, and in walks Judy and the happiest-looking clown I have ever seen. Tony laughs and goes to plant a kiss on her pasty white cheek. "Yuk, Daddy, you'll get it all over you," Jillian says, pulling away.

Small boys are filing into the restaurant, laughing and sliding chairs all over, screaming, cheering.

I come from around the bar and, looking at Jillian, say, "You look so cute. Did you eat breakfast?"

"Yeah."

"Do ya want a Coke or something, kid?" Tony asks, bringing a paper cup with Coca-Cola to her. She reaches out to take it, her big red Raggedy Anne hair flipping around. "Such a pretty little hand you have there." I laugh at the disparity of her small beautiful hand and long, tapered fingers, with this ridiculous-looking clown outfit.

"Yeah," she says again.

"I recognize those eyes, though. Those are my kid's eyes," Tony says, winking at her.

"Yeah," she says yet again.

"What time do you have to be there?" I ask her.

"Two," was her only response.

"You can go see the kids in the next room. They'll love that," I say.

"No, I don't think I want to do that."

"Really?" I am shocked. Jillian is one of the most exuberant people I have ever known. "Well, that's fine." The three of us are standing off to the side of the restaurant section, and the kids can't see her.

Judy is carting drinks and potato chips to the tables.

"Are you tired, Jillian?" I ask, more than a little concerned. "Do you have to work tomorrow?"

"No, I'll be home tonight and tomorrow."

"That's wonderful. I thought we'd have steak, so stop and pick up one on the way home."

"Mother look at me, I can't go to the store."

"True, true." I laugh. "You are tired."

"No, no, I just feel kinda funny."

"Are you sick?"

"No, it's…just…a strange feeling I have."

"Maybe you should just go home. I'll call them and tell them you can't come."

"No…it's not like that."

"Jillian…"

Tony appears from nowhere. "Aw, leave the loon alone. How are the bells, kid?"

"Oh…they're gone."

"Good," Tony and I reply in unison.

"I gotta go, Mother."

"I love you, be careful. Watch those balloons." I place my arm around her tiny little waist through the costume and give her a hug.

"I love you too, Mother."

Tony and I walk with her to the front door of the restaurant.

"See ya tonight," I holler back at her.

"Cara, we need four hamburgers and six pizzas," Judy shouts from the back of the bar.

"Right, I'm coming."

The noise of the children in the next room is distant, the nausea and weakness in my body so intense that I slump to the floor of the bar.

"Cara! Cara!" Judy and Tony shout at me in unison.

"Cara, what the hell…" Tony is lifting me to my feet. "What the hell is the matter with you? Snap out of it."

"Oh…I…don't know…I'm just so…so…sick. And weak."

"Jesus Christ, you're soaking wet. You look more like a white woman than ever. Can you stand up?" I hear his cane as it falls to the floor. "As he leans over me, I see his face as shocked as I feel.".

A glass of water is shoved in my face.

My words slur as I mutter, nearly incoherently. "I…don't…know." He has a bar towel now, and he is wiping the sweat from my face.

"Breathe, dammit, breathe." I look up at his face, and he is green with fear.

"I'm all right. I think I just need to sit down a minute. Maybe I'm just tired. What time is it?"

"What the hell difference does it make what time it is?" He is practically shouting at me in his fear.

"I don't know. I just need to know."

I turn to look at the old schoolhouse clock above the bar. One twenty-two. The nausea and weakness seem to have gone, but I am trembling.

"Do ya need to go to the doctor? What the hell's the matter with you?"

"I'm fine, Tony, I think I'm fine."

"Ya coulda fooled me. Have you eaten, ya skinny ol' thing?"

I laugh at our inside joke. Everyone thinks me to be skin and bones, and Tony and I know that beneath what appears to be an extremely thin person is a writhing, sensual body. He always says, "I'm never telling anyone. Let them think his ol' lady a skinny ol' thing."

"I'm okay. I don't know what happened. Really."

I return to my work of making more pizza; the little mishap gone unnoticed by the many little boys in the adjoining room.

For the next thirty-eight minutes, I slice and dice vegetables, seasoning pizza sauce, and tasting it till it is perfection.

Chapter 7

From the corner of my eye, I see a police car pull up to the curb. The policemen come in, and I recognize Tom Righetti. He goes straight to Tony, who is standing near the front of the restaurant. They whisper, I see Tony grab hold of the back of the chair he is standing next to; I watch as his knuckles whiten against the natural brown of his skin.

I stop what I am doing, walking around the bar. He is coming toward me. His foot and leg dragging with more intensity than is usual. His color, once again that gray-green color so recently, gone. His eyes down, concentrating on the difficulty of his walk.

"Cara, give me your car keys."

"What?..." I look up at him, shocked. He never drives. Why does he want my car keys?

"Give me your car keys, and come with me."

"But...what...Tony, I don't understand...What is it?"

"Just come with me, goddammit. For once, do as I tell you."

With Tony driving, we pull out onto Main Street. Tom, in his police car, pulls in front of us, as another police car takes up the rear. Sirens blaring, the traffic clearing the road. We go through red lights and careen through moving intersections.

Now on the freeway, I once again ask, in a small frightened voice, "Tony, please, tell me what it is."

He gives no answer.

"Tony," The tears sliding soundlessly down my cheeks, for it must be the most horrendous of things. "Tony, *please, please.*" Both hands on the steering wheel, he continues to look straight ahead.

The sirens blaring in our wake, as we speed relentlessly north on the freeway.

"Tony, *please.*"

"It's Jillian…the kid's been in an accident, and they won't do anything until we get there." His voice a soft whisper, his eyes never leaving the road.

"Oh my God, oh my Lord.," the sobs heaving my body. Terror affixes itself to my heart.

"Cara, get a hold of yourself! You just need to be all right when we get there. She must not see you like this."

"But, oh Tony, what…where…oh Tony, please, please don't let there be anything wrong. P*lease Tony, say it will be all right. Please Tony, please.*"

"Cara, stop." His voice is a whispered plea.

"Yes, yes, okay. I can do this." I reach in the glove box for a tissue.

Careening yet through more red lights, with cars pulling over at the sound of the sirens, we arrive at the emergency room. The letters are tall and red. They are very red. I never noticed before how very red they were.

He stops the car in front where it says ambulance only. Getting out of the car, he comes to open the door for me.

"No, no, Tony, no. I can't. Please, I can't. Please, Tony, no…"

"Cara, come on, I'll help you, we have to do this."

"But, Tony—"

"*Cara!*" His voice sharp, trembling.

My legs are so weak I nearly fall as I climb from the seat of the Cadillac. My white shirt is wet through from tears.

Tom Righetti is standing on one side of me, Tony on the other, as we enter the emergency room doors.

The smell is of disinfectant. The nurse on duty sits quietly behind the desk. Why is she just sitting there? I would think she would be scurrying around to help my daughter.

Tony tries to push me into a chair that leans up against the wall. It is chrome and turquoise.

"*No,*" I say and pull away from him.

"Wait here. Cara. Do as you are told."

"No! *Tony. Please.*"

The nurse from behind the desk miraculously appears at Tony's elbow. "Are you Hilary's parents?"

Oh, thank God, it isn't Jillian after all. My mind is racing. I knew this could not be true.

"Hilary Tesstorrio," I hear the nurse in the white uniform say.

"Oh no, where is she? Her name is Jillian, not Hilary. Where is my daughter?"

"I'm sorry, Mrs. Tesstorrio, but your daughter, well, you see, your daughter is dead. She was so badly hurt we couldn't save her. I'm so sorry." Her hand is on Tony's sleeve, and I can't stop sobbing.

"*No no no no no, Tony, oh please, Tony, oh, no....*" I slide to the floor, and for brief seconds, the blackness engulfs me. This can't be true, I have to fix it.

From the floor, I see Tony's face and know he has known from the time they came into the restaurant.

"*Where is she? I want to see her. I need to see my daughter. Please I need to see my baby. Don't you understand I need to see my baby. Now! Do you understand!*" I have gone from a weak, frightened, sobbing woman to a screaming, uncontrollable mother.

"*Now, you don't understand?*" I am sobbing again. "*She can't be dead! She is my baby, she is only eighteen years old. I need to see her now. Why did she die, what did you do?*"

I hear Tony's voice as he says, "Can you give her something?" I jerk my arm from his.

"*I don't want anything, I want to see my daughter, now. I mean now, I need to see her. Please, Tony, make them let me see her. Please,*"

Tony. Tony, please help me. Please, Tony. Oh, Tony, please…. Oh, God, how can you have taken my baby? Please, God, no, God please." Tears spill down, splashing on the gray-green of the nasty tile floor. As m*y body gives way to the despicable truth*, and I slide down his leg.

"Cara! Cara!" His big, muscular arms, for the first time, they are no help. They hold no promise. They hold no peace, no solace. As he wraps them tightly around me, holding me upright physically, he says, "They say we can't see her. It would be more upsetting. The car caught on fire."

"Oh my God…, oh… my baby! Oh, Tony, I just need to see her. I need to hold her in my arms. Please, Tony, make them let me. Please."

"Cara, come. There is nothing we can do here."

"I cannot leave my child in this awful place, I have to see her, please."

"Cara, please come. Try to stand, please."

I hear the nurse as she asks if there is any one to call to come and help. And I hear Tony say to call his mother.

Tom says, "I'll go get your mom, Tony, and bring her out to your house. Okay?"

"Yeah. Sure, thanks. We have to go tell Samantha."

"Oh no, Tony, we can't tell Samantha something so awful. We just can't. I can't. I won't. Please Tony, you can fix this, please."

"She has to know, and we need to tell her before she hears it from someone else."

"Yes, yes, that would be awful."

I turn calmly to the nurse and say, "Did my daughter say anything?"

"She said her name was Hilary Tesstorrio, and then she said she felt so sick to her stomach. The impact severed her vena cava and caused a massive coronary. The only reason she was still alive when she got here was more than likely, it must have clotted over because of her youth and her health. Her legs were both broken, and her eyes were full of glass."

"I'd like to see her now," I calmly said.

"I am sorry, but I have been given instructions that you remember her the way she was. You know, the clown thing makes it even worse."

I feel as if I am having an out-of-body experience. Everything is in slow motion as I move through the long hallway, my husband's hand at my elbow. The sun is shining as we emerge from the building. The sky is blue, there are cars driving by, and people are getting in and out of them. How can that be? The world is the same as when we went in, only flatter, less vibrant. If everyone died that someone loved so deeply, would the world cease to exist? Is *it* only a reflection of our love for one another?

People are just moving around as if nothing has happened. The car is moving through the stoplight, no sirens blaring, with people all acting as if things are normal.

"Cara." I hear the whispered sound of my name from the man sitting next to me. "Cara."

"Yes?...I was just wondering why everyone is not down on their knees weeping. For the Lord has taken our daughter. Why aren't they, Tony? Why aren't they?" Great sobs of grief issue forth from the small, little, me, who no longer exists. "Tony, please tell me why they are not all weeping."

"Because they don't know yet, Cara. No one has told them."

I look at my husband and see the white of his hair, the face that has aged in minutes. I say to him, "Do you know how she worries so much about her weight? Well, she weighs only 2.8 ounces now."

"What do you mean?" He looks at me, startled.

"That is the weight of the soul. I read that just the other day."

"My God, Cara."

Chapter 8

We somehow arrive at Samantha's small neat house. He turns the engine off, and we both sit in the paralytic silence of grief.

"Come on, Cara."

"No,…Tony. I just can't. I can't do this."

"Yes, you can, and you have been given no choice…Come on, Cara. We don't want her to hear it from someone else."

I read recently in some healthcare literature that people who have experienced a severe loss or trauma as a young person often feel watched and persecuted. My wonderful child has had enough trauma for several lifetimes. How will she ever deal with *this*?

The music of a twenty-one-year-old blares through the door, as out of habit, we rap at the door before entering.

Our stoic, solid Samantha Jeanne, who has, in the last three years, nursed me through cancer with her broken arm casted at a right angle to her shoulder. Still she helped dress me every day so I could go see Tony as he lay immobilized in traction for months. She was never complaining, never anything but tolerant and forgiving.

She stands now in her small orderly living room, golden red hair cascading around her perfect face, paling at the sight of her parents—the time, the day, out of character. Her eyes betraying a knowledge of things yet unknown.

She says nothing as the three of us stand closely to one another as if that would protect us from the terror that has come upon our lives.

Unshed tears fill her beautiful azure eyes, as she swallows hard, fighting for a control she is not physically aware she needs.

Both Tony's and my hands reach out simultaneously to touch her, and she steps back. She shakes her head. "No, Mother, no. Oh, Daddy…"

"It's Jillian, sweetheart. Jillian is dead. She was killed on her way to work this afternoon," the disembodied me says the words with alacrity.

"It was supposed to be me, it was supposed to be me."

"No, no, it wasn't supposed to be you. Why would you say that?"

"I don't know, but I know it was." Great heaving sobs engulf her as we cling to one another. The tears fall from Tony's eyes for the first time as he kisses the top of her head and says, "I love you so much, Samantha."

"I know you do, Daddy."

A profound statement from this man, as he has never said that to me, or to them.

***

The haze of the events that follow is nearly incomprehensible in their absurdity. It wasn't bad enough she was dead. Now they were going to do an autopsy. It was the law! She had not seen a doctor in the last month, and it was the law!

"You will not cut up my child!" I scream, a scream of insanity and grief unknown to anyone other than the Lord God himself as He watched as they tortured his son. The sacrifice one of tremendous significance for the first time.

"Tony, please, you cannot let them do this to her. Please, Tony, make it stop. Please don't let them cut up our child, I am begging you. You must not let this happen. I will die from this. We will all die from this horrendous pain." Screaming, I fall to my knees in front of him begging, pleading as the police and coroner stand watching. These men stand in my home, a home once filled with love and laughter. I look at the face of my Samantha; a face clouded with grief and fear, a surreal look lurks in the depths of her eyes. Any cognitive ability I ever possessed, now gone.

"There is nothing I can do. Cara, please, you're making yourself sick. We have no choice. It is the law." He bends and lifts me to my feet.

"Can I see her?" I plead. *"Please, I need to see her.* Can't you please understand I need to see my child?"

"I'm sorry, Mrs. Tesstorrio. We can't let you do that."

"Oh God, help me. Please help me. I am so sorry for your loss, God, I never knew…"

Tony's arms close around me tightly as he holds my hand to sign the fateful document that will dissect my child.

Father Anthony stands over me as I sit on the loveseat in the corner of the living room. Waiting, waiting, and watching for Jillian to come home. Every car that drives by, I raise my head to look, but she is not there. The house is filled with people, caring, kind people, trying to help. That's a joke. You can't fix this.

Father Mark stands next to Tony as they watch me, saying words I can't hear. Telling me things I find unimportant.

As my insanity reaches new heights hourly.

I am aware of the insanity that rages through my mind. I simply seem to have no control. My physical body seems to have shut down as well, with the exception of the enormous pain. A pain so intense that I would be at a loss for words to describe it. There is a hole in my heart, a blackness that is enormous, with an intensity of pain that abides there, one that surely will cause my death soon. And it will be over. The pain and suffering will be gone. The ache in my arms, where my child lay as a baby, will be gone, and I will know only blackness, for the Lord will take no one to Him with such pain in their heart and such insanity in their minds.

The newspaper has come for her picture. I am hysterical as I see Tony hand them her graduation picture. "No, they can't have that," I whine. As I pull it from his hand, I see how flat it is, how unlike Jillian really. There is no resemblance to the vibrancy that was her. And I hand it back to the reporter, who, shocked and uncomfortable, promises to return it this evening.

People whispering, Father Anthony sitting next to me, asking if I have any questions, Father Mark telling me Jillian was saved, she was fine, and I knew that. Ridiculous diatribe going on all around me.

Flowers and plants arriving in droves, with their fragrance permeating the entire house. One tree, nearly four foot tall, whose leaves dripped constantly, as if it too, weeps in grief.

I sit in the living room where I had sat with my children, where friends and family alike had gathered for Christmas and birthdays, their laughter forever echoing in this soft, beautiful room. A room in which we had slept in sleeping bags on the floor when we first built it, because there was no furniture. We had roasted marshmallows, in the yet unadorned fireplace, laughing and wiping sticky-sweet marshmallow from our faces.

A living room in which I did yoga every morning of every day for the last ten years, where, on one such morning not too long ago, Jillian, having gone through all the meditations with me, stated, "This must be what it feels like to be dead."

"Maybe," I had replied.

Now, this lovely room is steeped in the grief of her loss, the plant dripping endless tears at her absence.

I watch, and I can hear the words of comfort, the looks of help-lessness on the faces of my husband and daughter, as their grief is staid, because of me, and the intensity of my own, and I can do nothing to help. I am an inert physical being, of no importance. Lost to the world they live in. The world we once all inhabited.

Strange, how life changes in an instant.

I watch from my tightly curled position in the corner of the loveseat, as the procession of people file by. Jillian's friends, Samantha's friends, our friends. My sister and her family, my brother and his family.

My brother sits at my side, sobbing, "She is with the Lord now, she is safe." As he pulls me tightly to him, the hot tears scald my face as they stream silently, relentlessly. "Did you call Mom and Dad?" he whispers into my hair.

"Yes, and Mother screamed and threw the phone on the floor. I had to call back so many times." The sobs overwhelming now, as I try to tell him, "I told Daddy, and Mother said, 'Do you want us to come?' My God, my child is dead, did I want them to come? So different we are…"

"So…they are coming," Paul says uncertainly.

"Yes, they'll be here in the morning."

"Can I do anything for you?"

"No, I just need to see her. Paul, talk to Tony, make them let me see her. You know, it could be a mistake. You know it could be a really bad mistake."

Our doctor and friend, Doug, stand before me now, holding out medication. "Cara, I want you to take this, it'll help you."

"No, no, please, no. What if she comes home? I can't take anything, please. I'll eat and have some coffee, and I'll be fine."

"Come, Mother, let's go get something to eat. We'll wash our faces. Daddy, can you help her?" Samantha and Tony stand behind Doug, as he looks to Tony for some sign of what to do.

My parents and my brother and his wife have arrived from Seattle. Rick and his wife and Vera and Amos from Fort Worth. My handsome father is noticeably grief-stricken, his face nearly unrecognizable through the pain written so clearly upon it, his shoulders stooped, his hands visibly shaking. My mother stands behind Daddy, uncomfortable within the heaviness of the grief-stricken surroundings, fidgeting, unable to touch me, unable to express her sorrow. Daddy holds me close to him and I sob uncontrollably, the soft sounds of his sobbing mingling with that of my own.

My oldest brother ushers them into other rooms away from the heartache and intensity of the environment.

Rick stands before me, tall and handsome still, this man who is the biological father of my children. This man who maimed and beat me and my children, this man who, with the scissors of a fine seamstress, I nearly killed—and I would do it all over again.

His young, pretty wife, dressed in white fur, stands passively behind him. I look for signs of abuse on her heavily made up face. He reaches out to hug me and I pull away from him. After all these years, my anger is more intense, Jillian as a baby had never lived a life without trauma, and now her life was *over*—he was the culprit. *He* had caused me and my children more pain and suffering than most persons could bear. *How dare he enter our home.*

Vera and Amos have driven from Fort Worth, Texas, and the anguish is written on their faces. These people who have been so good to me through the devastating events of mine and my children's lives. Jillian and Samantha's grandparents, Ricks parents.

Vera wraps her arms around me and the tears spill from each of us. "Ah, girl, she is safe now...Mama's here fer you. Cry girl. Let it go."

I see Amos look away as the tears fall upon his red knit shirt, making small dark spots.

Out of sheer habit, I have washed my hair, and put on my makeup. The early morning light holding only fear and pain, as I peer into her room to find her not yet returned.

I look at the driveway; her car is still not there. How can that be?

The house is so full of people and so quiet all at the same time. The gardener brought a sheet cake and said how sorry he and his family were. The neighborhood has come, and the people Tony and I work with have come, all bringing food and flowers. Her teachers from high school, the people she worked with. How dare they? They are the people who wanted her dressed up like a clown. How dare they show their faces to me?

"Eat something," my mother is saying. She is so distraught, so unused to emotion of any kind. So shattered by my life, the drama with which it has unfolded. The emotional hardship of it, disturbing to her. Did she think I had orchestrated all the tragedy within my life? Was it disgust that played upon her face, or was it pity?

I had bargained with the Lord, but surely, he had understood my intentions, my heart. I shudder as the push of insanity invades my mind, I grasp for reason where there is none. If I were so powerful, couldn't I bring her home?

"Where is Daddy?" I ask Samantha. Her eyes dart from one person to another as she determines what to say.

My heart leaps for joy—they have found her. I knew they were mistaken.

Seeing the fleeting look of hope on my face, immediately, she says, "No, Mother. Daddy and Poppa went to take care of her car.

The numbness that has pervaded my soul returns as I wonder what could be wrong with her car. "What?" I ask, puzzled.

Time drifts by at an alarming rate when you are semi-conscious. People fixed me food; I pushed it around my plate. The phone rang incessantly, and I sat in silence as if I myself were dead. I sit curled in the loveseat waiting, waiting for my daughter to return.

I hear Tony, my father, and my brother Peter enter the house and nearly leap to greet them. "Did you find her? Did you find her, Tony? They were wrong, weren't they? Tell me you found her."

"Cara, we had to take care of the car. She's gone, Cara. Goddammit, she's dead, do you hear me? It's that goddamn car. You should have never let her take the bumpers off it. That's why she's dead."

"No, no, no!" We cling together, all of us, with great gasping sobs of, grief, pain, and anger.

"How can you say that to her?" I hear my Mother shout at Tony.

"'Cause, dammit, she let the kid do anything she wanted."

Samantha, who is standing in the background, is white with fatigue and grief. And now this, this accusation of death and destruction.

"*Can I see the car?* Maybe if I see her car—"

"No, Cara, you can't see that car. *It is burned to the frame. You don't want to see the fuckin' car.*"

Was she frightened? Did she know she was hurt? Did she know to go to the light? Did Grandma McDonald come to get her? No one else she knows is dead. Is she scared? What if she goes to the wrong place? Oh God, protect my child, show her the way and light. Send your Son to take her home. Forgive me for my sins. Forgive me for the pain I caused her.

An endless litany of prayers—Our Father, Hail Mary full of Grace—over and over, as I rock back and forth, crouched on the floor in the corner by the kitchen sink. They are prayers for my little girl to be shown the way and the light. People stoop to whisper things to me, to sit with me, to beg me to come, come with them as night turns to day and yet again another night. As I rock back and forth, in madness. Praying for the safety of my child.

On the third day, my fear subsided, whether steeped in the doctrine of Catholicism or because in fact she was safely *Home*, I did not know, I did not care.

And…after all, she still hasn't come home.

The fathers from the church have been here daily, and today we must make funeral arrangements. Imagine the preposterousness of making funeral arrangements for your child.

I am much calmer now, at least for minuet periods in time. I feel as Jillian did so long ago, standing in the corner. I smile as I think of her at the age of five being told she must sit in the corner and think about what she had done. The constant reminder to her that she was not to talk or sing. That she must sit quietly. "Okay, Mamma, you can make *this me* sit in the corner, but the *real me* is standing by you." I remember finding it difficult not to look for the *real* Jillian. The real me isn't here. Yet, I hug and console the people in the house as they come and go.

There would be a rosary Wednesday night, a High Mass to be held at the church, and then at the gravesite.

The *gravesite.* "We have no grave," I tell Tony, incredulous that we would really need one.

"We have to go buy one."

Thy Will Be Done

"I'll lend you for a little time a child of Mine," He said,

"For you to love the while she lives, and mourn for when she's dead.

It may be six or seven years or twenty-two or three,

But will you, till I call her back, take care of her for Me?

She'll bring her charms to gladden you, and should her stay be brief,

You'll have her memories as solace for your grief.

I cannot promise she will stay, since all from earth return,

But there are lessons taught down there I want this child to learn.

I've looked this wide world over in my search for teachers true,

And from the throngs that crown life's lanes, I have selected you.

Now will you give her all your love, nor think the labor vain,

Nor hate Me when I come to call to take her back again?"

I fancied that I heard them say, "Dear Lord, Thy will be done.

For all the joy Thy child shall bring, the risk of grief we'll run.

We'll shelter her with tenderness, we'll love her while we may,

And for the happiness we've known forever grateful stay.

But should the angels call her much sooner than we've planned,

We'll brave the bitter grief that comes and try to understand."

—Edgar Guest

Chapter 9

Still, the 'real' me sits curled in a fetal position on the loveseat, watching, waiting.

As I do as I am told.

The five of us, —Tony driving, my mother, father, and Samantha— sit in the back of the Cadillac, as we turn down the street to go to the funeral home.

Sitting in the front seat, I am thinking that I will never have the strength to exit this automobile. *This is more than you can ask of anyone, Lord. Please don't let this be true. Make this some horrible nightmare, and please let me wake now.*

As I raise my head and look out the windshield of the car, Jillian is there. Vibrant in a gossamer hue of pink and gold, luminous, shimmering as if she has a light of her very own. Her hand extended to me, she says, "I'm all right, Mother. Come, let me help you."

"Oh my God, it is her. It's Jillian."

"Look, look!" Great sobs of relief flood my very being as Tony screams, "Dammit, Cara," and careens to the side of the road.

"It's her. Did you see her? It was Jillian."

"Jeez." His hands on the steering wheel, he drops his head to hang between his arms.

Samantha leans over the seat and pats me on the shoulder. She says, "What did she look like?" My mother and father sat sobbing in the backseat of the car.

The casket is white mother-of-pearl with violets painted daintily on all corners, a large gold cross on the lid. *She can wear her prom dress. It is beautiful—lavender, scoop neck, flowing.*

"Mother, please," she had begged as we shopped for the perfect dress. "That's it."

"But, Jillian, it is nearly three hundred dollars."

"Okay, we can look some more."

I stood looking at her. Remembering the hardships of her travels to this point, and said, "I think you've earned it."

"Oh, Mother, really? Oh Mother, thank you, thank you."

I am brought back to the present by the sound of my eldest daughters voice.

"She can wear my underwear," Samantha is saying as I remember what we are doing. We laugh. The sound is foreign, somehow out of place, irreverent. But the memory of Jillian getting into the drawers that housed Samantha's fancy underwear and wearing it without permission, it is funny. "She'll be thrilled," I say with a smile.

The funeral director, having surreptitiously entered the room, stands to our left.

"Mr. and Mrs. Tesstorrio, you can come see your daughter in the morning if you like."

"Really?" The heaving sobs begin at once, these, ones of relief.

"You ain't gonna go see the kid," Tony says, his anger and fear palatable.

"I have to see her, Tony. Please come with me. I have to see her."

"It won't do any good. No good can come of you seeing her. Give me those clothes, and I'll take them down."

Samantha and I gather up her clothing to give to him.

He looks at me, sadness lining his face, great pouches beneath his eyes., "She can't wear this, Cara, *remember they cut her all up.* She has to have something that ties around her neck." Sobs, erupt from this man. Sobs that are so great with hidden grief, I think the sound of them will cause my death.

"Oh, Tony, I am so sorry, oh, sweetheart, come let me help you. Sit down."

"No…shit, I gotta take this shit down there. I'm fine," he says, wiping his eyes and nose with the back of his hand. "Come on, help me get her something to wear."

We stand together in this, our daughter's bedroom going through her things. The smell of them, the smell of her room, causing more pain that is ineffable. "We have to cover her up. She liked pants, and that blouse. She can wear Samantha's underwear and that blouse and those pants," he says, as we wipe away tears from one another's face. The blouse is cream silk, and the pants slubbed silk.

⁕

From my now-permanent position in the living room, I watch as Rick approaches Tony, talking softly. I watch to see Rick push a large wad of bills toward Tony's hand, and Tony, saying something, pushes it away from him, turns and walks away.

Vera and my mother are standing before me. "Cara, let Butch pay for the funeral. He surely wants to, let 'im," Vera implores, her voice soft and gentle, pleading. Pleading for the rights of her *Butch*, Rick to lay claim to a child he neither wanted nor deserved.

My mother is saying, "It is only right he does so, Cara. After all…."

"*After all* what, Mother? *After all* he has done for her in life, I don't think so. That will not happen."

"But, Cara, you have to forgive him sometime," my mother's voice gentle, not angry, only a plea for my own well-being.

"Forgiveness is for the Lord to decide, Mother, and as for me, I don't even think of him. I forgave him long ago. But he will not buy his way out of this at the price of Tony's and my child. He gave up his rights years ago."

My mother backs away, once again, disturbed by the quiet intensity of my emotion.

"I will go with you to see her. I would want to see her too. You can't go alone," Jenny says. She and Paul have been so kind. Everyone, so kind and considerate.

So grateful it isn't them, or their child.

"Thank you, Jenny. Thank you." I look at Tony for approval, I find none as he leaves the room.

Jenny and I arrive at the funeral home. Why do they call it a home? Ridiculous. The flowers are amazing. There is not a spot available that doesn't have flowers. I have had orchids flown in from Hawaii. They are her favorite flower, and I want her to have everything perfect.

This, after all, was the last thing I would ever do for my child.

As we enter the chapel, the coffin sits against the altar on a pedestal. It seems an interminable distance, and I can't seem to pick up my feet.

The music is soft and gentle, the room is brightly lit, with the sun shining through the glass of the cathedral windows, causing the casket of mother-of-pearl to sparkle. How many feet is it I wonder? I can't seem to get past the door. My knees are weak, and the tears come unbidden, for I need to see. The tears are blinding.

"Come on, Cara, you'll feel better if you see her. Come on, I'm with you all the way."

"I don't know, Jenny. I don't know. I don't think I can do this." My body is heavy with the darkness of grief. Legs that will not carry me. A mind numbed in the locked recesses of torment and pain, slow to give commands to the extremities that would propel me down to that distant place.

Tiny Jenny, all five foot of her, is stoic and determined to help me through this task set upon me by our God.

The walk is long, and as the casket becomes closer and closer, I sit down in the pew, weak and drained of all that has driven me throughout my tumultuous life. This I cannot do, Lord. Why, Lord, I don't understand.

Jenny, ever tender and gentle, kneels at the edge of the pew and softly says, "Cara, can you do this?"

"I have to, Jenny. I need to see her. Lord," I sob, "please give me the strength."

"He's with you. I know he is," Jenny says with unwavering confidence.

I stand in front of the coffin. She is unmarked by a casual glance. She has no burns that are obvious. Her legs lie long and straight in the white satin of the coffin. There are slight telltale marks through the miraculous makeup, so expertly applied, but she appears whole to my searching mother's heart.

She lies, as if sleeping, her great blue eyes now forever closed, her hands folded softly across her abdomen, holding a single orchid. Her blonde hair, more curled than she would like. I want so badly to touch her. But when I do, she is cold, and stiff, and I recoil in shocked silence. Her neck is swollen so large, she looks fat. The massive coronary, I think. My clinical knowledge kicking in from deep within the recesses of my shattered mind.

It is just her body. *She isn't in there.* I am so relieved she isn't in there. My daughter isn't *in there.* She did go *Home.* Lord, keep her safe until I get there. For the first time, I am saddened that I will perhaps have a long life.

I slide to the floor and sob. Unable to rise to my feet. "How can He ask this of me? How can I live like this?"

"The Lord will help you. He'll carry you, Cara. He will," Jenny says, kneeling at my side.

Kneeling, Hail Mary's reverberate in my head, the music, a soft ghostly sound. The gauzy effect of the curtain separates us from the people who came to pay their respects. I watch as for hours people continue to parade past the coffin that holds the remains of my daughter. I lean to Tony and whisper, "Can you tell them not to go by any more times?"

"What do you mean?" he whispers back.

"They just keep going up and looking."

"Cara, they are all different people. There must be thousands of them."

Vera asks if she can wear white.

"Of course, I wish I could. I just can't."

Tony's mother, Myrna, makes a heavy black veil for the hat I will wear. I cannot look at anyone, and I don't want to see them.

The "other me" attends the funeral, and but for brief moments in time, the memory is not within the contents of my mind, only etched deeply in the recesses of my heart.

The house is empty now. Everyone gladly having returned to their customary lives.

With the exception of the two of us. Tony and I, alone. The house is filled to overpouring with darkness and the sadness of grief. I have tried to return to work, but I simply cannot function. I can't concentrate; therefore, I cannot make the decisions necessary to keep the hospitals running. Better they know they have no leader, than one who is inept. Maybe next week I'll be better.

The telephone seldom rings, and I am reminded of the curfews for telephone time on the never-ending conversations of Jillian and her friends as she sat at the kitchen counter for hours on end, laughing, chattering away. Animated conversations that she looked forward to with such enthusiasm.

The mail comes in droves. The death certificate states the time of death, *1:22 p.m.* I feel the knowledge, more than a knowing, that I too died at that hour. Never will that part of me experience life here on earth; that part of me will reside with Jillian for all eternity. By its very strangeness, it gives me peace, peace to know I am with her.

I resume my vigil, watching, waiting, unable to internalize the fact that she is not coming home. I read the many cards and letters from friends as well as those persons I was never aware of. Letters arriving expounding the joy and help Jillian had given them. The gift of herself, to persons I knew nothing of. A Jillian that I had not known, a Jillian I would never know. And the hole in my heart blackens for the lack of my ability to see clearly the gift of her presence.

I went to the beach today, certain that as in times now gone, I would find solace there. The brilliance has left the sun. It, too, hangs helpless in the cloudless sky. The thunder of the ocean waves left me without awe. The sand empty of her footprints as I fell to my knees in profound agony. Do I contemplate suicide? I see no need, as the physical and psychological pain will surely kill me, and it will be over.

I need only wait.

Exhaustion from grief each night brings with it a sense of calmness, a sense of some peace, and in that calmness, she comes, without emotion, only a natural sense of herself. Is it my imagination? I do not believe it is. An apparition perhaps, but she is truly here.

I sense her in the car with me as I again go to work. I can smell the fragrance of who she is, and her presence fills the car to overflowing. I try to remain calm as the result of my emotional outbursts causes the veil between us to once more fall. I truly understand that she exists on another plane, and I try to understand that to miss her is like missing the baby she had been, when she was an adult, but that knowledge is lost on this mother's heart.

No longer afraid for her, as there seems nothing I can do, save offer constant prayers to the Father who took her. I, more selfish now than I have ever before been, fear for myself. Living is more than I can do, Lord. Am I to continually re-invent myself, seeking wider and, more comprehensive forms of who I am, to live in a world of platitudes? I don't understand why You ask this of me. As The word 'why' is now ever-present in my vocabulary.

How can You can ask this of me? Is it that you wish to stretch my soul to the very width and breadth of my limits? You have found them, Lord, *you have found them*.

She comes each night at bedtime, as she had done for years, to stand, the essence of her, leaning against the door of our bedroom, to say 'good night'.

With the light of morning being the worst time of day for me, for it revealed anew each and every morning, that it was true, she was indeed gone. Nothing had changed. Nothing was going to change.

And Tony drank and drank, coming home less frequently.

Certain that he too was dead, upon his return, I would cry and cling to him, like some broken thing.

He told me, "Get over it. She's dead. There was nothing to do. You should be glad, she was always making trouble. Better she's dead."

"You son of a bitch! How dare you say that to me?" I screamed. He left and didn't come home until the following night. We didn't speak of it.

I heard rumors of my own interment at the local mental health facility. I found it both frightening and humorous.

I have tried to read the Bible, and put it down, I have picked up the green book, and put in down. They held no solace for me. I could find no answers to my questions there.

I write in a journal of my feelings, thinking this will help. I cannot bear to read the words of agony on the pages, the ink smeared, the words distorted from the tears that mar the paper.

I long to speak of her to Tony, to anyone, as I am obsessed with her. The loss of her. I see it too painful for him, but as with the tides of the ocean, I am compelled, arousing his anger, his revulsion, his helplessness.

I long for the comfort of my husband's arms, the banter of verbal foreplay that would lead so quickly to the physical. My shame and fear of his rejection not allowing me to make those advances that would surely bring disgust and loathing at my weakness and tears. The new me. Lost, forlorn, and saddened. Weak and broken. Only a shell survives, unable to rise from the ashes of despair.

He too is lost to me. Or is he only hiding? Hiding from the grief he feels as well? I smell the cloying sweetness of the perfume of another, as he crawls into our bed before dawn each day. Mingled with the smell of drink and the staleness of tobacco. I recoil and am repelled by his betrayal. Am I so easily replaced that he can find my essence in the arms of another, or can he, only then, find himself?

I would be brokenhearted, but I have no heart, only a black hole in my chest. The aching of my arms, a constant physical reminder, should I at last lose myself to the madness that cloaks my mind, and forget.

The fear of forgetting is a very real thing. As I can no longer remember what she looks like. The touch of her hand. The laughter of her voice eludes my senses. What did she like to eat? The torture goes on in the endlessness of doubt and fear.

Now I too, hide. I hide in the books that delve into the mysteries of the *other side*, finding some solace in thinking I know where she is. Always a voracious reader of books, I am driven to inhabit the world in which my daughter resides. Reading of the plans we as souls make before our journey to earth, I hear again Samantha's words—"It was supposed to be me"—and I wonder at the truth of those words, having come unguarded at a moment of extreme stress. I wonder at the probability of the truth in those words. Could, in fact, we have chosen this, has the Lord a "game of life" that we are all participants in?

I can see how, resting in the light and the presence of the Lord, you could look at this life here on earth, and say, "Yes, look how brief a time it is compared to eternity," and think, "yes, yes, Lord, I can do that. To learn, to grow, to serve you as no other."

The feeling of insanity and physical pain only diminishes in the company of Samantha. And I fear the Lord will come for her as well. Surely I will have then suffered enough for whatever grief I have caused.

Chapter 10

· · · · · · · · · · · · · · · · · · ·

Locked tightly in my heart, —or is it in the depths of my soul?—, lies the fear that will forever hold truth to me. The single rose the Lord had left me, the red rose of my dream, for I identified that rose as the beauty in my life, the devil had taken all else from me. Now…Tony is gone, and Jillian is gone…That leaves my Samantha…My fear rises like bile as I beat it down, searching within me for the 'little box' to put my grief, horror, and fear. I live alone, I eat alone. Solitude envelops me. Tony is absent from my bed. Samantha, the only thing who lies between myself and oblivion.

"You will get better," everyone says. "You must try." Once more, my mother's words come unbidden, yet again, to haunt me: "*Can't never did anything.*" But I *can't* find the strength within me. Only the *little box*. Each morning I continue my vigil in the sanctity of the church. I wait to hear His voice, to feel His presence in my heart that will assure me of his motive. Oddly enough, I have never felt persecuted, only *tested*, as was Job. Ah…but now that I knew…He held my daughters hostage, my faith only increased. The thread that holds my sanity has pulled taut.

Daily I go through the motions of living. Smiling. Making trite conversation. Working. Working is apparently the only occupation that diminishes the fear and grief.

Our friend Dom Castillo's mother has died, and I have gone to the funeral alone.

I have stood throughout the services unyielding, fighting the desolation that comes with a fractured heart. Knowing how important it is that you have support from the friends and family you have formed over the years, I have made myself attend.

But now, in the aftermath of the service, I feel disembodied, unable to get in touch with the reality of the situation. This was an old, sick woman, but all I feel is the pain and the reality of my child's death.

Kneeling at my baby's gravesite. I have no recollection of how I got here, only the sight of the still-mounded earth. Lord, this is too much, too much to ask. *How will I ever survive this?* As I kneel on the ground, praying, my wide-brimmed black hat shielding my face as I sob uncontrollably. *I can't do this, Lord.* I cannot bear the pain. The constant, unyielding pain. *I can't.*

I feel his hand on my shoulder, and his presence envelopes me. "Let me help you. Come on, get up," he says as he takes my hand and pulls me up. "You're so thin." He pulls me to him, holding me as I sob.

"I can't do this, Tony, I just can't do this."

"You have no choice. Come, let me drive you home."

"I have my car here."

"I know, we'll take care of that, but you have to let me drive you home, or come to Dom's. Everyone will be there. You shouldn't be alone."

In the car, he laid his hand on my lap, and I pick it up and hold it. Such a beautiful, strong hand, broad and thick. My mind wanders; I once saw him drive an enormous splinter all the way through the palm of his hand, because he couldn't pull it out, and he was not going to go to "some damn hospital." I turn it over and look at the thick, fleshy open palm—this hand that had caressed me both in passion and in solace, and I bend my head to it and kiss it softly, lightly, smelling the fragrance of this man I love so very much. "I miss you so much, every moment of every day."

For a brief moment he looks at me. His eyes fill with love, clouded by the pain we have caused each other. He caresses my cheek as I hold his hand in mine.

There is silence between us. A silence of peaceful understanding. Softly he says, "Why wouldn't you look at me in court?"

"Because I knew if I did, I wouldn't be able to do this, and we are destroying each other."

"But I love you," he said. He has never before articulated those words to me—with one exception, it was always, "I married you, didn't I?" or something of that nature, always alluding to the possibility.

"But you have never told me that. I thought you were still in love with your ex-wife."

"Not since I met you. Why would you stay, if that is what you thought?"

"Because I love you so much I didn't care if I was first or last, only that I could be with you, that one day you would love me…and then the gun. How could you do that, for hours you sat on that couch playing Russian roulette with a .357 Magnum revolver? My God, Tony, what about Samantha?"

"I was just tryin' to do what you wanted, for once."

"What I wanted. That is the craziest thing I've ever heard. I didn't want you to kill us."

"Yeah, you said you did."

"When? When did I ever say that?"

"On the kid's headstone, ya said it loud and clear."

I think back to what is written on the headstone.

<hr />

It had been difficult to say anything at all except her name and the dates, but I just couldn't let that be it. I couldn't let her life not be valid in the years to come when someone would look at that stone.

I went to official after official until I got permission to put a verse and her picture on the flat stone. No more statues and mausoleums to the dead, only a flat insignificant stone. It just was not acceptable, so I lobbied to change the rules.

I then labored to write something that would do her justice. I would read it to him in bed as I wrote one prose or poem after another. His response was utter revulsion.

"Just let it rest. Forget it." He admonished me with anger, turning his back to me.

"I wish I could. I just don't seem to be able to do that," I told him.

"It" finally arrived on the sixth on January. She had been gone three months to the day.

Her picture sets to one side in black and white—her graduation picture, the beginning of her adult life.

On it these words try to describe our child:

Her smile a ray of sunshine, to everybody near
Her eyes so bright and sparkling
Her chatter ever dear.
She lived life to the fullest
Lord, we should have known
That Angels are from heaven,
And You'd come to take her home.
Until again we're granted the sunshine of her smile
Keep her safe and love her, Lord, I'll see her in a while.

As I think of the words on the headstone, I look up at him. He is so serious, so broken.

"Oh, honey, I only meant that time would go by and we would see her again."

"Well, that's not what I thought you meant."

I had no inkling that he had even gone to see the headstone. He had never said a word. But it had been a long time since any words had been exchanged between us.

The memory of that day seeps into my mind…

I had gone to church, came home, took my boots off, and put them on the washing machine in the laundry room along with my purse.

It's February, and although it is not cold, we think it winter, as that is what the calendar says. The house feels awful. Dead. Sad. Dark. I hate that feeling. But if that's how the people who live there feel, what else can happen?

It's my birthday. It's been four months to the day since she was killed. I am existing in a fog. Just one foot in front of the other. I go to church every day. I kneel and pray. Often sobbing uncontrollably.

Tony says, "Get over it." He can't stand it.

I tell him, "I try. I just can't."

My mother did always say, "'*Can't*' never did anything." But I truly cannot find inside me, what it takes to do this.

Tony is sitting on the couch. He is always sitting on the couch these days. He doesn't bathe or change his clothes. If he goes to work, he doesn't come home until morning. With my ineffably inept ability to comprehend the differences in our thinking processes, I am simultaneously angry with him and frightened for us.

Intellectually as well as professionally, I know that he is depressed. He has all the classic symptoms, but he refuses to go to counseling, only sulking or leaving when the subject is broached. I am in no better condition.

The room is brown and orange. *His room.* Earthy, masculine. The rest of the house is formal and soft. With books and music. There is an enormous rock fireplace covering an entire wall, a bar, and a TV. A massive tree trunk for a coffee table sits atop a carpet of oranges, browns, and gold. Unwashed shirts hang on the backs of bar stools. Boots lined in an orderly fashion in front of the fireplace. "Leave them be," he would proclaim as I endeavored to put his clothing in the closet or the laundry. It has taken me years to learn he simply liked the convenience of being able to just grab a shirt or his boots. The light glints off the wire and glass of the gun cabinet behind the bar. Funny, I never have seen things so clearly. Or through such a thick fog.

The TV is off. That never happens.

"Hi, I'm home," I holler. A constant attempt to create normality.

Walking into the room, I stand before him. Our tiny black Pomeranians are lying on the thick, overstuffed brown sectional couch with him.

He is holding an enormous .357 Magnum in his hand. Letting it hang between his legs. With the barrel pointing downward at the floor.

"My God, Tony, what are you doing? Have you eaten? I'll fix you breakfast."

He doesn't say anything.

"Tony, are you all right?"

He looks up at me.

"Tony, what is the matter? Are you all right?" His eyes are filled with tears. I kneel before him. Reach out to touch him.

He immediately waves the back of the gun at me, leaning forward. "Don't touch me!" he nearly shouts.

I jump back, frightened of him for the first time in my life. "All right, all right," I say as I kneel on my haunches on the floor before him. I reach out to lay my hand on his knee. "Can I do something for you? Do you want me to call someone?"

"Get back." He waves the gun again.

The silence in the house is deafening. I have a sense of leaving my body. I stand slowly and tell him, "I'm going to change my clothes."

"No, stay here!"

"No, Tony, I am going to change my clothes. I'll be right back."

"I said...you are not going anywhere." His speech quiet, clipped.

"Okay, okay," I say, thinking, this too will pass. Lord, help me help him.

I slowly stand. The kitchen is really an adjoining room, and he can see me as I slowly back away.

"I'm going to get some water. Do you want anything?"

"No," he says. I look—he has no coffee, no cigarettes. He is dressed in jeans and a long-sleeved wool shirt. He is pale, that dusty greenish color Latin's get when they are sick.

"Are you sick?" I ask

"Probably," he says.

I walk toward him. "Can I help you? Can we talk about this?"

"I said, get back!" Again, he waves the gun at me.

My knees are weak, and I am sweating. Shaking. My palms are moist, my hands trembling, as I walk to the kitchen. I feel that line, that line that exists between sanity and insanity. It is so fine, yet it is raging in our home, with just the two of us to deal with it.

God, oh my Lord, I pray. Help him, help us. I look at the clock over the oven. It says it's just 12:30. How can this have happened in such a short time? He's been telling me that the "man upstairs" is trying to tell us something. We've had four automobile accidents, he's crippled, I've had cancer, and Samantha broke her arm. Jillian is dead.

"Do the math," he says. "Look at it. He's trying to tell us something."

Now this. Oh Lord, I don't have the strength for this. I don't. Lord, you have to understand.

I pour me a cup of water from the refrigerator and put lemon juice in it. I know I should eat—I am so thin—but I can't.

I'll sew. The sewing machine is right here. He has always wanted me in the same room. Fabric strewn about is commonplace. I am making bridesmaids dresses for a wedding, in which Jillian was to be the maid of honor. Jillian's friend had asked me to stand in for her. I was so honored to do that for both she and Jillian. If I can just keep busy.

I turn from the counter.

My god, he is holding the gun with both hands, pointing it at his head.

"Tony," I say so softly, I can barely hear it.

I hear the hammer on the gun click.

"Tony," I whisper, through those terrified, tearless sobs, known only by the insane.

"*Shut the fuck up!*" he says as he suddenly wields the gun in my direction. "Sit down, and shut the fuck up!" His voice was hard, quiet and, yes, cold.

The house reverberates in darkness. Evil permeating our very existence.

Trembling, I go to the sewing machine and sit down. "Just let me sew," I whisper.

My heart is beating arrythmically. I'm taking halting breaths. Breathe, just breathe, I tell myself as I sit in the chair, my eyes closed, silently asking the Lord, How did we get here to this dark, dangerous, evil place? Lord, fill me with your presence please. Put a white light around me. Fill him with your Holy Spirit. I can't, I won't believe this man is evil, Lord. I love him, I know 'who' he is.

What is the passage in the Bible about being unevenly yoked?

2 Corinthians 6:14—"Do not be yoked together with unbelievers. For what do righteousness and wickedness have in common? Or what fellowship can light have with darkness"

This can't be us, Lord. For I have seen the goodness in this man, the tenderness. Save him, Lord, from our transgressions. Lord, save him in this, our hour of need.

The tears are streaming down my face, and I'm trying so hard not to be seen or heard.

I hear the cylinder roll and the pistol cock. I look over at him

He is pointing the gun at our little dog. She only weighs three pounds, a little black Pomeranian. He loves that dog. What is he doing?

"Oh Tony, no."

"I said s*hut up!*"

He pulls the trigger. No bullets. She is still alive. I can't believe he is doing this. He is a gunsmith by trade. He would never dry fire a gun, never.

The tension is tangible. It is as if a wire has been pulled taut through him. A thin, fine wire of fear, insanity, and psychosis.

"Tony, please let me call someone, someone who can help us."

"Nobody can help us now, it's over."

"No, honey, no. What about Samantha?"

I push the chair back, and start to get up.

"I said...sit down and be quiet," he says. A voice filled with no emotion, only quiet resolve.

I don't know how this happened, but I know, instinctively, that he means it. My hands shake as I try to hold the material together, and they are so moist and cold. The silence, deafening. I glance at my watch. It's a quarter to two. In my peripheral vision, I can see him sitting on the sofa, in his regular spot in the corner by the end table. His head is hanging, and the gun is dangling from both his hands between his legs

Lord, help us. Lord, help us.

He aims the gun at his head. He is holding it with both hands, and I can hear him pull back the hammer.

Bizarre thoughts are now taking hold of my mind, as I join in his insanity.

I think of the new painting I bought last month in Los Angeles. It is hanging on the wall in the living room that separates this room. He'll ruin the painting, and there will be blood all over everything.

Oh God, now I'm crazy too.

He pulls the trigger. I jump and start crying hysterically.

"No, no, please don't do this, please," I whimper.

"Stop it!" he says, but his voice is quiet and cold. "*I said, to shut the fuck up!*"

He points the gun at me, and I understand this is it; this is what our life has become. This is how it is going to end. I understand now, He has put two bullets in the cylinder of the gun and he knows that the next shots will achieve his goal.

Samantha, my love, my child, how will she survive all this tragedy? She can't. It's just too much for her to bear. No one will know because no one comes here any more. It has just become a house of death and pain.

We will lie here with blood and guts, and she will be the one who has to clean it up. No one will know until I don't show up for work in the morning.

I am so sorry for all the heartache I have caused. Samantha, forgive me. Lord, forgive him, for he knows not what he does.

He fires. I look up, and the barrel of the gun is still pointing at me. And I hang my head, tears dripping down my face.

He cocks it again. I hear the barrel roll. I hear him dropping the bullets in the cylinder. At first I wasn't sure, but now I am certain. He intends to kill us both. So he has at least two bullets in it.

How many times has he shot it? Three or four. I can't remember.

I'm not afraid to die. If Jillian can do it, I can too. She was just a little girl. I've lived a long time, comparatively speaking.

But a .357—what a mess it will make. He just wants it done right. No mistakes.

My body is cold and visibly shaking, I feel weak and so tired, so very, very tired.

Samantha, please, remember how very much I love you and that I would have never done this. And try to forgive Daddy. He is just so upset. Forgive us, Samantha, and please try and be happy, my little baby girl.

I look at my watch, it's 3:14. Funny, I was born at two. So I will die on my birthday.

The phone rings. I get up to answer it. Barely able to stand, I'm amazed at the feeling of liquidity that encompasses my body.

"Don't answer it," he says.

"I'm answering it," I tell him. My voice weak, shaking.

"Hello?"

"Mother, have you been calling me? Are you all right?"

"Yes...but no..."

"Mother, what is it!"

"Oh, I can't."

"You can't what, Mother? Are you all right?"

"Well no, not really...I..."

"It's Daddy, isn't it?"

"Yes, but—"

"Mother, come here now!"

"No, I can't now."

"Yes, Mother. Now, he will hurt you."

"How do you know?"

"I don't know, I just know. Come here now."

"I can't."

I am speaking in monosyllables. My voice weak, trying desperately not to offend him. For I now know how tenuous the balance is between sanity and insanity.

"Yes, Mother, now. If you are not here in fifteen minutes, I'm coming there."

"No, no." My voice was as soft as I can make it, for he's watching and listening. *What can I do? I can't let her come out here. He'll kill her too.*

"Yes...okay," I say. And hang up.

I look at him. Nothing has changed. Nothing is going to change. He has made up his mind. For him, it is the only solution to our life together.

"I have to go to the bathroom," I say to him softly.

"Stay right here," he says. The gun wavers in his hand.

"I'll be right back. I really will, and we will finish this thing. I will help you."

I walk to the hallway.

He's watching me; I turn. "Really, I'll be right back, and we'll do this thing."

"Okay." He drops his head to rest on his chest as if in relief.

I turn quickly, grab my boots, and my purse. Thank you, Lord, I had put nothing away. The keys to the car are lying next to the boots.

I push the opener for the garage door. Lord, help me not to make any mistakes. I'm in the car and pulling out of the garage.

He's there at the utility room door. The garage door comes crashing down across the hood of the car. I step on the accelerator. Tires screeching out of the driveway.

I hear his voice, and am pulled back to the present.

"I thought you wanted to die. You said you would see her in a little while. On the headstone you said that."

"Oh, Tony," I sighed. "Her time, not ours. This time on earth will go by in the twinkling of an eye. And I will see her soon, because of that. You know that deep in your soul. You know that."

But I knew in my heart he was a scared and a scarred little boy, really.

When Jillian died, I needed him. He couldn't or wouldn't offer me solace or understanding. Nor acceptance.

He told me, "You should be happy she is dead. She was just one problem after another. And after all, if you hadn't let her take the bumpers off her car, she'd still be alive."

Because I was not whole without him, I thought he knew I needed him and would be there for him as well, that he too was not whole without me.

A heartbroken mother and woman, or a pathetic romantic.

Chapter 11

The sun is setting on the great Pacific Ocean, with its majestic waves rushing against the golden sands as I stand gazing out the kitchen window. It is some ten miles away, but perched atop the hill in the elite *silk stocking* district, I can see all across the valley, its farmlands, verdant with strawberry fields, broccoli, and lettuce. The smell of rotting sugar beet weaves in the cool winter air. There is no sizzle to the sunset at this time of year, only a soft, warm, orange glow. The fountain in front of the windows bubbles in its enormous basin, as orchids lift their winter-weary heads for the last time.

The kitchen is abuzz with the caterers setting up the food, the dinnerware. The glasses all sparkle upon the counters. Cabinet doors, with their antique glass, stand open to inspection. Cabinets that I had had beaten with chains and whitewashed. This massive kitchen with its enormous Wolf range, is filled beyond belief.

The sounds of a string quartet accompanied by the concert grand piano drift into the kitchen from the living room where they are tuning up for the evening.

The doorman and parking attendants will be arriving soon. Have I forgotten anything? I am suddenly aware that I am clutching the white tile of the counter.

Relax, I tell myself, this will be fun. You want to do this. 'It' does come with the territory. This is for all the invitations I turn down all year long. For all the amends I need to make socially.

One of these days, I am going to not feel this social obligation. I will live quietly. With my demons, my fears, my losses. I have worked to near exhaustion, run to the far corners of the earth in search of absolution, to erase the ever-present physical pain, that small, fine thread of insanity that beckons me to the darkness. Never finding reprieve. To return once more to find that 'it' truly had happened. The unspeakable had indeed befallen our family.

The tears of desperations and grief slide down without restraint as I see *her* standing before me. *"Mother, you must stop this. Would you wish for me to mourn for you in this manner?"* She shimmers in the darkness of the room, and I feel ashamed for my lack of trust, of faith. For truly I would wish this on no one, least of all my children. I *will* get better!

The invitations went out four weeks ago, two hundred and fifty of them. Some of my immediate family have flown in from Seattle, and will stay through the holidays.

I am sure they are upstairs now readying for the evening, grumbling about this enormous display of wealth. Actually, Peter is more than likely the only one disturbed by it. The rest of them are excited, not knowing what to expect. All with the exception of my mother, who will love it.

The caterer is going over the menu now. Pay attention, I think.

"Yes, yes, that's very good," I say as I taste the caviar and the watercress. The salmon mousse is beautiful, and there are platters of meats and cold salmon with a wonderful sauce. Breads, cheeses, and beautiful desserts.

There are three waiters all in black tuxedos, and kitchen help in little black Playboy costumes.

"It looks wonderful, it tastes wonderful," I say. One hour to go, and the first of the guests will be arriving.

I take one last look at the house to see that everything is perfect. The invitation stated formal attire, so I truly want this to be a 'formal affair'.

The family room is warm and cozy with its hunter-green walls and the lovely hardwood of the floors. A massive used brick fireplace, draped with garland, is ablaze with the crackle of wood burning. The Christmas tree is pretty, with all the toys my children have made over the years.

The bar is beautiful, with carved wood epitaphs of the winemaking process mounted above the massive maroon granite countertop. The walls, a mural of grapevines I myself painted into the pale morning light. The tuxedo-clad bartender looks up as I approach. "Do you have everything you need?" I ask.

"Si, gracias, senora." He looks uncomfortable.

"Juan, you can take off your jacket. Your white shirt and vest are fine."

"Thank you, thank you. Yes, much better."

"Remember there are cases of mix, glasses, and liquor in the utility room. The waiters will serve the champagne on trays. Wine and mixed drinks are all you are responsible for."

"Oh, si, senora, gracias, senorita...."

I turn the lights on in the hallway leading to the library. The library is off limits tonight. It is a lovely room with the soft lights glimmering through the glass-paned door. Books in profusion line the mahogany shelves. Paneling and carvings which took a year to complete. Large, glass french doors lead to the patio of soft pink tiles overlooking the long, rectangular reflecting pond with its statuary at the end.

The house has been four years in its manifestation. But a healing one.

Two houses were just too much for me to care for. I would pay for the gardener, but when I got there it was obvious he hadn't come. So my so-called 'vacation' home on the lake became one of obligation to clean and garden. Things I didn't do at home.

Tony wanted none of them, nothing that would remind him of our lives as they had once been. So, what to do? I was determined to do as my daughter, *from the other side, had requested. I will make the best of this.*

As a very young girl, I had drawn house plans, elaborate house plans. With nooks and crannies, wonderful facades. Why not, I thought. I can do this. I sold both houses and properties, and this is the culmination of lots of time, money, and great attention to detail.

The foyer is of massive dimensions, lit with the crystal chandelier from a grand old hotel they were tearing down in Los Angeles. A friend of mine found it for me, its chain covered in white velvet scrunched to the ceiling. The fifty small flame-like bulbs shimmer against the twenty-four-foot ceilings. The smooth rounded walls are covered in a soft ivory damask. As I step up onto the wood floors, the eighteen-foot Christmas tree is a vision of beauty, with wide rose-crushed velvet ribbons cascading gracefully from top to bottom, white casa blanca lilies lying amid softly dusted branches, white and gold porcelain angels, Wallace sterling bells, and the thousand lights glow like tiny stars twinkling against Mother Nature's natural beauty. The circular stairway to the second floor is adrift in the same theme of lilies, ribbons, and evergreens, as the garland gracefully drapes the banister to the elegant mezzanine above. The wall sconces of gold and crystal are draped in the same velvet ribbons and greenery.

The grand entrance, with its oval etched glass door, portrays a Victorian theme in the otherwise Greek exterior. With its massive cantilever portico over the twenty-foot-wide cobbled stones of the circular drive. Flanked by regal Italian cypresses, with giant old oak trees settled in the distance. It too is ablaze in miniature lighting. The lampposts that announce the drive can be seen alight over the distant expanse of the manicured lawn.

Music drifts in from the living room, aglow from the light of the beautiful marble fireplace, casting a lovely patina on rich mahogany paneling, ornate with hand carvings and festoons. The grand piano sits amid the cellos, violins, and bass. Performers in their black and white intent on the rapture they are providing. Crystal vases of red roses and white lilies fill the elegant room. Their fragrance mingles with the fragrance of all the Christmases past.

The Christmases past. I feel that familiar nostalgia as my heart skips a beat, tears welling in my eyes. They were never this. This ostentation, never this opulent.

Trees decorated by my children. Resplendent in beauty. The laughter of them poking fun at each other as we made cookies and wrapped presents. Present's that were really without monetary value. But with value placed on the time and effort given to each one. A shared love and laughter, with family and friends. Gone to me forever in an instant.

Pull yourself together, I silently scolded myself. This is wonderful. It is simply different.

Now to the dining room. As I pivot in the foyer, the sun shows its face for the last time this day, casting an orange-purple sheen on the eight-foot arched mullioned windows that cover the front of the house.

The crystal chandelier in the dining room as well as the crystal sconces on the walls all glazed in the prismatic hue. Candles everywhere, waiting to be lit, the table, a mountain of linen, crystal, china and sterling. The draperies of ecru-watered silk fall gracefully, puddling on the white carpet, the subtle beige pattern of oriental branches cascade across the walls of soft ivory. Plates hung in a collage of lovely roses, dogwoods, and birds. Some of them I painted myself, others left to me by great-grandmothers and aunts.

I should have had someone to take pictures, I think as I continue on through the door to the kitchen to ascend the back stairway to my rooms. I really must dress. But first, let me see that my guests have everything they need. I cross the long mezzanine and rap softly at my parents' rooms. Ah, they look marvelous.

"No," my mother says, wringing her hands in nervousness and excitement, "maybe I won't go down. I think I better not go down."

"Oh, Mother, don't be silly, you look lovely. You'll have a wonderful time."

"I don't know," she whines.

I put my arm around her and kiss the top of her head. "You look beautiful. Come on, it will be fun." I look across the room to my father, standing very stately in his tuxedo.

"And you, sir, look very handsome." I wink at him. "Agnes has fixed you a light supper you can take in the breakfast room," I say as I close the door.

I rap at my nieces' rooms as I enter. The room is filled with clothing strewn about and the giggling of young girls. How very old-fashioned they look in their black velvet dresses and patent leather shoes. The bathroom doors are agape with the remnants of their ablutions.

My brother Peter and his wife Ellie rest on the bed. As I quietly close the door, I issue the same message of food, as I have to the others. The pomp and circumstance too much for them, in their elite, politically correct world of academia. Peter is having a difficult time dealing with my life, which is always so foreign to him, so fraught with drama. Still he finds it of great interest.

My Samantha's door stands ajar. I can see her reflection in the large antique mirror overlooking the pretty, feminine room. Awash in Ralph Lauren pink and rose cabbage roses, it is me that is reflected in this room, not her.

My breath catches for an instant. I am never prepared for her uncompromised beauty. Her presence. She is far more elegant and contemporary than cabbage roses. She stands tall and regal, her lovely figure draped in a simple gown of chocolate velvet and chiffon. Her soft ivory skin rises above the bodice of the gown, on her neck lays a necklace of emeralds, rubies, amethyst, golden topaz, and sapphires. The matching earrings hang suspended from her earlobes, framing a face of glorious perfection, a face that stops the hearts of men and women alike. She is sought after by the famous couture and fashion divas of the world. Her mass of strawberry blonde hair piled upon her head, with tendrils of curls plummeting down the nape of her lovely neck and around her perfect oval face in organized disarray

Thank you, Lord, for this blessing, this wonderful, kind, loyal, loving daughter, I pray silently. This is the only Christmas gift I shall ever need. Thank you, Lord.

"I'm hurrying, Mother. I am almost ready," she says as she bends down to place a chocolate velvet pump on her tiny foot. Perpetually late, this daughter of mine.

"You look wonderful, and look at me. I'm not even dressed yet."

I proceed back across to my rooms. I see the maid coming toward me. "Marisa, can you please see that the rooms are tidied up after everyone goes downstairs? Oh, and can you be sure all the lights are on, even the balcony lights?"

The balcony across the back of the house is the most beautiful thing. With heavy cement balustrades, pink tile, and large potted sago palms.

"Oh yes, senora." She smiles and curtsies.

There are far too many servants here tonight, I think. What do really wealthy people do?

My rooms are as lovely as all the rest—with a his-and-her bath and his-and-her closets. Closets that are as big as the bedrooms in the houses I've lived before, with cabinetry specifically designed to show off your clothing as well as store it. There are drawers and counters, lovely carpets, and full-length mirrors.

The gentlemen's bath on the far side of the room looks out over the water. With rich brown tiles, with tiles of gold to trim the massive shower stall.

Philippe, I think as I glance across the expanse of my elegant bedroom, into the bathroom beyond.

Careful what you wish for! No more men for me. Never again, I vow, as I turn and go in to get dressed.

I can hear the beautiful Windsor chimes as they announce the half hour. Now I *will* have to hurry.

My makeup is on and, my eyelashes glued, what underwear I intend to wear is on. A pair of panty hose. A standard joke among my daughters, I am never without pantyhose.

I love them. They freed me from a girdle as a girl, and I will be faithful forever more.

The jeweled and sequined Bob Mackey gown fits me like a glove. I step into its vibrant red fabric. It has a large keyhole neckline, with a button at my neck to hold it up. It plummets to the base of my long, slim back. Perfect, but heavy, I think, as I survey the results in the mirror. A splash of perfume. Diamonds at my ears, wrists and fingers, silver Stuart Weitzman's—I am ready. A bit ostentatious to be sure, but I love it. Let the party begin.

My palms are sweating, and I'm freezing. Anxiety or excitement, I am never sure. Nine times out of ten, this is how any social event begins for me. I know why. It is simply not me to be social. Yet I can put on this act and do fine. Even have a good time.

I hear the strings of "Winter Wonderland" as the music fills the house. Hear the chatter of the first guests as they arrive.

"Mother, you are beautiful."

I look up and there stands my exquisitely beautiful Samantha. What on earth would I do without her?

"Come," she says. "It's time." knowing of my aberration of anything 'social'.

At the top of the spiral staircase, we pause for a moment to take it all in.

There are valets parking cars. A small young man dressed in a tuxedo taking coats of guests. Black-and-white-clad servers with Santa caps and silver trays loaded with glasses filled with champagne. The halls are truly decked. The house is beautiful, and suddenly filled with people.

My youngest brother, Paul, with Jenny and Gabrielle, are very festive in their finery, standing at the bottom of the stairs as we descend gracefully downward. "Now, this is a party!" he proclaims. All fears and anxiety dissipate as he has always spoken the truth.

As I move among the guests, I am feeling more and more at ease. It *is* nice. Ah, there is Paige. "I am so glad you could come. You look wonderful," I say as I give her a hug. She is most attractive. Handsome, I believe is the word. She would become even more so as she aged.

"Yessss," she says, with mischief in her eyes. "And I brought someone who wants to meet you." I have to fight my immediate rising anger. She has been trying to get me to date for the last four years. And no matter how much I proclaim my fear of the classifieds, and wherever else she gets her dates, she simply can't leave it alone.

"Oh," I say, "did you tell him I was poison and wasn't at all interested?"

"Cara," she says, "be nice. Skip, this is Cara. Cara, this is Skip, and he has been dying to meet you." He is tall, taller than me by about three inches. So about six foot two. His eyes are beautiful blue, and clear—perhaps not clear, but cold, I think. White curly hair and snow-white close-cropped full beard. Not bad-looking. Thin, with sloping shoulders, but my gawd, he has on a *powder-blue tuxedo*.

I reach out to shake his hand. I am so shocked I can barely keep from saying something. He has the largest hands I have ever seen.

"How nice to meet you, Skip. I'm glad you could come. There is food in the dining room and drinks at the bar."

He is still holding my hand. I try to extract it from his grip, but he gently pulls it up, lowers his head, and kisses the back of my hand ever so gently.

"I want nothing but you," he says as his eyes meet mine.

For a moment I am too stunned to speak. "I am very flattered, just not interested. Please make yourselves at home. I must see to my other guests." I turn and walk away.

"Cara, that was so rude of you," Paige is saying as she is following me to the living room.

"Paige, how many times have I told you, I do not want to date?"

"He's wonderful, Cara. Perfect for you."

"If he is so perfect, why don't you keep him?" It is hard to believe we are speaking of a human being and not a dog, I think as I proceed to the living room, with Paige still in tow.

"Because, he doesn't want anyone with children, and all he can talk about is you."

"Where did you meet this one?" I chide her. "Really, Paige, I can't. I am just not interested."

"In the personal column, but I've talked to lots of people who know him. And they all think he is wonderful. Come on, Cara, how long has it been since you've had a date, or sex? Just be nice to him."

"How nice can he be if he doesn't like your children?"

"Oh, Cara, you know how my girls are."

I feel myself become a kind, caring person again., I turn and look at my friend, and I smile as I think of her girls. They have been a handful, to say the least. I have taken a butcher knife out of a five-year-old's hand, because, "she wouldn't give it to me."

I've gone up every morning and helped her put her pantyhose on, because she broke her arm chasing one of them on a bike, "because they wouldn't come back."

And, Jillian, who was baby-sitting for them on one occasion, called me and said, "'The middle one is possessed."

Her husband left her for his secretary when Jillian was killed. She was so devastated she never once asked how I was. She only wept on my shoulder, desolate.

I love her. She is well-intentioned and highly intelligent.

"Okay, I'll be nice." Placing my arm around her shoulder, I give her a gentle squeeze. "How old is he? Is he married? Does he have any children? And where in the world did he get that suit?"

She laughs. "It is a bit much, isn't it?"

My nieces descend the stairs, clapping their hands in delight. They are beautiful girls, dressed in pilgrim-like clothing of black velvet and lace. They have big round dark eyes and thick near-black hair cut in stylish bobs. Their excitement is palatable. Their parents come resolutely behind. Peter is elegant in a dark pinstriped suit, and Ellie is dressed nicely in a very sedate dress of dark plum, and a white Peter Pan collar sets off her remarkably beautiful face. She wears sensible pumps upon her feet.

My father holds the elbow of my mother as they too come to join the throngs of the personages who have been part and parcel to my life. Mother's eyes twinkle, the shy smile upon her lips. Excitement obvious in her manner.

The chatter of friends and family once more grace my home. The music filters through the house, with the sounds of carols being sung. The melodious sound of my mother's soprano voice drifts through the air as she sings in choral perfection to the strings of "O Holy Night."

Samantha's, as well as Jillian's, friends have come. My many friends, from our old neighborhoods, as well as people I had met and formed relationships within my work have arrived too. The house is filled to bursting. Kyle and Lynne and their boys, Janice and Mark and their children, Dom and Maria. Each gathering in small, intimate groups to talk and laugh. Their children chatter among themselves as waiters fill any wanting glasses. I drift from one to another, chatting, welcoming them, wishing them the happiest of holidays, thanking them for coming. For truly I am blessed to have so many dear friends.

My Antonio is not here...he didn't come...I will think of that tomorrow...

Chapter 12

I turn in the bed, the morning sunlight drifts cautiously across the coverlet. The phone is ringing. I glance at the clock and am astonished to see it says ten o'clock.

"Good morning, . . . " I mumble into the telephone.

"Oh, I woke you, I am so sorry. I'll call back later."

"Who is this?" I ask.

"Skip. I just wanted to say thank you. The party was really wonderful, and your home is beautiful, as is your daughter. I really enjoyed myself."

"Oh, you're welcome," I say sleepily.

"I'll call you from Africa sometime next week, if that's all right with you."

"I guess."

"Okay, then you have a nice time today." He hangs up.

Africa, what is he going to Africa for? I ponder to myself as I pull the peignoir over my shoulders. I can smell coffee. Wonderful Agnes, hopefully she has fed everyone breakfast. It was a wonderful party, and I am glad I did it.

Christmas Day arrives, without snow, but a beautiful, sunny California day.

Amazingly, I am still quiet and self-possessed, having had company for more than ten days, as well as an amazing party. I must confess I will be happy when it is all over. They are all leaving tomorrow, and finally the house will be mine again. But will I ever get it clean?

Everyone is happy with the gift exchange, and dinner was wonderful. The wild rice dressing and salmon is superb, even by my Northwest relatives' standards. However much a delicacy, we in the Southland consider it a luxury. They are used to it.

The crown-roasted pork and dressing was wonderful too, and I would have the gravy spilled over the Queen Anne chairs for years to come. As my sister's husband James tripped with the gravy boat as he was trying to navigate the overflowing dining room, to get to the foyer, where yet another table sits filled with people. Even as large as the dining room is, twenty-two people for dinner is somewhat overwhelming.

<hr />

It is seven o'clock in the evening, and the telephone is ringing.

"It is for you," my mother says. "A man," she whispers.

"A man," I say, my face all scrunched up.

"Yes," my mother says as she hands me the phone.

"Merry Christmas," I say into the telephone.

"Merry Christmas to you," says this very deep voice.

There is silence. "This is Skip," he says, "I just thought I'd call and tell you Merry Christmas and to tell you I am looking at something more beautiful than you."

"Excuse me?" I say. This is the most forward man I have ever encountered.

"I am standing at the bottom of Victoria Falls, and I thought how wonderful it would be if I could share this moment with you. Have you ever been here?"

"No, I haven't," I respond. "But I have heard it is breathtaking."

"I have been lots of places in the world, but this is spectacular," he says. "So, how is your Christmas going? Is your family still visiting? I really enjoyed talking to your father and brothers the night of the party."

We talked for a few more minutes, and then again he hung up.

"Does he live in Africa?" my mother said when I related the conversation to her.

"I don't know." I shrugged, "I don't think so."

The week between Christmas and New Year flew by. Everything at the hospital is very good. I am so happy to be back into a normal routine again.

The house is once again orderly and quiet, with the sound of classical music wafting throughout.

———⟨≈●≋⟩———

It is New Year's Day, and Samantha is coming down to spend the day with me.

"Happy New Year!" the voice on the other end shouts. Ah, this time I recognize his voice.

"Where are you now?" I ask.

He laughs, an infectious, deep laughter, "Oh, I'm home."

"And where is home?" I ask.

"Lompoc," he replies.

"So how long were you in Africa?" I ask.

"I got home yesterday. We had our last hunt on Thursday and flew back to New York, and I landed in LAX early yesterday evening."

"So did you like Africa?" I ask. Always interested in geography, and loving to travel, I was fascinated. We had a pleasant conversation for about half an hour, and he again wishes me a Happy New Year, and hangs up.

———⟨≈●≋⟩———

"So,…have you heard from Skip?" Paige asks, as she is picking at her salad. We are having lunch, and she is remonstrating over the trials and tribulations befalling her and the men in her life, as well as filling each other in on our children and our holidays.

"Yes, as a matter of fact, he has called three times, spoken briefly. Very polite. He was in Africa. So what do you know about him?"

"*Welllll,*" she says, grinning, "I have been poking around for you, and it seems he owns his own business in Lompoc, belongs to all the altruistic clubs—Elks, Rotary, Chamber, you know— and that he has been married and divorced several years ago. Drives a Cadillac, belongs to the gym there, works out five days a week, and—you will be glad to know—doesn't drink or smoke."

"Really," I say. "And just how did you find this out? Where did you find him?"

"Well, you know me. I got him out of the personals in the paper—Oh, don't be so prudish. Not all of us want to sit home alone. As far as the info, welllll, I work in Lompoc one day a week, and I know a lot of people there. It is a very small community. Sooo, I can find out nearly anything your little heart desires…are you going to go out with him?" She laughs and looks at me with a smug little smile. "I knew you would like him."

"Well, he really hasn't asked me."

"He will." She laughs and leans back in her chair, her hands holding the linen napkin, spread in glee. "You like him. I knew you would."

"Oh, I don't know. There is no chemistry there."

"Oh, Christ, Cara, that only comes once in a lifetime. I've got to run." She applies her lipstick and places the money for her lunch on the table. "Call me…"

"I don't know…there is that blue tuxedo…" We both laugh.

<hr />

Two weeks pass, with life as usual. Yoga classes, work, cleaning, yard work.

I love my job, and it is 24-7. Being the owner/administrator of the thriving Cambridge Care Center is, to say the least, demanding. But from the day I started, I have loved it. It tests my senses in every manner.

I have to be financially astute as the money is an astronomical challenge. The expenses are enormous. The payees are diverse, and with the government involved, unwilling to pay simply on my say so. Then of course, there are all the rules and regulations brought to bear by the state and federal government. So it is constant reading, seminars, and inspections. With me at the helm, I am ultimately responsible for the final outcome. Overwhelming at times, bringing me to my knees and to tears on more than one occasion. However, the rewards are infinite. Everyone here truly needs help. They are sick and frightened for the most part, with some of them alone and lonely.

I try to keep it at least 45 percent private pay. That keeps enough money coming in to care for everyone, even when Medicare doesn't pay, which unfortunately is frequent. There are the families, the physicians, therapists, and of course, the employees to be cared for and assuaged. Just an enormous family.

The yoga I teach two nights a week—that too I love. Although I charge for the classes, I give it all to Compassionate Friends, an organization for bereaved parents.

Really, I don't know when I would find time to date.

It is six o'clock in the morning. The telephone is ringing. Lord, don't let this be the kitchen, I simply can't cook for a hundred people this morning. "Good morning." Long years of being on call make me alert and businesslike immediately.

"Good morning," a male voice replies. "I'll be in town today and thought maybe you would have lunch with me. Dutch, of course."

"Who is this?" I say in a not altogether friendly tone.

"Skip," he says, his voice irritated, no doubt in response to mine.

"Oh, hi, sorry. It's early. Don't you sleep?" I reply.

"Sorry, is this too early to call you?"

"Yes, it is early. And I don't go out to lunch."

"You don't eat?"

"Well, yes, but I eat at the hospital. I only go out for meetings."

"Really," he says, sounding perplexed. "I have some beautiful pictures of my trip, and I thought you would like to see them. How about an early dinner on Saturday? I could come and pick you up, and we could just grab a quick bite to eat."

"I don't know. I don't date, you know. I am much too busy and am simply not interested in a relationship."

"Me either, but I find you interesting, and I had such a good time talking to you I would love to show you my pictures. To be honest, sometimes I would just like to have a date for social events."

"That is true," I said. "Okay, Saturday about six," I finally acquiesce.

<hr />

He is dressed in Levi's and boots, a beautiful baby blue cashmere sweater. The sleeves are pushed up on his arms, revealing tanned muscular forearms, decorated by two bracelets of gleaming gold. A Rolex graces his other wrist. A bit flashy for my taste, but after all, my entire goal here is to be accepting of other people.

He's quick and funny. Utterly charming. His enormous hands look rough and callused. He is very polite and very much the gentleman—opening the car door for me, pulling out my chair.

He speaks of his parents with great regard and tells me he has been estranged from his children since his divorce some twenty years previous. His eyes, the clear blue of Santa Claus. With the hair and beard to match. Are his eyes cold, now...I can't tell.

The evening is pleasant, and the photographs of Africa are beautiful, and his narration is stimulating.

In one stunning photo at a game park, a very elegant giraffe is pictured. The giraffe is twenty-four years of age, and this giraffe has isolated itself from its peers, and will remain in seclusion of sorts until he dies. This is customary.

"I can understand that," I tell him, laughing. "There are many times I wish to isolate myself from the rest of my peers." His glance is perplexed, but no comment is made.

The check for dinner comes, and he looks at it and says, "Your half is thirty-six dollars."

Rather than being appalled at this lack of gallantry on his part, I am pleased. We had an agreement; he has kept his word.

Over the ensuing months of spring and summer, there are art gallery openings, cocktail parties, business dinners, lavish charity events that are formal and exclusive.

His friends are both powerful and influential in the Santa Barbara and Santa Ynez Valley as well as suppliers of film and production in Los Angeles. People with lavish homes and owners of hotels along the coast of California.

I get to dress and be wined and dined in a fashion and atmosphere reserved for the rich and famous. He reveals little of himself but apparently listens intently as I chatter away.

When asked pointed questions, he dodges them artfully. Do I notice? Certainly. I can feel intuitively that this is not right. And I quickly shove it to the back of my mind. After all, he is more than a gentleman. His kiss, a brief good night, and his sexual demands are nonexistent. His hand is always at my back, ushering me through the many throngs of people we encounter in the many and varied social affairs. Always pleasant and polite.

I decide he is gay, and after Philippe, that is pleasant respite. Sex is not something I am interested in, having been used as a repository of sperm multiple times a day in every orifice of my body during a brief but enlightening marriage to the master of sexual delights, torture, and domination.

Be careful what you ask for.

Philippe—he seems but an distant bystander in this drama of my life. If I dared to tell the truth of my brief marriage to him, 'they' would in most cases not believe it, and if they did believe it, I would be considered stupid and vile, and he a spawn of Satan.

I had known him for years. I knew his wife and their four children. I had worked with him at Wellenes Furniture Store, years ago. He went to the same church as I did, and I saw him every Sunday.

Needing a new truck for the hospital, I had gone to a local dealership where he worked, thinking that I should at least give someone I knew the business.

"Philippe, how are you doing?"

"Well, I'm divorced, and well, things change. I heard about Jillian. I went to the funeral, but I never got a chance to see you. I can't tell you how sorry I am."

Philippe was kind and attentive. With soulful dark eyes. A big teddy bear of a man.

Polite conversation followed, old acquaintances spoken of, after which, he asked me to dinner. I had not dated anyone since my divorce from Tony three years ago, and I thought yes, why not.

He loved to dance and was an excellent dancer. He was well-dressed and being more than sympathetic to my occasional ramblings concerning Tony and Jillian. Ah, someone I could speak to of Jillian. Someone who provided continuity. He had, after all, known them both.

He was madly in love in no time. Wanting nothing but to marry me.

There was a wedding in the grandest of fashion. All of our acquaintances turned out. My family arrived from their respective abodes to wish me well. Hoping against all hope that this would provide some semblance of sanity and peace for me.

Samantha planned the wedding, and it was perfection in every detail. Black and white in its entirety.

I took my mother shopping and she was resplendent in lavender, with hat and shoes to match. My handsome father, in his rented tuxedo, walked me down the aisle.

Only the bride was not radiant as she knew a mistake was in the making. My intuition rabid, remembering my innate desire to please, to be accepted by my mother and the *father* of my children. Would I continuously take whatever was offered up? Was there no thread that connected me to anyone I could truly love? Had that thread truly unraveled with Antonio?

It appeared it had.

Tony having never exhibited a rabid libido. I had joked with an intimate female friend on more than one occasion, that in the next life I would have someone that wanted to ravish my body more frequently. We had laughed with both of us declaring, "Good luck on that one. Once they got ya, they don't want ya." I believed this and understood to a great extent that the differences in Tony's and my hours, his crippling injury, and quite possibly his dalliances were to blame. For when the time came, ravish my body he did, with great tenderness and care.

I should have known from looking at Theresa, Philippe's ex-wife, that things were not what they were said to be. She was old beyond her years, sad, and distant.

He was a handsome man, of Mexican heritage. Looming tall, at six foot four inches, weighing 205 pounds, and lean. The epitome of tall, dark, and handsome. With an uncharacteristic gracefulness. His eyes dark, and he was amused at most things.

He was, however, possessed of a sexual nature only found in sinister, erotic places. The vile and repulsive things known only to those of a black soul. The need to possess and overpower, a compulsion within his mind and body. Pain and possession was his forte. Whips, chains, and suffocation, mere foreplay. The dark eyes would become hooded with desire, a desire to control as well as to cause pain. His manhood of monstrous and painful proportions as black as if he were of Nubian descent.

At first fascinated, I quickly learned to be frightened of his desire as the perpetuity of it was intense, demeaning, and painful. Worse than that, I found him to be strangely erotic, and soon longed for him to demean, torture, and possess me. For during that brief period I felt accepted and cherished. Our sexual adventures became something I both dreaded and felt addicted to. I pleaded with him to seek help. And found more "punishment."

After three months, I was done. I asked him to leave my home, and to his credit he went gracefully. He filed for the divorce himself, never asking for anything of me. I can understand his concerns, what would become of his life, were the truth of it be told.

Chapter 13

It had started simply enough really, and ended in something that can only be *spoken* of to be aware of the nature of its destruction and humiliation; its power of debasing. There can be no subtleties that would transmit the ability of a person to use and abuse one so graphically.

During our two years of courtship he was ever the gentleman. Soft, gentle lovemaking, and only on very rare occasions.

I, starved for attention and intimacy. So many traumas in my life, Tony's accident had left him physically unable to perform, not just physically, but the emotional trauma to his manhood had left him without desire, with a deep fear of rejection. Jillian's sudden death had traumatized us both beyond any ability to enjoy or resume our sexuality. It had been years since I had enjoyed any intimacy, intimacy of any kind.

Philippe's and my stunningly lavish wedding left me *apprehensive*...again those *'funny feelings'* that I could find no justification for.

His first unusual request was that while we were at home, I wear no undergarments. And only dresses or skirts. I found this request only mildly discomforting. And I thought, *he will tire of this*. He was adamant that his request be honored. He checked frequently during the evening hours we spent at home. No fondling, no groping, only an inspection.

On the third week of our marriage, his displeasure at finding I had on underwear upset him beyond belief. He was hurt that I disobeyed him. "This has been my only request." Lifting me gently in his arms, he carried me to the bedroom. He very tenderly removed all my clothing and laid me gently on the bed.

I laughed and squirmed as I was certain he could not be serious about this. He softly said, "Lie still, my darling, I just want to look at you. If you won't abide by my wishes, you will not wear any clothing."

"You can't be serious," I said, trying to rise from the bed. Softly with his great strength, he gently pushes me to the bed.

Smiling, he said, "Do as I ask. You belong to me."

"Okay, okay, just let me up. I have things to do."

"No, my darling, you must learn to do as I say." With extreme tenderness, his large, strong hands stroke my body. "Just lay still."

I lay on the bed in my nakedness for two hours while he undressed, and laid beside me naked, all the while he stroked and fondled my body.

Suddenly he rises, telling me to get up and get dressed.

Doing as he asked, I reach for my underwear. He cleared his throat and stood abruptly, rising to his full six foot four inches. I drop them.

Really, what could it hurt?

On each day, very early in the morning he stood at the end of the bed and began to apply the shaving foam to the area of his desire. My legs are weak with fear and arousal. *This man is a nut*, I think to myself as I dare not move. Castration of my female parts might be at hand. Why would I find this in the least arousing? Am I sick? A perfect submissive. I am.

A powerful woman, respected and held in high esteem by my peers, I generally frightened men, and I looked to men for their power. This, however, was not really what I had in mind.

Chapter 14

Philippe has a very ornately engraved silver plated large box that holds many toys, toys I have not heard of, *toys and tools*, I have never thought of. Toys of pleasure, tools of pain. Toys that produce pleasure through pain. A concept totally foreign to me. A concept heaped in guilt.

I wish to speak to someone of this, however my only confidant being my daughter, my ex-husband, and my dear friend. What would they think? I cannot fathom.

When I try to talk to Philippe of it, his only reply was that he wished to make me happy.

The lights are out. I feel certain he is sleeping as I crawl into our bed. It is late, and I have just come from working late this evening. I no longer bathe at night, as Philippe wants to "taste me." Not soap and perfume. I do miss the warm, sudsy water—although he has an array of lovely fragrances and oils that he lavishes on my body, and their fragrances are sometimes medicinal in aroma.

Nearly asleep, I turn and sigh as I feel his great bulk come closer to me. The smell of his masculinity is strong, and I am aware of his desire. Pulling me to him, he softly whispers, "Do you need the ropes tonight, my darling, or will you do my bidding?"

"This isn't working, Philippe, I can't live like this, I thought you would get over this, this obsession. I am sooo tired."

"There, there. You are not hurt, are you?"

"No, no amazingly enough, you have never really hurt me, it is just so, so…I don't know, so nasty, so unnecessary, so, so unusually demeaning."

"There, there, I'll clean you up and you rest, you're just tired."

Chapter 15

Philippe has called and said he was picking me up after work tonight. He has a surprise for me. He has been so attentive this week, and so normal. He seems to flit from the benign, to the treacherous eroticism of a malevolent captor. Certainly the previous weeks of our marriage have proven I know nothing of this man.

We have been driving for nearly two hours now, and he has finally told me where we are going. I have never stayed there before, but I am familiar with the hotel, and it is lovely. Rustic, hidden in the trees above San Simeon. With a lovely view of the ocean.

He has brought flowers and perhaps champagne, and has packed my clothing for two days. It just seems he should have asked first. "We have dinner reservations at eight," he says as he glances at me.

"That's nice," I say. I am still more than a little miffed. Ungrateful wretch I am. A surprise romantic weekend most women would love.

The room is large and spacious, a fire flickers in the fireplace, a dining table and chairs sit to the right as we enter, and the bed is already turned down.

"I'm going in to freshen up and change my clothes," I say, as I head for the bathroom, luggage in hand.

"Good darling, I will unpack and we can go to dinner. Would you like a glass of champagne?"

"You brought champagne?"

"I did." He smiles, he is so handsome. And just as I had thought, he is a kind man. A kind man with strange and alarming sexual proclivities. *Unspeakable proclivities.*

"The champagne tastes funny," I holler at him from the bathroom.

"When did you have champagne last?" he laughs.

"True," I say.

As we leave to go to dinner I see the *silver box.*

Dinner is lovely, a small orchestra is playing big band music, and we dance for nearly two hours. I love to dance with him. Such a strong lead, and so smooth. There is a place just north of us, with wonderful music and the smoothest dance floor, that we go to dance at least once a week.

Having returned to our room, I go into the bathroom, and begin taking off my clothing. "Here, let me do that," he says, his hands gentle, as they remove the necklace I wear and unzip the 'little black dress' he had packed for me. He does think of everything.

"I am very tired Philippe, I think I will just take a quick shower."

"Let me, my darling, let me bathe you, I would love to bathe you," his lips soft against the back of my neck, the soft kisses lingering on my shoulders. "Your skin is so soft my darling, let me bathe you. Come," his muscular arms lifting me from the floor.

Laying me on the bed, pillows propped up behind my head, he brings me a glass of the champagne. "No, no, I think I've had enough."

"No, my darling, it will help to relax," his strong hands and lips caressing as he undresses me, slowly, lovingly. I can hear water running, as the steam flows from the small bathroom.

I must have drifted off, as I start at the silken ropes being tied to my wrist. "No, not tonight, I am so tired. Did you place a sedative in the champagne I feel very strange."

"I did-you will do my bidding tonight my darling."

I beg him to stop, as hour after hour the pain and debasement continues. "Please just let me sleep." I beg. As yet another silken rope is placed securely. Another silken gag stuffed in my mouth. I would call to the Lord…I fear only Satan resides within this room.

"I know, my darling, but we must get you cleaned up, and then you can sleep. You can sleep all day tomorrow. I promise."

The silk is blue this time, with ropes of firmer fabric, as he places the silk on each of my wrists and legs, securing them to the posters of the rustic bed. "Really, Philippe, you don't need those."

"I know, darling, but I like them and it helps you, yes."

Consenting adults, consenting adults. The phrase flows through my mind like water.

As I cease resistance. The sedative; alarmingly intense. I am allergic to most drugs, and angered that he has done this…this….I wonder at the strange taste of the champagne earlier in the evening. If I could just think…

"No no no," I whimper. "No more."

"Yes, darling, say you want this."

"No, Philippe, no."

"Shush, my darling." The gag is again slipped into my mouth. I shake my head no.

My physical, mental and emotional exhaustion is profound as I lapse into a near-comatose sleep.

The sunshine fills the room with warm brilliant light, the small dust motes giving it a life of its own, as my eyes open to the rustic décor of the large, unfamiliar space. Philippe sits seated at the small dining table, the remains of breakfast before him. The white of his Egyptian cotton shirt a deep contrast to the dark of his Spanish ancestry. The collar of his shirt open, the cuffs turned up clean at each wrist, he holds a porcelain tea cup in his hand, and raising it to his lips I wonder at the grace and elegance of a man of such great physical stature. He is clean shaven, and his black hair impeccably coifed. The graying at his temples adds to his elegant demeanor. He is wearing dark slacks and his ankle rests across one knee, his Ferragamo loafers visible. He holds the newspaper before him, as Brubeck plays softly in the background.

"Ah, my angel, at last you are awake," he says, lowering the paper to look over at me.

"What time is it?" I say sleepily, stretching my long arms and legs. Was this a dream, an incredibly horrifying nightmare?

"It is eleven, did you sleep well. Would you like me to order breakfast for you? What would you like?"

With terror so complete, the memories of the previous night wash over me, as I peer above the linens to the elegant man who sits so demurely at the table, as if he were a normal human being. Or are my experiences in life so sheltered that this is normal? Even in the romantic novels of drugstore variety, I have never encountered such as this. I am at once frightened and angered.

"No, Philippe, I think I would like to go home now. I will call a taxi to take me, if you will not allow that *I will* call the police and have them come." Reaching for the telephone at the bedside table, my hand shakes as I do so. In part from fear and anger, in part from exhaustion.

"But my darling, you can't mean that," rising to cross the room to where I lay, naked beneath the linens of this bed, vulnerable to his touch, the sound of his voice.

"Stay away from me. I trust neither you nor myself. This is not how I chose to live my life, so you do whatever you have to do, but this is over now." I now sit perched upon the bed with the sheets pulled tightly around my body in protection. The trembling of my extremities apparent as I fight for control of this situation I have found myself in, the receiver held tightly in my hand, I hear the voice of the desk clerk, "Yes, may I help you?"

"Yes, Thank you, can you have a taxi here for me in 15 minutes?' the treble of my voice a distant echo in my ears as I watch Philippe fast approaching me.

"Certainly, I will call for you now," the voice on the other end of the line mimicking my panic.

My resolve apparent to him, he backs away as I crawl from the bed, dragging linens in my path, the newspaper he had held in his hands flutters to the floor, as his massive shoulders slump in defeat. I wonder at the number of women who endure treatment such as this at the hands of those they trusted? I wondered who had provided him with such eroticism during his long courtship of me. Wondered if I would ever recover from this this abhorrent abuse. *This time, I had no broken bones, no missing teeth, no visible injury only my mind battered and bruised. My trust shattered.*

Chapter 16

. . . .

November comes softly to the California coast, with its imitation of winter—cold, clear nights, trees naked of leaves, lawns browned by summer sun, to become greened with the torrential rains, days that turn to bright sunshine, and chilly winter skies.

Alas, Skip is not gay, only impotent. He is clumsy and rough, with kisses that are hard and brutal, with hands that grope and bruise, rather than caress and worship the flesh. He is both demanding and persistent in his pursuit of an erection and satisfaction.

I, like so many others before me, am only paying a debt. A debt of companionship and money spent on me and my family, a debt of expectation in a world of men. A soulless payment for deeds unknown. But does love, true love, ever happen twice in a lifetime? I doubt it. Paige thinks I am a fool to continue thinking it does. She continued to laud Skip and reiterate that in fact, he was a good choice.

After a pleasant summer evening of dinner and a movie, he asks, "Would you like to see my house?" I always wondered where he lived. When asked, his response was always, "I'll show you one of these days."

Okay, I think to myself. "Yes, that would be nice."

We drive to a very exclusive neighborhood in Santa Ynez, the large, wrought-iron gates loom before an enormous Mediterranean façade of ivory stucco, the red-tiled roof a dazzling sight in the sparkling summer sun.

With the press of a button, the gates swing open, and the garage door slides up, revealing the massive dual wheels of his red phallic-sized pickup truck and his powder-blue corvette residing on an ornate expanse of intricately tiled floors.

The door to an impressive bath stands ajar at the end of the immense space.

"That's the bathroom I use," he says.

I am surprised, shocked, a bit overwhelmed…why wouldn't he have brought me here before?

We enter through the back door. There is a laundry room, a large butler's pantry, and a small office, then the kitchen—with every known modern accompaniment. A large breakfast area, with bamboo and glass table set for two. It overlooks a patio with a fountain and gazebo. Beyond this lies a formal dining room with crystal and china ensconced in a hutch of massive dimensions.

The floors are of rich ivory ceramic tile; the sunken living room to the left with plush carpet, elegant fireplace, white sofas, and inviting easy chairs.

The next room stops my heart, then accelerates it at an alarming rate. It is dark by comparison, and its enormous dimensions are filled with life-sized elephants, giraffes, cougars, lions, head's of rhino, deer, elk, and antelope. Every conceivable animal is on display in all their glory. Dead and mounted as a testimony to his cruelties.

Guns, bows, and arrows cover the wall around a sixty-inch TV screen, with a massive, very used, black leather chair facing it.

My palms are sweating; every instinct I possess is screaming. But my intellect prevails. This is after all just a man. All men like to hunt. Tony hunted, albeit for food, but hunted nonetheless, and we too had a big deer head over the fireplace.

This man is nice to you and your family.

"What do you think?" he asks.

"Well…" I hesitate, searching my mind for words. I am overwhelmed…"You killed all these animals. Why?"

"It is a culling effort by the African government," he says. "Our fees cover the expenses of caring for the animal preserves, as well as a means of keeping the strongest of the animal population abundant."

"Really," I stammer. "I have never heard that before. What about those ivory tusks, are they really from an elephant?"

"Yes, ma'am," he says proudly. "I killed it at about one thousand yards. They provide a large tractor-like Cat to help the natives skin them. They fasten big hooks in the skin, and pull with the tractor. The meat is then divided among the natives, who are otherwise starving." He is both enthusiastic and articulate in his explanation—or excuse.

I am standing just inside the doorway, with my hand over my heart, trying to quell the nausea that is threatening to overtake me. "I didn't know that," I said, backing out of the room.

"You don't like the room, Cara."

"No, I don't think I do. I didn't know you did this. Is this what you have been doing on all of these trips you take?"

"Yes, yes." He sounded animated and excited. "I always wanted to do this. I love it. I've been to Tibet, lived in a yurt and hunted mountain goat! Alaska for polar bears—"

"I thought you couldn't kill polar bears," I say, pulling back from him.

"Oh," he says with a chuckle, "if there's a will, there's a way."

He takes me by the elbow and escorts me through the rest of the house. My mind in a fog, I follow him through bedrooms and bathrooms. The master bedroom is a stark, orderly affair with a king-sized bed, unmade, with a large plush-looking comforter on it.

The door to the walk-in closet is ajar, with the neatness of his clothing nearly as much a shock as the dead animals. Every item, according to style and color; every hanger, the same space from the next. Eerie.

The master bath, a profusion in shades of brown rocks, with a never-ending waterfall flowing serenely over the stones. Giant

ferns sublimely lift their fronds to the gentle mists. "This is lovely,"
I tell him. "Remarkably lovely. But I'd like to go home now."

The ride home was silent, heavy with thoughts, emotions
not verbalized.

He slides the big red Cadillac under the expanse of my front
portico, the large bronze Kramer lost-wax lions gaze at me
benignly. "You're mad at me," he states.

"Oh, I don't know. I am shocked, surprised, and somewhat
sickened. I don't know. It is repugnant to me, I guess."

"Why, Cara, we can't all be the same, you know. We have so
much in common. You can't let this interfere in what we have.
We're bound to have different hobbies. I don't want to read and
paint and sew. Men do what men do."

"I guess. I just need some time, okay."

"Can I call you tonight?"

But it was two days before he called. The shock pushed away,
and his parting words still rings in my mind: "Men will be men."
Did I really want to throw away what we had over his 'hobby'?

When he called, I acquiesced. I simply would not think
about it.

We take constant trips to Los Angeles for football games
and parties. Football games, I tolerate, but I hate for the violence
inflicted. A childish sport of men. Observed from a box reserved
for those of money and influence, where drinks are served and
trays of hors d'oeuvres lie uneaten while the shouts of the observers ring in my ears.

I think I am tired of this pretension. But do I wish to return
to my life as it was? I don't know. Am I afraid to be by myself?
To grow old alone? Do I wish to live a life filled with superficial superlatives? A life without love, a life without desire?
Without gentleness?

There lies the problem. In it, center stage, is always and forever
Tony. I love him. But do I wish to live that life again? I knew
I would be forever punished emotionally for having left him.
"Threw him away like an old shoe," he said.

I can look across the hills and see where he lives, a small hovel amidst the clamor of elegant homes.

***

"Can you live here?" Tony asks me, as I sit nude upon his bed, unashamed in his presence, among the litter of gun magazines and dirty dishes. I survey the surrounding small studio that adjoins a sumptuous house, and say, "Yes, but I would take down these dreadful red velvet draperies, make new curtains, and paint it all white."

"Why can't you just be content to be with me, Cara?"

"I am content to be with you. I just don't know why you are living this way."

As ambition is not intrinsic to nature, it must surely be a sin. Was I ambitious, or merely seeking security? Or is it merely beauty I seek?

When am I not going to go to him when he calls? I ask myself, knowing I always will. He won't come to my bed anymore since I moved away from the home we shared for so many years. Oh, he comes. We talk, laugh, and flirt. But he won't go to my bed.

And, I am too proud to ask him.

Tony and I are giving Samantha a big garden party for her birthday. He had called and asked if he could bring his girlfriend. I said certainly. After all, Skip would be there.

Marsha is in awe of the house, commenting on the cost of everything.

Finally, tiring of the conversation, I look at him, wink, and say, "Marsha, you know this is a community property state. He has the same amount of money I do."

He glares at me. "But I intend to hang on to mine," his voice only a glimmer of the anger I know, as his wife, lies there.

As always, the electricity between us fended off all interlopers and tended to cause difficulties with what we preferred to call our lovers.

Lovers, hell, we are the lovers.

"He is much too superficial for you, Cara. Don't marry him," Tony said as he took Marsha by the hand to leave. Always observant, always right.

This time, I hope he is wrong.

Chapter 17

Christmas has once more come and gone. Another year looms bleakly in the future. My relationship with Skip continues with very little change.

Well, there is that night I spent at his home.

I had agreed to stay at his house only if I could drive myself. On the pretense of work calling. The thought of staying at his home caused me such anxiety I needed an escape route.

I could not sleep. The house was freezing cold. I got up to go to the bathroom; the toilet didn't flush. I went to get a drink of water; there was no water in the kitchen. Nor was there water in the faucets or in any of the bathrooms. It was the weirdest thing I had ever encountered.

I looked at the clock; it said 3:00 a.m. I grabbed my clothes, and left. I went home, took the phone off the hook, and slept until two the next afternoon. When I finally replaced the receiver back in its cradle, the phone rang for hours.

Around nine that evening, I answered it. "Please Cara, I love you. I need you. Why did you leave?"

"I just couldn't stay there with all that weirdness, the animals, no water. What is that? Why don't you have any running water in the house? What do you use for a bathroom? Is that really your house, or is it a model home we stayed in last night?"

"Of course it's my house," he replied, his voice showing signs of anger now.

"So tell me about the water."

"Well, I just use the bathroom in the garage. I don't use anything in the house. I don't want it to get old."

My god, what have I got myself into? I thought.

But he was obviously so upset. "Please, Cara, please let me see you. I can be there in fifteen minutes."

"No."

The next day, two dozen red roses arrived at work, with a note that said he'll pick me up at nine o'clock in the morning the following Saturday. "We are going shopping," the note said.

Tuesday, one dozen pink roses are delivered to my office. Wednesday, one dozen yellow roses, Thursday one dozen white roses, Friday, one dozen red roses, each with a card, in his handwriting no less: "I love you, I love you, I love you."

Everyone in the hospital is entranced by my love life, all offering their profound advice.

"Men like that don't grow on trees."

"You deserve someone to be good to you."

"I know him, and he's a really nice guy."

It went on and on.

Friday evening, he called to confirm our date.

Of course, I forgave him. After all, he really had done nothing wrong. Living in a beautiful house without water was not necessarily a sin. And I shushed my intuitive feelings, having decided that the most successful areas of my life lie in my work. Therefore, it would behoove me to make decisions based on my intellect and not on my emotions.

He picked me up and took me to the airport where we boarded a plane bound for Las Vegas. Upon arrival, a limo takes us to Caesars Palace.

"I have no clothes or make up," I complained. "I can't do this."

"Of course you can, we will buy those things."

Buy those things, we did. Underwear, makeup, a beautiful pants suit, with shoes to match. We shopped and shopped. He liked to shop. He bought me gorgeous shoes and didn't scoff at the price tag for my narrow foot.

Last but certainly not least, a full-length white mink coat, with fox sleeves and collar, with a hat to match. This is like the movies, I think as I lie in bed that night, listening to the sound of his snoring. Lord, forgive me. I *could* be bought.

In the morning, I awaken to the delicious smell of rich, fragrant coffee.

I open one eye and peer out over the sumptuous linens. There stands Skip, with coffee in hand and a very large envelope. "Open it," he says.

I open the large manila envelope, and I am shocked to see the contents: two round-trip tickets to Italy. Fourteen glorious days in Milan, Venice, Rome, the Isle of Capri, Sorrento, and Assisi. He is excited as he sits on the bed and watches me reading the itinerary.

"Have you ever been there?" he asks.

"Yes, I have. But I would love to go again."

"It's settled, then," he says. "We go in April. I love you so much, Cara. I want you to be my wife. Please...say yes."

"I...I...I...don't know," I stutter., "There are so many things I don't know about you."

"Please, I love you. That's really all you need to know, but I'll tell you whatever you want to hear."

"Skip, I told you when we met I am really not interested in getting married. I am paying alimony now, and I certainly don't need that again. Then, too, there are the hospitals. It is a full-time job, and I don't have the time it takes to devote to a relationship."

"Please, think about it. I love you. I need you, someone like you to share my life with."

As I climb out from beneath the covers, the small spaghetti straps of the emerald green silk full-length gown slip from my shoulders. I can feel the sweat, as it trickles between my full breasts.

"Please, Cara," he begs, "think about it."

I look at him. He is nice-looking, clean, well-built, funny, and yes, charming. He seems to have the finances to provide a nice lifestyle without my money. He is well liked by his friends, and his parents seemingly adore him.

So what is the problem? Am I just afraid, afraid to fail again? "I don't think so. I don't know, Skip. I just don't know."

His face is long and sad. He looks as if he'll cry. "I'll wait," he says.

Surprisingly, the rest of the weekend was glorious. We ate, gambled, and we went to a show that evening. The next day a jet whisked us back home.

Again, I didn't hear from him until the following Thursday. Strange, how he can seem so enamored of me and still go days without so much as a phone call. It did leave me with time to think and time to get on with my life. After all, that is what I had always said I needed, each time we had discussed it. So maybe that was what he was doing. I had never met a man with so much restraint; however there was always a first.

April came, and I enthusiastically packed for Italy.

Chapter 18

Italy is the most beautiful of countries, its beauty having not diminished in the two years since I was last there.

We were up at the crack of dawn and on a tour bus. With microphone in hand, the tour guide filled our minds and imaginations with information about the history and the peoples of this splendid land. He explains that all tour guides must have a classical education in the arts and history, a topic only another lover of history, architecture, and the gross national profit of countries can understand.

As I sit in rapt silence listening and watching the magnificent countryside glide by us, Skip sits, head thrown back, mouth agape, snoring loudly. "Shush," I whisper to him. He starts at the sound of my voice. And for a few more minutes, he is quiet.

"Aren't you interested in this?" I ask.

"No, not really," he replies.

He, however, loved the shopping in Florence. He had three pairs of leather pants made, with jackets to match. He bought hats and gloves.

Meanwhile, I am wandering the streets in search of vendors with small paintings of the lovely Firenza skyline, with its red tile roofs and the Duomo shooting skyward.

We traverse the countryside with the guide pointing out large fortresses built around the great castles on top of tall hills. He tells of the marriages of the common man who lived under the auspices of the lords of the castles, how the wives were all taken to the lord of the fortress on their wedding night. Then if he approved, they would be given to the groom later.

We cross into Switzerland to a lovely little town resting on the shores of Lake Majjorie, nestled in the Swiss mountains. Could anything be so delightful? Only the Isla Bella, with its white peacocks, strutting in display of their glistening white plumage. The castle is lovely, old and lovely.

I was once told that I descended from the Savoys, so I was very interested in this particular part of the country. The eleventh century was certainly a long time ago, but the Savoy dynasty ruled the Piemonte-Sardinia area, and Napoleon and King Louis XIV –both invaded it repeatedly because of its strategic position.

Venice is lovely, musty and lovely. It is situated on 120 islands formed by 177 canals in the lagoon between the mouths of the Po and Piave rivers, at the northern extremity of the Adriatic Sea. There is a railroad and a highway that connect it with the mainland, and the islands that the city is built on are connected by some four hundred bridges. The Grand Canal that divides the city is approximately two miles long. Skip and I took a gondola ride through this glorious ancient city. With the Doge's Palace, *Palazzsso Ducale*, and Saint Mark's Square—everything I thought it would be. Saint Mark's Cathedral is considered to be an outstanding example of Byzantine architecture. It is both Italian and Gothic, with some early Renaissance elements. It is hard to believe that this was constructed over one thousand years ago. The beauty is remarkable; the attention to detail, unsurpassed— with the exception of Michelangelo's *David* and the last *Pietà*.

I was so touched, so moved, by these works of creation, that I could have knelt in worship before them. Their very essence, one of supreme love and devotion, of grief and heartbreak. I was there two years after Jillian was killed, and with the emotion of losing a child so fresh, so profoundly paralytic that had I been alone, and not among a throng of strangers, I most certainly would have fallen to my knees. Tears fell, unbidden, my eyes blinded to the exquisite beauty before me.

In the years that had followed Jillian's death and the divorce, I ran and ran...taking Samantha with me, afraid to leave her. We explored the world and all its marvels. Returning home was always a shock as the truth hits me—Tony was indeed gone; Jillian, dead.

Ultimately I learned acceptance. The grief I had, I could live with. I could function. I had found a "place" to keep it, and after all, it was all I had left of her. My life was but a house of cards. Fragile; beyond imagination.

I did not go back there this time. Skip has no interest (I can't imagine, but true it is), and I would not ever wish to have that emotional reaction that resides in me to a work of art replaced by something less than miraculous.

But I digress—back to Venice. The bell tower of Saint Mark, the campanile, is about three hundred feet tall. Imagine. There is so much history here. I could stay forever.

However, we must shop.

Skip wanted to shop, and shop he did. Venetian crystal, linens, Murano glass, and more Venetian crystal. I bought a purple wine decanter and wine glasses and champagne glasses, with delicate flowers of pastel ceramic embellished on them. Skip bought as if he was just now furnishing his home.

In Assisi, we stayed in the monastery. It was clean, simple, and ancient, with the most delicious food I have ever eaten. Common fare, but would have delighted the taste of any gourmand.

In the land of Romeo and Juliet, we were both amused and aghast at the bathroom facilities. One must stand over a grated trough and "go." It was rather too public and too wet for my tastes, however interesting the practice. But it was the only thing available, so that is what we did.

On to Pompeii, something I had always dreamed of and had never done. The ruins of Pompeii. I was so excited I didn't sleep the night before. As we traveled through the valley of Anzio and the battlegrounds of World War II, I was amazed at how much it didn't look a likely place for a battleground. There among the riches of a fertile valley lay the remnants of a war so terrible as to take the lives of thousands of people. Rusted jeeps and long lengths of barbed wire inhabited the surrounding countryside. It has the largest United States military cemetery in Italy.

Pompeii has been deemed a historical site. It is manicured; it is staged as one would in a theater. Having seen the Coliseum, the Trevi fountain, and the rest of the ruins around Italy, I was surprised to find it so, and disappointed, to a small extent. What did I expect—mummified people, lying with baskets at their hands, faces of shock and desperation? Yes, I think, I did.

Sorrento is a modern city and filled with shops. "We are going to buy for the store here," Skip says.

"What store?" I ask.

"The gift shop on the beach," he says, not even glancing at me.

"Whose gift shop is this?" I ask, interested.

"Mine," he says with a grin.

"You didn't tell me that. Where is it, and what are we going to buy?" I am perplexed. Why has he not mentioned this before now? "'*We*' are not going to buy anything. '*You*' are going to buy for the store. Knick-knacks, statues, crystal, linens."

"Is that what you came here for?" I ask.

"No, I came here to please you, but yes, as long as we are here, we are going to buy for the store. So…you just busy yourself with things you think are as lovely as you, and I will go talk to this man here and make all the necessary arrangements for the exportation of everything."

Like a child in a candy store, I perused everything in the ware-house. I bought beautiful porcelain statues and dishes, embel-lished and unembellished. Magnificent inlaid wood trays, tea carts, jewels, and more crystal and linen. At the end of a very long day, we are escorted into the office of the purveyor of the establishment. Before him lay the bill of lading. The amount is fifty-five thousand dollars; American.

I feel I will choke, but I sit as if I did this every day. Skip signs on the dotted line: Marvin Homer Borhen. So that's his real name. I'm tired and it's hard not to laugh. No wonder he is "Skip."

The gentleman slides the paper across in front of me. "And you, Madame, sign here."

"Oh, no," I say. The only smart thing I was to do for months to come.

He raises his eyebrow and looks at Skip. Skip says, "Oh, I am responsible."

So he owns a business in Lompoc, a gift store on the beach that sells magnificent gifts, not unlike the Madonna Inn in San Luis, evidently. I have known him for more than a year, and I knew nothing of this. What an enigma this man is.

Early the next day, we take a boat to the Isle of Capri. We queue up along with a long line of tourists to take the tiny rowboat, with their native Italian rowers to explore the cave of the 'Blue Grotto'; the water level at the opening of cave appears to be far too high to accomplish this feat, as the four tourists exclaim to our Italian rower. ""No, no, lay down flat in the bottom of the boat, we get in before tide rises," he exclaims in relatively good English. We all obediently huddle at the base of the small row-boat with me being the 'lightest in weight'. The boat rocks precariously as we enter the massive cave, its crystal clear water true to its name. I am at once entranced with the story of the steps arising from the depths of the waters to the castle above, where at low tide, ascent is a possible use in entrance and escape for clandestine adventures.

With all of us leaning over the side to look at the steps going up to the castle, I fall from the small rowboat and into the water. Splashing and sputtering, I do resurface, only to endure the grueling job of being pulled once more into the rock-ing boat, teeth chattering and laughing. The Italian in charge shouts, "Hurry, hurry, the tide is coming in. We will be stuck."

Onlookers from the many other rowboats look on with laughter and encouragement.

Funny as it is, I was soaked to the skin. I was freezing and wet, shivering, Laughing and shaking from cold all at the same time, I say to Skip, "Please, just go to one of the tourist stands and buy me some sweats."

Wanting badly to cover me, he does as I ask. "They're fifteen dollars. When we get to the car, if you have the fifteen dollars, I could use it," he says.

What a silly thing to say, or to want. Fifteen dollars, after having spent all that money yesterday. Oh well, maybe it was *because* he had spent all that money yesterday.

Chapter 19

It is Friday night, and I am going to ask Skip to spend the weekend with Samantha and me here at the house. She is coming down from the beach, and maybe it would be nice to just *be*. Nothing to do, nowhere to go. I'll cook, and we can see how this goes.

We have eaten breakfast of sausage, eggs, fried potatoes, and biscuits. You can't seem to fill him up. I love to cook, and it is fun to cook for someone who likes to eat.

I am standing at the sink, just finishing up the dishes. His arms encircle my waist, nuzzling my neck. He says, "What shall we do today?"

I roll my head into his chest, smiling at the warmth of it. Love isn't everything, I think to myself. "Nothing," I say, "absolutely nothing."

"Really?"

"Yep, really."

Samantha is lying on a chaise lounge by the pool, and I am sitting in a wicker chair on the pink paved tiles, the balcony shading my head from the hot midday sun. The water sparkles as if a million little diamonds float on its surface. Fragrances of jasmine and orange blossoms hang in the air. What a perfect day—with one small exception. Skip doesn't seem to know what to do with himself. His discomfort is almost palatable.

"Come sit by me," I say. He sits, only able to do so for a few minutes.

"Really, don't you want to do something?" he says, in utter disbelief.

"No, this is what I want to do. Swim, read, lay in the sun, watch television."

Another half hour goes by. "I think I better call work," he said.

"It's Saturday. I thought your shop was closed on Saturday."

"Oh, I have a special job today."

He comes back and says he has to go to work and that he'll call me tomorrow. I was flabbergasted. But if my work called, I would go too.

In the next few months, he flew to Alaska to hunt. After a brief seven days at home, on to Tibet, where he again became enamored of yurts. This, perhaps, was having-it-all companionship, with the rare ability life offers to live your own life.

In August, we flew to Scotland.

We've been in the Scottish Highlands for ten days. It is remarkably beautiful. Much like the Pacific Northwest in many ways. The years of habitation, making the Pacific Northwest look still primitive and untamed by comparison. The roads are well maintained. The forest management is supreme in that they cull the timber, removing any and all dead wood, even though it may still be standing. The government determines what color your home will be, with only two or three choices, and never colors in close proximity.

The rivers are wonderfully full and seem to rise right to the edge, in the precise disciplined design of Mother Nature. The brown waters flow at a speed that keeps the mud turned up at the bottom, making it difficult to see deeply into the water.

Fishing rights must be purchased, something I found very interesting, It is generally 'let' on a weekly basis, usually one or two miles in length and often only the right or left bank. Seldom are both banks 'let' by the same person. The most prime rivers, commanding as much as five-hundred pounds a day.

The trees are wonderfully tall and majestic, both evergreen and deciduous, making a canopy of dappled light, as it bounces along the rippling water. Where red stag deer and the roe deer, grouse, white hares, capercaillie, and other game abound. Hunting is something that is an 'art' in this country. They feel that the key to well-balanced population lies in the correct control of the females. Much wiser, I think. The United States seldom, if ever, lets you hunt females.

Their pedigree Highland cattle are the largest cattle I have ever seen, with their thick bodies and shaggy red hair thatched in profusion over their foreheads. And the pigs, I will never be more amazed than at the size of them. Absolutely the largest pigs I have ever seen. There is a beautiful cow called the belted Galloway. It is all black, with a large white band all around the middle of its body, like a saddle.

The mountains are sharp, craggy granite, with scarcely any vegetation on them. I can see goats in the distance, only upon close scrutiny, looking for small white dots, and not looking for something the size and shape of goats. It's desolate, as we wind through the road to the Isle of Sky. I believe that's where we are going today. Yesterday we went to a distillery, Scotch whisky, namely, Glenmorangie, and Glenfiddish. The Scots started this little hobby in about the fifteenth century, and they do have it mastered. Eighty-five percent of it is sent around the world.

We have made *all* the castle tours and gone to all the woolen mills, of which I was sorely in need. A beautiful cable knit wool cardigan, a black wool straight skirt, and a couple of sweaters, and a new pair of shoes, and I was warm and cozy, ready for the Scottish summer.

We are staying with Laird and Lady Ian Chisholm, who are distant relatives of mine on my mother's side. They have a lovely house in the little town of Drumnadrochit at the northern-most tip of Loch Ness, nestled on a wooded hillock just above the Loch.

When I had asked Ian what kind of clothing to bring, his reply was, "Well, lassie, we are the same as you, in the middle of summer."

Just for the record, August in California is *verra* different than August in Scotland.

The evenings have been wonderfully entertaining. Ian and Mary have had friends drop by with fiddlers, and we have danced the Shottish, sang old folk songs, and drank Glenmorangie scotch, with stilton cheese and fresh picked pears.

We have taken this old relic of a pickup truck up into the hills and picnicked in the heather, while the cows and pigs meander all about us.

'Tis true of the Scottish mist. It seems to be a constant thing. But it is, to me, very much like home. However I must exclude the beds, single beds with thin hard mattresses, which are reminiscent of Venice, with the exception of the warm down comforter.

Tonight is the Grouse Ball, which I have been looking forward to it since the airplane ride over here. I knew we were to go and had packed a black velvet halter top, floor-length Valentino, and convinced Skip to buy a new black tuxedo. "Unless of course you want to wear a kilt." I had laughed.

"No," he said. "I think I'd look better in a straight skirt." He is funny.

The person who sat next to me on the plane was astonished that we would be invited to go to the Grouse Ball, as it is very exclusive.

"Really?" I said. "My relatives didn't say anything about it. Only that it was an annual event and we were all going."

Skip has been fun. He is more than willing to try almost anything—with the exception of haggis, I couldn't get him to try that. It really is disgusting. But the gravy is delicious.

Preparations for the Ball have been going on all day, the excitement and anticipation mounting with each passing hour. My hair is beautiful, if I do say so myself. Mary, being Ian's wife, did my hair pieces, and she mixed them with my hair until they were soft and shiny as burnished copper, with soft ringlets, hanging around my face and down my neck.

The dress is simple and elegant, with a plunging back just above the base of my spine. A simple cameo at my throat. Black high heels, a small, emerald-green velvet evening bag with black braided shoulder strap and clasp.

Skip looks very elegant in his tuxedo as I place the cabochon ruby studs on the white pleated shirt. His hair and beard a sparkling white in contrast to the black tuxedo. *Much better than powder blue.* Will I never forget that?

"'Verra handsome," I say in my best Scottish brogue. "Ye'll do nicely."

He laughs and takes me in his arms. "You too, lassie."

The ball starts at nine. However, being so far north, the sun has not yet set, and the drive there is spectacular. Through winding Scottish Highlands, we traverse the ancient roadways, with houses dotted along the roadway that are six hundred years old. A canopy of rhododendrons, as tall as any trees, hang over the roadways in what must be a glorious sight in the springtime.

Ian tells us, "The government will give you approximately ten thousand pounds if you rebuild something that has long been derelict." Good business, I think to myself.

We arrive at a real stone, four-story castle, –*Innes House, at Elgin.* It appears to be about the mid-sixteenth century. There is a moat, a bridge, and a small (in comparison) courtyard. The doors are massive wooden planks with large, hand-forged hinges.

As we enter, we are all given a program for the auction, as well as a dance card.

As if in a dream, I follow the sound of the music drifting through the doorway.

I stop, stock-still at the sight before me. My first impression is that of an old painting with women in the most elegant of evening gowns, in the softest of chiffon, and the palest of pastel hues, many with white, elbow-length gloves, the buttons covered, tightly securing them. In their gloved hands, they hold crystal champagne flutes bubbling with the effervescent fluid. The room is of immense proportions, the walls of stone soar at least fifty feet, the great ceiling timbers stretch out in a gothic arch in support of the roof, and the floors are of stone as well. Smooth, and polished, through years of use.

There are long sideboards placed about the perimeter of the room, and they too are of rough-hewn material with benches to match, An ancient "gathering room," I think. I am completely delighted. I am brought to the present by Ian's hand as he touches my elbow.

"Ye ken close yer mouth now, lassie." As he chuckles. "Nuthin' the likes 'o this in America, eh?" he added, slipping into the ancient Scottish brogue for effect.

"Oh my gosh, I…I…don't know what to say."

"The men, my God, the men are gorgeous."

The room is filled with the most beautifully dressed men I have yet to see. Every plaid is there it seems. Every clan represented. I have never seen such beautifully dressed men in all my life. Who would have thought that men in skirts could be so very sexy? The kilts are of varied lengths, and I smile at that thought. (It is said that they wear nothing beneath them, their length determined by necessity.) They are complete with sporran and dirk, knee-length woolen hose, and patent leather shoes, with velvet waist coats in various rich colors of emerald green, ruby red, and a sapphire blue, as well as black and brown. The lace of the jabots are delicate and intricate, the lace hangs from the sleeves of their weskit as well. Some are sporting tams.

Again, I am brought to the present by the serving wench before me. "Champagne mi-lady?" she says. "Come, let me introduce you." Mary takes me by the arm and we make the rounds, as the music of a lighthearted Gaelic tune drifts through the air. Upon closer inspection, the women's clothing is old and threadbare. I am surprised and ask Mary about the circumstances for this as it seems somehow *out of place*.

"The taxes, darlin', the taxes."

We danced until dawn, with a midnight supper of herring, oat cakes, and coddled eggs, with great hams, venison, and beef laid out on the sideboard.

A night of glorious memories.

Sleep and a flight to Paris. At de Gaulle airport in Paris, we rent a small Citron.

Skip folds his six-foot-three-inch frame into the driver's seat with great difficulty as I burst into laughter. "Maybe you should let me drive," I tell him.

"No, you have to tell me where to go. I've never been here before, and you have." He hands me the map.

He is so cramped in the seat of the small automobile, it is with great difficulty he steers the small Citron. His knees push out around the steering wheel, and his elbows drag on his knees. "We are staying on the Champs Elysees," I tell him. "Just follow the signs to downtown…and remember the circles."

"What circles?" he says irritably. It is nearing eight o'clock, dark, and the traffic is horrific as it is a Friday evening.

"I'll watch the signs, and you just drive, okay?"

"Okay," he says. But the sweat is glistening on his forehead, and I know this is going to be difficult for him. Horns are honking, cars are careening all around us, car windows are rolled down, and drivers are shouting. Funny, he can kill an elephant, but he is afraid to drive in Paris.

"Do you want me to drive?" I counter one more time.

"No!" he shouts.

We have now made our fourth pass around the Eiffel Tower. I have tried to tell him where to go. But to no avail. He is simply too nervous to hear me.

"If you just get in the outside of the circle and turn to the left, we will be fine," I say in my most calm voice.

"Just how the fuck do you expect me to do that?" His voice is hysterical amongst the traffic and blare of horns.

Arrival at our destination brings nothing but more hysteria. There are no parking places for the little automobile, and try as he might, he must continually turn around. His frustration is palatable. The smell of nervous sweat permeates the little car. At last he finds a parking place he can back into. Rolling down the window and leaning his head out for better visibility, he proceeds to back the car into the parking place, when alas, somehow, he lays his massive hand on the window button, the window rolls up locking his head in the window.

"Get me the fuck out of here!" he screams.

Hours of frustration and tired from traveling, all I can do is laugh hysterically. Tears stream down my face, leaving me unable to either speak or respond to his hysterical screams for help.

"Do something!" he shouts. "This isn't funny."

"Okay, okay," I say trying to control my sobs of laughter. "Roll the window back down," I tell him.

"I can't. I don't know where it is."

"Well," I say between chuckles, "it must be on the door, don't you think?"

"If I knew, don't ya think I'd roll the fuckin' thing down?" he shouts to the outside of the car, his head helplessly ensconced in the window of this car. Getting out of the car, I go around to the driver's side.

"Can we open the door?" I say, between side-splitting laughter.

"No, I don't know where the handle is."

I crawl back in the car, surreptitiously searching for the door handle among his gargantuan limbs. "Ah, I've found it," I say as I tug on the door handle. It springs free, dragging Skip's head with it as the doors swings outward, accompanied by screams of pain and curses.

Walking again to the driver's door, I can now see, through tears of laughter, the buttons that control the window. "Here it is," I say.

"Quit your goddamn laughing and get me out of here!" he says through clenched teeth as well as clenched head.

"Okay, I'm going to," I reach in and push the window. It goes up. He screams, spewing more foul language. "I'm sorry," I say, fighting for control and hoping no one is around to witness this most unlikely event. "I can't see it either," I tell him.

The very red skin of his cheek now hangs over the glass of the car window as it hugs his face tightly within its once-benign jaws.

"Now I'm going to push the other way. Okay?"

"Just do it!" he screams. The window descends to its previous, nonlethal position as I push down on the button. He extracts his head from the window, and I see it indeed has broken the skin on the side of his face.

"Oh, I'm *so* sorry. Are you alright?" His dignity is beyond repair, however, and has in fact been replaced by unsuppressed anger.

The anger abated after a day or two, the open wound on the side of his face was to remain for nearly two weeks. And we were never to speak of it again.

The remainder of the trip paling in comparison, we stayed in Paris only a few days as he hated it. Then we drove on to Bruges, where we spent a peaceful few days among the ancient little city with its quaint shops and women making lace on street corners.

Chapter 20

Having been home but two days, my suitcases still piled on the floor with mounds of laundry and every manner of memorabilia piled in chaotic disorder, he wants me to meet him in Santa Ynez at a Wine Festival. "Oh, Skip, I really can't," I plead. "Work has been terrible. I've never been gone so much. I haven't even unpacked yet."

"You can do that tomorrow, Cara. Come on, I need you to come to this. Come on. There will always be work to do. There are a lot of people you need to meet here."

Never being one who "needs" to meet people, I have my doubts, but as usual, I acquiesce. As he so often reminds me, "That is part of a relationship."

The winery is located in the beautiful Foxen Canyon, just north of Santa Ynez Valley, and I have always loved the drive. Golden brown hills dotted with cattle rise against the azure blue sky, billowing cotton white clouds nowhere to be seen.

Beautiful old oak trees, with their gnarled torsos, skirt the old country road, leaving it dappled in sunlight. With streams running along the side of the old two-lane road making quiet gurgling noises. The air is soft with the sweet smell of tall grasses, moist earth and unfettered nature. I am not certain what road to take, but I have never minded being lost.

The Mercedes cruises smoothly along the country road as I feel my shoulders relax and my mind clear. It is always like this in the car. The car is big and solid, reliable, with its timeless design, it hugs the road and just goes. I more than likely will not hear from him for the next week, I think to myself. And then I can get caught up at work and at home. I told Samantha I would wallpaper her living room too. I like doing that. Really, I like to work. To produce. To be of service.

There are small signs on the roadside, "Wine Festival Ahead." So that takes the "lost" out of my thoughts.

I turn to the right, with the always-impressive oak trees lining a roadway that is complete with yellow line, the split-rail fence flanking the roadside leading up to a magnificent stone building reminiscent of Scotland's castles. The vineyards are in their neat rows of perfect order and seem to go on forever. With the occasional sun-browned Mexican stooping to tend to the gnarled branches of the beautifully leafed vine. The still-hard clusters of green grapes glisten in the sunlight. Chardonnay, the small sign says.

As I turn the corner, I see Skip resting against the powder blue of his Corvette. He has saved a parking place for me, and I pull the big gold Mercedes in next to his small sleek automobile. He comes to open the door for me and gives me a big hug as I get out of the car. His enthusiasm, as always, is contagious.

"You look wonderful," he says as he surveys my white pants and halter top, with my pink high-heeled sandals, the large brimmed picture hat matching the pink of the sandals.

The muffled sounds of music and laughter drift to us from inside the winery. "Everyone is here today," he says excitedly.

"And *who* is everyone?" I ask, grinning.

"Fess Parker, James Brolin, Jim Arness."

"Really?"

"Yeah, well, they all own wineries in the area, so they're all here to push their product." We walk the expanse of the parking lot, and immediately people are clamoring to talk and to have us taste the wine.

The wines and champagne flow in no distinguishing order. The hors d' oeuvres are carried on large sterling silver trays by men in tuxedos. The music is delightful.

All in all, I am having a wonderful time.

But as dusk starts to settle on the idyllic setting, the heat and the wine have given me a headache, and I simply must go home. Disengaging myself from this last man to corner me, I look around the room for Skip. Pushing through the throngs of people, who by now are all pretty much inebriated, I finally find him, actually I *hear* his booming voice in the far corner of the room. As I stand close to him, he reaches out and pulls me, rather roughly, to him. "And this, gentlemen, is my soon-to-be wife," he says, his voice booming and boisterous.

"Tell them, say yes," he says, his bright blue Santa Claus eyes hard with the glint of defiance in them. I turn to look at him, shocked. Standing on tip-toe, I whisper in his ear, "I'm going to go home now."

"Not now," he says. "We are just getting started." His elbow encircled around my neck and roughly pulled me to him. "Tell them you're going to marry me."

"No, I'm going now. Do you want to walk me to the car?" I extract myself from the head lock he has on me. I hate it when he drinks. Actually, I hate it when anyone drinks. He is loud and rough.

"Okay, okay," he says.

Walking to the car, I say, "What is that all about? Me going to be your wife?"

"You are, Cara."

"I haven't ever said I would marry you. Remember, I said I never wanted to get married. You said that too. Remember?"

"But, Cara, I can't do this too much longer. You have to decide, or I have to move on."

The door shuts on the car. I am so shocked, I can't move. I look at his back as he walks back up the small incline to the winery. Did he just give me an ultimatum? He did.

He can't wait any longer...what is that supposed to mean? The anger wells up inside me as I start the car. The nerve of him. To say that in front of all those people. To taunt and try to embarrass me. What did he mean when he said, *"I can't do this too much longer?"*

The car scoots down the road toward home, the incident replaying in my mind. Suddenly something begins to mix with the anger. Panic comes to sit hard in the pit of my stomach. Both hands grip the top of the steering wheel as I careen around curves. Tears welling up in my eyes, I can no longer see. Coming to my senses finally, I pull off the side of the road. The tears spill out in a torrential cascade down my face as my body shudders in great heaving sobs. I can't marry him, I just can't. I love Tony. I will always love Tony. I miss him so much. I would give up all the movie stars, all the trips to Europe just to have him back. Please, God, help me.

I sniffle, raise my sobbing face from the steering wheel, and reach in the glove compartment for a napkin. Get a grip, I tell myself, as I blow my nose noisily into the scratchy napkin.

The drive home brings despair and anger, again replaced by panic. Panic that once again I will be alone. Without a man. Socially unacceptable. Society says they don't care, but they do. Life is geared for men and women together. Women alone are both pitied and feared. The panic is all-consuming, accompanying me well into the night. If I don't marry him, he will leave, and my life will go back to its previous ho-hum. Work, work, and more work. With some social encounters, some wonderful vacations, but essentially, I will be by myself. Or I could marry him. To be trapped forever in his lifestyle, with him. I hated it...to have him in my bed.

The early morning light filters slowly through the bedroom windows, and as I pull the covers over my head, I think, he was drunk, he won't remember, and I won't ever mention it.

Again, it is Thursday before I hear from him. "Cara, how are you?" he says in his jovial, booming voice.

"I am fine, how are you? What have you been up to?"

"Thought we'd go to dinner tonight. Okay?"

"Sure," is my only response.

"Okay, I'll pick you up about six thirty."

"That's fine." I hang up the telephone. My nerves, taut with anxiety. So I guess I can't forget it happened. We'll see if he says anything.

He said something, all right.

"I love you. I want you. Make up your mind. I want to be your husband. I want to take care of you." The evening drones on with his argument always being, "Things change, we get along well together. You will learn to love me because I am going to be so good to you, you will think you've died and gone to heaven." He begged, he pleaded, he cried.

I finally said I would go to my parents, I would think about it, and when I came back, I would let him know. Funny that I should think by going away I could make up my mind. I have a bad habit of doing that. Running away.

Chapter 21

As the plane makes its descent into Seattle, my heart leaps at the beauty that unfolds below me. Emerald green evergreens, snow-covered majestic mountains surrounded by the vast expanse of blue waters, glistening as if tiny diamonds had been scattered over them. The ferry makes its way across the Sound, as the Olympic Mountains rise, jutting up in protest against the pink and purple of the sunset.

My daughters always thought this is what heaven would be like.

Is it, Jillian? I ask as the pain tugs at my heart and tears start to well in my eyes. It is far more beautiful, I am sure, because you are there.

Beauty and pain seem to be the same emotion. Breathe deeply, everything is fine.

Even the airport is clean by comparison, but who comes here? You could shoot a cannon through the city streets, as my father expertly maneuvers us through the city, sweeping up and down the steep hills of Seattle to the ferry dock.

Only forty miles away, it will take us over two hours to traverse the ferry, the country roads, the Hood Canal Bridge, with more country roads before arriving at their home. It is perched on the northern tip of the Quimper Peninsula on the Admiralty Inlet. The Hood Canal and Puget Sound converge as they travel on in their separate directions. With the Cascades on one side and the Olympics on the other, it is a sight that makes driving dangerous as one is struck dumb and unable to think by the shocking beauty of it all.

There are few services available. An international airport boasts a dirt runway with cows grazing on its nubbins of grass. The deer wander freely among the downtown shops. With gaily-colored baskets swinging from the light poles of the eighteenth-century-converted gas lanterns. The buildings are primarily of Victorian architecture, with brick that is slowly losing its mortar and window casements adorned with peeling white paint. They are still as resplendent as a great Victorian lady—copper-clad roof turrets that turned turquoise over years of salt sea air and gargoyles leaping beneath fascia of shell motif and dentil molding. Lentils of elaborate design grace each building in succession, with a color palette of rich red, creams, and turquoise. Thinking it to be the center of commerce for the state, the forefathers took great care in its design. The courthouse is of a grandeur and size unexpected in an area so remote. As is the post office. The clock tower can be seen for miles as it tolls the passing of time.

As all seafaring traffic must come by here and since the bay was adequate for deep-hulled ships, it was the perfect spot for the founding fathers of Central City to be certain their investments were safe. They took great care in the planning and building of their homes and places of worship. The homes still sit in all their grandeur amidst lavish lawns and garden architecture. With views of the Pacific Ocean, the shipping canals and the majestic mountain ranges to the west and east. Snow-capped mountains on a clear day are able to set your heart to flutter, leaving you breathless.

The Asian people came on the boats from the east and lived in the underground tunnels that connect the city with the World War I army base of Fort Worden. The ones that stayed were used harshly to work on the docks and serve the gentry of the hopeful people of the city. But with the passing of time it was apparent that this was not to be. The ships found it easier to unload at the docks of Seattle, as the railroad was there, and it was in fact, on the mainland.

The city dwindled to a mere ghost town, gradually becoming only a tourist attraction for its old world charm and historic value. With the passing of time, it has become a popular place for Hollywood to film, for artists and writers to stimulate their imagination. Because of this, it is not unusual to see famous personages within its realm.

Boasting only one grocery store, a hardware store, and mom-and-pop stores, denying admission of any chains of a retail nature, it leaves you living in the past. Remote and isolated, it remains a world unto itself. Still, my parents found comfort and solace here. With time and a small but adequate income, they could travel to the "other side" if the desire or necessity were to arise. Mother drew house plans on the back of an envelope, and my father built the house.

The house is comfortable and homey, and the wood stove makes it both warm and inviting. Windows abound as the view is spectacular, with the water and sky changing colors as the day progresses. Sunsets to delight even the most discerning of observers.

We fish and crab and dig for razor back clams. We eat clam fritters and oysters fried perfectly, with fresh shelled green peas and corn on the cob from their vegetable garden. Flowers of sweet peas graced the table, and the pleasure of their fragrance will forever remind me of my parents. We play cards and talk, talk of great and small things. Both of importance and of little importance. And I was reminded of the briefness of life. Of desires unfulfilled. Of the regret of the things not done. Of courage lost from fear of failure or from the fear of what others will think.

I listen to them and am reminded of my inheritance, the gift of courage to be anything I wanted to be. I dreamed of having been raised without prejudice as to my gender or those around me, to not be limited by the fact that I was a woman in a man's world, longed for a relationship of loyalty and kindness between a man and a woman. A relationship of the equality of their very natures. A relationship built on trust and respect for each other and the sanctity of their union. Their roles perhaps definitive. He the provider and the protector, she the nurturer and the keeper of the hearth. To nurture and respect each other. To find solace in each other. To be friends.

I wanted that, I deserved that. I was also afraid of another failure.

"You're strong, you're capable. What's the worst thing that could happen?" my mother says with great conviction. "You know what they say; what doesn't kill you makes you stronger."

"If that is true I should be tough as nails. I don't know Mother, I could not be able to love him…I could get another divorce…" I say, dish towel in hand, as I am drying the dishes.

My mother, standing at the sink, with her hands immersed in sudsy dish water, stops her dishwashing, leans her hand on the edge of the sink, and looks up at me from her small round hazel eyes blazing of intelligence. She says, "Oh, posh, so what? Your life has been fraught with losses and hardships. You are strong, and if you don't take this chance now, you will forever be alone. Love is a romantic notion of the young. Friendship is what you need and well, trust. Mind you, alone is okay. Marriage is not for everyone, but if you think he is a good person and can support himself, we don't want anymore of the other kind. Do it. Your great-grandmother was married six times. Just go to a lawyer first so that what you have does not become his. You've worked far too hard to have that happen."

My, how she had changed, perhaps wisdom does come with age. *Or* perhaps she too would like for me to have *a respectable life?*

Chapter 22

The wedding was on. The prenuptial was a grating problem as he has refused to sign one. However, faced with the fact that I would not marry without him signing on the dotted line, he very quickly signed on that dotted line.

We were married in Michael Jackson's hotel in Los Olivas at Christmastime, with only my Samantha and a friend of his in attendance. The holidays are busy times at work and at home. Friends and family came, and we celebrated the holidays. The honeymoon would wait.

He hasn't moved his things into my home and has stayed only infrequently. His excuse was, "My house cannot be left alone, and I am closer to work."

On several occasions, we have planned to have dinner together. Having prepared it and waited for several hours, I put the untouched food away.

He has offered no money for living expenses, and I feel uncomfortable approaching him concerning this. I am certain it has merely slipped his mind.

We have been married nearly two months, and one evening having just returned from dinner, he stands in the garage looking longingly at my Mercedes. "Is the Mercedes paid for?" he asks.

"Yes, it is. Both that and the El Camino are paid for, why?"

"Well, I think I would like to own half of it," he replies, placing his arm around me.

I glance up at him and say, "Why? You have all those cars."

"Well, I let the Cadillac go back. It was only leased. So I think it would be best if I just owned half of your car. I would be happy to pay you for my half."

"No, it's my car, and I like having my own car," I tell him. "But I *would* like you to give me the household money we discussed."

"Oh sure, I will, I'm just a little short this month. But I'll make it up to you the end of this month. I've got a big job and it's nearly done."

This seems reasonable to me.

In March, we made an appointment to do our taxes with his tax consultant as mine was in San Francisco. Skip thought it necessary to file jointly. "It's more cost effective," he said.

A pleasant man, Jeff Bloomquist peers over his glasses at me and asks, "How much do you know of his affairs?"

"Only what he has told me." I glance at Skip, who is squirming in his chair.

"And that is…" Jeff says.

"That he owns some apartment buildings, a home, a couple of lots, and a business and the land it is on. Oh, and the gift shop…the cabin at the lake."

The silence is thick. I glance back and forth at the two of them.

"Isn't that correct? That is what you listed on the pre-nup as assets." The palms of my hands are suddenly moist and clammy.

"What did he say his income was?" Jeff asks.

"Eight thousand a month. He said he would give me four of that for our household," I blurt out, me being the one squirming now, the silk of my blouse beginning to stick to my back under the tailored black of my suit.

"Do you know his bookkeeper has retired?"

"Well certainly, we had a retirement party for her at my home just last month. But I…I don't know what that has to do with anything. Employees change all the time." Suddenly the small, snippy words of the bookkeeper of ten years creep into my mind. "I'm tired of taking care of Skip Borhen. He can just find someone else to do his dirty work."

At the time, I had thought, what a nasty thing to say about someone you had worked for, for ten years. I feel the straightening of my back, the set of my mouth, as I look first to Skip and then to Jeff. "Let's just get this over with. Tell me the real story of his assets."

So it begins.

The ride home is silent and endless. "Are you ever going to talk to me?" he says.

"I have nothing to say."

That night he begs and pleads, he is so sorry. He will do whatever I want him to do. He loves me. He can't live without me. "Please, please, we can do this. Anything you say, I promise." His eyes welling with unshed tears.

"How could you do this to me? How could you lie? How will I ever trust you?" The tears of grief and despair spill over my cheeks. "You have nothing, not even the shirt on your back is yours!" I scream at him.

"I do! I have all those things, you know I do. They are just mortgaged to the hilt. I had a little bit of trouble, that's all."

"A little bit of trouble! Is that what you call this? You have mortgaged everything to go on hunting trips and vacations. To support yourself while your business floundered as you played the rich tycoon."

"I took you to Europe," he says. He is pacing the floor and wringing his large, bony hands.

"Yes, and you put that all on credit cards that are at this moment delinquent. I am so shocked I can't think of anything to say to you. Nothing, nothing at all! You are over a million dollars in debt, with no means of repaying that. How did you think I would react?"

"It is only money," he says. "*We* are more important than money. Don't you see that? Is money the only thing you think about?" His voice is booming and accusing.

"Mercenary," my mother had called me at one time. She has also told me I was generous to a fault. Aren't these completely contradictory statements? Is money all that important? I don't know. You can't do many things without it, the most essential of things. I certainly have a great respect for money. Unlike Peter, it does not represent power to me, only comfort and security. I am jolted back to the present by his booming voice.

He's talking, hollering. I need him to just leave. Leave me to think this thing through.

Sitting on the sofa in the family room, money looks back at me at every turn. Money spent on luxurious surroundings. Unnecessary things. Elbows resting on knees, my head held in my hands, I lift my tear-streaked face to him and say. "Skip, tonight go to your house. I need some time to think. I just need to be alone."

Suddenly, he is quiet. "Really, you'll think about it? Oh thank you, thank you. I love you so much I can't tell you how much I love you." He is kneeling before me now, his arms clasped around my knees, head in my lap. He is crying. "Please believe me, Cara, I am so sorry. I'll do whatever you say." I stand, pulling him to his feet, leaning my head into his chest. He lightly holds me by the shoulders and softly kisses my head. "I am so very sorry. I just wanted you so badly. I'll do anything you say."

"Just go. Just go and let me think."

I watch as he turns to leave. He has no things here. All he has to do is turn and go. Why is that? "Wait, Skip, why haven't you moved anything into this house? Why are you not really living with me?"

His back is to me and he turns and says, "I'm waiting."

"Waiting for what?" I ask.

"I don't know. I'll call you tomorrow," he says. I hear the garage door close and the roar of the Corvette's engine as he backs down the drive.

Tomorrow, how in the world is one day enough to figure out what to do with a problem as big as this? My God, what next, Lord? What is it you want of me? Slipping my shoes off, I wander to the foyer and look out over the expanse of the rolling verdant hills, the ocean waves a soft white foam in the distance. "If money be your only problem, you have none." Who said that? I think he was an idiot. Standing, I look about the house, my home and my refuge, and with the flat of my hand, I brush away the falling tears. Is it the money or the betrayal?

I know...it is the betrayal.

But it is done. And in my arrogance, I am determined to fix the money. The betrayal, we will put aside, and try to forget. Time heals, and he says he loves me. I had often told Tony that love was a verb. Do I love him? No, but he is my husband. I simply cannot fail again.

I wander to the kitchen. Food is always a good equalizer. Comfort and solace. And something to busy yourself with while you are preparing it. Wine, scotch—no, that doesn't sound good.

A bath. Ah, that sounded good. Seldom am I truly dirty. I bathe for therapeutic reasons. The warmth of the water as it seeps into your bones, warming and relaxing taut, aching, muscles, the scent of the soap and the bubbles, as the fragrances lull you into forgiving calmness.

As Scarlett would say, tomorrow is another day.

<hr/>

The desk is deep in the profusion of papers. Seeming disorder rests across the cluttered workspace. Files stacked atop the depth of color in the oriental carpet. The tape spews continuously out of the mouth of the adding machine as the *rat-a-tat, rat-a-tat* of it echoes in the otherwise soundless room. A room I am comfortable in. A room I have spent more hours of my life than even my home.

There are no problems, only challenges. The cliché rings in my mind. I can do this. I asked that I not be disturbed during the next few hours, and if it looks at all feasible, I'll do it. As I lay in bed last night, I thought, what price do you put on companionship, on love, on family? When all is said and done, what else is there?

The hours fly by. I am in my element. Truly, numbers do not lie, and I am close to the end of this long and arduous task.

He said he would do whatever I said. I wonder if that's true. I can see it is possible to recoup some of his assets by selling off the most costly ones. Would he agree to that?

Then of course, there is the not-diminutive problem of his credit card debt. That tends to be a habit pattern. It is so hard to grasp the knowledge that I didn't see this. That I never thought to look.

Hours go by, and the clock chimes eleven. It is done, at least all I can do. Now it is up to him.

Chapter 23

Looking at the clock on the nightstand, its bold red letters read five o'clock. The telephone continues its incessant ringing. Oh Lord, not this morning, I think. Has a cook not shown up, an RN? I reach for the phone. "Good morning."

"Cara, my darling, can I come home?" My heart skips a beat. He has never referred to this as home.

"Of course," I reply. "I'll be home for dinner, and we can talk then."

"Okay, I'll see you tonight. I love you."

I rise from bed, stretching. The golden morning sunlight shines through the paladin window above the headboard as it glints on the thin gold wedding band on my finger.

The strangest marriage I've had by far, I think to myself. If we don't consider Philippe, and we won't go there...I think of Skip again, I am certainly glad I didn't want that three carat diamond he wanted to buy me.

I light the ivory candle and start the Raja yoga tape, and start as always with the sun salutation.

I dress, have toast and coffee, and drive the fifteen minutes it takes me to get to work, through strawberry fields and fields of freshly planted lettuce.

I am greeted at the front door by a very old, small man who has need of the bank to open. "Could you please do this promptly? I have business to conduct."

"Certainly, Mr. Baird, just give me a moment to open the vault. Here, you can sit down here and make out your check." Mr. Baird is a small, immaculate man of some eighty-odd years. His hair is slicked down with Brylcreem. He is dressed formally in a suit and tie and black wing tips on his feet. He suffers from senile dementia. He thinks that I am the manager of the bank and greets me each morning with the same request, that I cash a check for him for fifty dollars. I print out checks for him. Daily he writes them for fifty dollars, a tidy sum in a time when you made four dollars a week. The night shift nurses collect the money, putting it back in the office. We have continued this charade for the last ten years. It makes him happy and that, after all, is what we are here for.

The rest of the day goes by as usual. I make rounds, review charts, do the bank reconciliations, consult with department heads, review menus, orders for supplies and groceries, as well as maintenance records. I've ordered a new generator, and it hasn't arrived yet. For ten thousand dollars you would think they would be more prompt. Thank God the other one is still working.

A patient in the north wing has flushed a diaper down the toilet. I hate that. And the daughter of Mrs. McLeod in room 324 is hysterical because her mother fell this morning.

A relatively typical day in the life of a skilled nursing facility administrator, with most problems solved with investigative patience and tenacity in seeing that they do not occur again. It is not often I watch the clock, but…today I don't want to go home. I very much dislike that feeling.

I load the two boxes of files supplied by Jeff into the trunk of my car and place the adding machine tapes with spreadsheets neatly typed on top.

———— ✺ ————

Dinner goes by quickly if quietly. He is acquiescent and somewhat brooding.

But having survived the meal, I drag him, kicking and scream-ing, —at least mentally, —into the family room where the boxes await. He sits perched on the edge of the chair. Elbows on knees, his head in his hands, nearly jerking at his thinning white hair. "I can't believe this, it isn't true,…How can it be…" he stammers, stood up, and pacing the floor, then, back in the chair again. He paced yet again and again, all the while shouting. "It's her fault, Betty's,! It's her fault! She should have told me."

"No, Skip," I say, trying desperately to be calm. "These are your things. You have spent the money. You have to hold yourself accountable. You have an income of approximately four thou-sand dollars a month, with debts amounting to well over ten thousand a month. That makes no provisions for living expenses. And…your employees say you don't show up for work. So…" My pause is pregnant with hostility. I am angry all over again. "So what are you going to do?"

He is pacing again, running his hand through his hair, pulling it over his face, his long legs shaking beneath the heavy denim of the Levi's he wears. His cowboy boots, handmade of croco-dile, tapping on the birch hardwood floor. They must have cost a pretty penny.

"I don't know, Cara. I don't know. Honestly, I didn't know this was so bad. Honest. Cara, please believe me." He is kneel-ing before me, pleading as if for his life. "Please tell me what to do. I'll do anything. We could sell everything. We could move to Washington. We could start all over again. You could handle the money, all of it. I would work, and we could do this together. We could do this, Cara. I know I'm not young anymore, but I am strong and can work, and I'd only spend what you wanted me to."

I feel unclean, somehow, like I was blackmailing someone with love and affection. Do my will, and I will love you. I will let you live with me. Philippe flashes through my mind.

Skip's is kneeling, with his head once again on my lap. Sobbing. I am touched beyond belief. Perhaps starting all over is the right thing to do. A very romantic notion, to be sure. But practical nonetheless.

As if he can read my thoughts, he raises his head from my lap. He looks ancient.

"We could. We could start all over. It would be fun. It's a good idea, Cara. Let's fly up there and buy some property, and we can start all over. I love you so much, Cara. I just want you to be happy."

"I don't know, Skip. What about Samantha? I can't leave her. I won't leave her."

"She'll come. I know she will, and besides, she is a grown woman with a home and life of her own. You wouldn't be leaving a child."

<hr />

His hands are rough on my skin as he fumbles my breasts. The stubble of his beard is harsh against my skin. His hands grope amid the tenderness of my thighs as he explores the very intimacy of my body. His arousal is there; I can feel it pressing firmly against my thigh. Instinctively I know this too will not come to fruition. Is it my fault? I think as I lay beside him. Does he sense my lack of passion for him? The lack of passion that now mingles with hurt, anger and betrayal.

His kisses are bruising as they try to possess my mouth, to force his tongue deep into my throat. I know it is my obligation. I want to respond, but the pounding of my heart next to his chest is for another, for a man who caresses my body with the tenderness and strength of love, of a passion that consumes the two of us. The lips soft with tenderness, softly biting, a tongue that explored the very depths of my being. A man that so wished to own my own soul he was willing to sacrifice his own so that the coupling of our bodies was a spiritual encounter. Binding us for all eternity as our souls heated to a burning passion. A passion that burned in an eternal flame with an intensity that left us as one entity, one being, locked forever above the throngs of humanity. Afloat on a sea of intense light that fills our souls and our hearts that fuses us forever into one. One being suspended, diminishing all but the realms of God our Creator. Demanding that we love, honor and cherish. A passion reserved for the love of someone I would lay down my life for. Tony, oh Tony, I miss you so. I feel the tears as they slide down my face and into my hair. At the same moment, I feel the sticky wetness of his seed as it spurts between my legs, knowing that again, he could not wait. It doesn't matter. I don't think he knows. I don't think he cares. As Tony had said, "He is too superficial for you, Cara."

Who here has betrayed whom?

I lie with the great weight of this man on top of me, prostrate in exhaustion, and long for another, a man who will always hold my heart in his heart, my soul in his soul.

But that can never be. The world is filled with lines so fine as to not be distinguishable but by the sight given by God. We had crossed that line. Unintentional as it was, the line of trust was forever breached, and there is no going back. Only that thread of our lives remained.

Thinking I liked to be married, I married again, a dangerous liaison that proved to be, nearly costing me what remained of my sanity *Philippe*. Without the ability to share even the slightest hint of his perversions, only to hold those moments and hours of abuse within the depths of my soul.

Now this. I had once more fallen into the midst of a disastrous situation. Now, too late, I know.

I miss *my husband*. Marriage to him was what I longed for. Too late, I understand. The sobs tear at me silently as the man I am bound to rolls from my body.

"That was good, babe." He sleeps. An exhausted, triumphant sleep.

I put the house up for sale today, and I bought airline tickets to Washington. We'll go visit my parents as well as look at property.

"I haven't been this excited since I meet you," he says so enthusiastically as to be transmissible.

The plane has landed, and Skip has gone to rent a car as I collect our luggage.

Arriving at the rental agency, they bring the car around to us, a Cadillac.

"Why in the world would you rent a Cadillac?" I nearly shout as we climb into the car. "You're broke, for goodness sake." My anger mounts to dangerous heights yet again. The last months of trying to deal with his financial problems has left me exhausted and cranky, to say the least.

Chapter 24

· · · · · · · · · · · · · · · · · · ·

"Can you keep the books for the business, just until I get someone else?" he asks one night. With the stacks of papers already
sitting in my library. Do I wish for him to descend further into
the depths of financial ruin? No. That thought being unbearable,
as it seems I am to be the recipient of all the problems plagued
by this man.

It seems he has made plans for us to go to his cabin at the
lake when we return from Washington, and he has invited all his
children there to meet me. His *estranged* children. Interesting.

Monday of last week, standing in the kitchen, I heard the back
door open and the tiny patter of running little feet. "Gamma,
Gamma," came this wee, high voice.

I went to the laundry room door, where I am besieged by the
tiny groping hands of a small little girl, clinging to my knees,
exclaiming, "Pick me, pick me, Gamma."

I had no choice; I bent and picked her up. Seeing above her
head and tiny fat hands, I saw the face of my husband; grinning
from ear to ear. "And who is this?" I asked.

"This is JR," he said. "I told Meryle you would be glad to
watch her for a while."

"Really," I said. "And what is this 'Gamma'? Where did she
get that?"

"Well, that's what you are now."

Her hard little shoes dig into my stomach. I stooped to put her
on the floor. She was the spitting image of her grandfather. With

bright blue eyes and a homely little face. Thin wisps of brown hair and hands and feet, not unlike the monstrous ones of her grandsire. There was no denying that this was, in fact, his grandchild.

The stories of his children are varied and numerous. From drug use to suicide, children of varied fathers, to children of unknown fathers. He had a son that although bore his name, was not his flesh and blood; but the son of a man his wife had had an affair with.

"How come you never told me all this before?" I asked in a most accusatory fashion. "I am trying to be understanding. But this is a bit much. And *grandma*. That, I was not prepared to do at all."

I am jolted out of my reverie as he says, "Cara, where do we go from here?"

"Do you want me to drive?" I ask.

"No," his response is immediate. "Just tell me where to go."

Memories of Europe flash through my mind, and I see his head rolled up in the window.

I stifle a giggle and say, "Just stay on the interstate. We'll take the Edmonds ferry." As if going back in time, we meander two-lane country roads. We see the small mom-and-pop stores, with their antiquated store fronts, signs that say Mercantile and Hardware, and gas stations with round individual pumps. Skip is enchanted; *a place "no one will know him."*

Our arrival is greeted with heartfelt joy. I can see that my mother is smitten with this giant of a man as he takes her hand in his and gently kisses the back of it.

Looking at her with those sparkling blue eyes, "I can plainly see where your daughter gets her beauty." he says to my now besotted mother. He takes my father's small hand in his great paw and shakes it in genuine glee at having finally met my father. Shaking my father to his toes, nearly knocking him off balance in his enthusiasm. "I am so glad to finally meet you," he exclaims as my father scurries for balance, giving a soft chuckle as he does so.

"You never told me he was so big," my mother whispers as we climb the steps to their home. Soft, young-girl giggles, coming from her.

I hear his booming voice as he tells my father of our plans and extols the beauty of the country. His enthusiasm for this new adventure, yet again, is captivating and contagious.

Chapter 25

The land is damp, the thick carpet of dead and decaying leaves a spongy path beneath our feet as we trudge through land that is both virgin and untamed. The sound of bright red-headed wood-peckers pecking rhythmically at their work, the small skittering of tiny animals as they scurry to get out of our path. Making the shrill whistling sounds of their species, Eagles soar overhead in all their majestic beauty.

I would, in times to come, hear their screams, sheltering my little dog, as prey I was sure she would be.

The osprey gliding on the rising air currents were nearly indis-tinguishable from the eagles, and it would be some time before I was able to discern at a glance which was which. Only then would I think how silly it was not to see the difference immediately.

The fragrance of the ancient cedar, spruce, hemlock, and fir trees tower heavenward, creating a canopy above us of lush emer-ald green velvet. The peacefulness is pervasive in the gentleness of the forest, and I wondered at the many times I had visited and thought it to be suffocating, now finding only beauty.

A regal buck stands to our left as we make our way through the thick sword ferns, their fronds reaching to nearly my shoul-ders. His antlers are great in size, sporting six points each. His chest is massive. A soft snort echoes through the forest as the coolness of the air exposes the soft white mist of his breath. His coat is of the softest buckskin color; his tail a flag of white stand-ing straight above his heavily muscled flanks. He stands, unafraid, knowing instinctively that no danger presides here in this, his realm of glory.

There is a small stand of alders, a sign of water nearby. The western maples stand with their massive height as the only rival to their brothers, the evergreens. They would turn golden in the months to come and spread their dying leaves on the forest floor, leaving a carpet of rich colors that would soon nourish the flora for all time. Elderberry trees reach for the sunlight, with their oriental spaciousness, and ovoid, shiny leaves. Raccoons hang from the trees, not unlike the koala of Australia, with their little masked faces, and curious, intelligent eyes.

The early morning dew sits atop the leaves and fronds as the filtering sunlight touches it and turns it to the sparkle of crystal. The fungi sit amid the trunks of long-fallen trees and sports implausible colors and textures. As the logs themselves become parents to a new tree, its seedling is dropped at random, to help spawn and nurture. These are called "nurse" logs, I would soon learn. The moss, thick and resplendent under our feet, climbs the towering trunks of these majestic trees.

I am at once filled with joy, a joy so profound as to have no words, a joy so replete in its depth as to cause the tears to fill my eyes and my heart to bursting. A splash of the purest white catches my eye, bringing me out of my reverie. I look down, and there before me on the floor of this majestic forest is the most perfect flower I have ever encountered. It has three pointed petals, very broad at the base, and anteims of purest white poking out of it, as if in protection. The leaves are the same, only a deep forest green, the flower being about eight inches across and five inches deep.

"Look, look," I whisper, unable or unwilling to raise my voice loud enough to be heard in this, God's cathedral, "it's a trillium." Do they care? They do not. *Oh, well, I had better catch up.*

I can hear the lapping of the water in the distance, and as the forest opens, the sight of a waterfall looms before me...It is approximately five feet across, and a good fifty feet high. It falls downward in a roar of spring like power as it descends to the basin of the canyon amid ferns and decaying logs. The red of the elderberries making a dramatic sight to behold. This side of the canyon is much less steep as I scurry down the bank, the ferns protruding to give me some measure of control over my descent.

Sunlight spewing life into beautiful rhododendrons, which have glorious blooms of soft pink, their throats filled with the deep color of magenta. Their thick leather-like leaves, their sprawling arms interfering greatly with my wish to gracefully proceed to the bottom of this canyon. But alas, descend I do. On my bottom for the most part, with my mind trying to determine how I am ever going to get back up. I am now aware that I have indeed lost my companions in my preoccupation with the flora and fauna. I am not certain Skip or the real estate agent will look for me, but I feel certain *my father will*.

Arriving rather undignified at the bottom of the canyon, my tall, black rubber boots, now seemingly filled with any manner of things, my bottom thoroughly soaked from the sodden forest floor, I proceed to try and extract myself from the tangle of an evergreen berry bush I have landed in. Crawling my way around, I discover the largest, slimiest slugs I have ever seen. Yuck, I think, as I pull my hand away and look at the thick slime it has left on my mittens. Trying unsuccessfully to scrape this residue off with the leaves on the ground, I then proceed to dislodge another creepy little critter from his resting spot on a rotting log, a small, seemingly skinless reptilian thing, with great eyes, and a long tail reminiscent of a dragon. "Oh my goodness!" I scream.

"Cara? Cara, is that you?" I can hear someone shouting for me amidst the gulls overhead with their endless cacophony of noise.

"Yes, yes, I'm up here." As I stand, yet another majestic sight unfolds before me—the azure blue of the water with its tiny imitation waves dance at the edge of the sandy shore. Like yellow diamonds, the water glistens on the bay, and in the distance, looming below a cloudless powder blue sky rise the massive peaks of the Olympic Mountains.

I walk out onto the beach. To my right are the Cascades, with Mount Baker resplendent in its snow-covered glory. The beach stretches for several hundred yards until it reaches its rocky point, goes back the other way, and ends at a small, privately owned marina. The sand is the dark gray of northern beaches and coarse to the touch; the water salty and crystal clear.

"This is it, this is *it!*" he shouts. "Please say yes, Cara. Please say yes." Running down the beach, he is now upon me, and I am swooped up into his huge strong arms, as he whirls me around. "Say yes, Cara, say yes!" Too many whirls, we lay laughing in a heap on the beach, the real estate person aghast but laughing. Daddy is grinning and taking a pinch of snuff.

So much for bargaining power, I think.

Skip and I untangled our laughing, joyous bodies from the tangle of our fall, and the sparkle of delight is undeniable as I look into his glistening, clear blue eyes. We sit at the edge of lapping waves against the wet sand. The water is crystal clear, with the stones and rocks of ages clearly seen beneath the water.

With mud, leaves, and slug slime stuck to me, dirt smeared on my face, and my red stocking cap askew, I look up at him and say, "Yes, yes, we can do this."

In an instant, he is atop me, kissing, hugging, laughing like a small child. "I love you, Cara! I love you. Thank you, Cara, thank you."

The decision is made. We will buy this property with the money I get from the sale of my house, as well as something small to live in while we are building a home here. The real estate agent "just happens" to know of an old family house in town, and it will be perfect for Skip's work and a place for us to live in the meantime.

The house sits on the corner of nearly a city block, if things were judged by urban standards (which they are not). It was built one hundred years ago. From the street, you see a very large old shack the color of weathered dried mustard. I just want to cry. That particular feeling did not diminish as we became more familiar with the structure. It has been built in sections of small, inadequate rooms over a period of one hundred years, the additions placed at whatever angle or end of the house presented itself first. The first portion is a small kitchen area and a sleeping room, and upon opening the doors to inspect them, the cupboards are bare wood, rough-hewn one-by-fours, with knot holes in profusion. The insulation peeks through at regular intervals, revealing newspapers of the late eighteen hundreds. Mouse droppings litter the rough-hewn, unpainted surfaces. The floor is slanted, and the pattern of the vintage linoleum is worn away, exposing gray-colored asbestos, the pattern at the edge a bright yellow and orange, which is rolling away from the walls. This room now serves as the pantry of the house.

The sleeping and living room has been converted into a kitchen, boasting a real wood-burning pot bellied stove—vintage, who knows, but it is renowned to be the only source of heat in the house, which now hosts four additional rooms as well as two bathrooms. These rooms have been added in a helter-skelter sort of way. Windows on inside walls, and floors dropping off at odd angles; the windows in all but the bedrooms fixed in place, with no way of opening them.

A kitchen sink hangs on the wall with its drain board attached, and the faucets suspended from high above it. Vintage, probably 1940. The window above it, cracked—the casement sporting years of paint layered upon older cracked paint. It was déjà vu as my mind leaps back through the years to the house in Biloxi, and my heart leaps into my throat. I swallow hard, telling myself that this is only temporary. Another adventure.

There is a bedroom large enough to accommodate my bedroom furniture and a full basement where we can store all the things that will not fit in the house.

There are numerous outbuildings, with six empty lots adjacent to the house that all come at a 'steal of a price.' The plaster walls of the living room are cracked, and the push-button light switches, when pushed, seem to cause no response. Three old metal cabinets are anchored to the wall on either side of the kitchen window, and a small free-standing metal cabinet to one side of the ancient electric stove. A relatively new refrigerator stands to the side of the stove, and inside it are light gray hairs of indeterminable origin.

I hear the voices of my mother, father, the real estate agent, and Skip, as they run from room to room in their apparent excitement. I pull at the back door—it is hanging askew and sticks as I jerk hard to exit this nightmare.

Once in the yard, which is overgrown and indeterminable in its composition, I see the huge old lilacs of deep purple and white as they cascade over the end of the house. There are apple trees and pear trees, snowball bushes, and oriental poppies wending their way through the weeds to the sunlight. Smoke bushes, rhododendrons, and azaleas, spirea, and hydrangea abound, overgrown with limbs hanging from weather and wind. Someone loved this house once, I think to myself. For the plantings are done with grace and care.

There is an old woodshed that could be used for a potting shed. The floor is dirt, but smooth and hard from years of use. The walls have only the same boards of the pantry cabinets on them, and the sunlight filters through the cracks. This door too hangs at an oblique angle and sticks, causing you to have to hold the white porcelain handle and push with your hip.

Entry into the garage is the same experience, but ah, this is by far the oldest of all the buildings. Electricity added with no necessity to cover the wires that are strung across at dissimilar angles are attached to white ceramic conductors of a sort unknown to me.

"...a prominent family. They lived here all their lives. The mother and father each in turn dying, and the children and their children living here," Bob our real estate agent is saying as they come out of the house.

"How long has the house been on the market?" I ask him.

"Um...only for about five years," he says.

Well, I think to myself, so maybe I can negotiate here to make up for Eagle Point. Obviously, there won't be much negotiating there. Would living here be worth living there at Eagle Point? Can I really leave Samantha down there by herself? She really is not by herself. She has her father and grandmother, my sister and brother, and all her many friends.

How many times would this litany form those words in my head…in my heart?

The truth was in fact, could I live without her up here? My life has always been my children, with the exception of Tony. No one has ever been more important. I have never loved anyone so passionately as those two little girls. And since Jillian's death, I have such a fear of losing Samantha as well; it is at times paralytic.

Perhaps she would be set free to live her life, free from my dependence upon her, from the grave responsibility she feels for my emotional well-being. My cloying need to protect her. This is the child who stayed behind (remembering her words, when told of Jillian's death) to help me through life's treacherous path, as in the beginning, she saw I was ill equipped. Why was that? Why, why___ a staccato in my heart, in my mind.

It's only two hours by plane, I tell myself for the thousandth time. "It is only two hours to Los Angeles from Seattle, is that right?" I ask Bob.

"Don't know, never been."

"Oh, you have never been to LA?"

"No, never been to Seattle."

Daddy looks at me, "It's longer than you think, first you have to *get* to Sea-Tac. The small two-passenger plane that commutes between here and the airport is not equipped to fly in fog or snow, and then only during daylight hours. To, Chicken, there are no taxis, then, the bridges and ferries, ya never know 'bout them."

An arm goes around my shoulders and gently pulls me to him. "Come on, Cara. It's perfect, and it will only be for a year at the very most."

"I don't think I can do this," I say as I slide the toe of my boot over the dirt of the floor. The scurrying noise of the rats causes goose bumps to rise upon my skin, my meaning not clear to him.

"Sure ya can. You won't have to do anything. I can do it all. Just say yes."

Dinner that evening is an animated affair, with Skip and Daddy making plans to cut trees and build roads. They calculate how much money we would make from the timber cut and what the sale of that 'old house' would bring, the sale of the lots. Neither of them considering that the house had been on the market for five years, and obviously real estate was not in high demand here. Oh,... Skip had big plans, but it would take my money, my home, and I would be leaving everything I held dear. To say nothing of my financial security.

Mother rubs my shoulder as I wash dishes, "Do what you must. But I think he is a nice man. And a nice man you can learn to love. And love and companionship are worth something, don't you think?"

I shrug. "I don't know, Mother. What does *he* love, me or my money?"

"I think he loves you, Cara. He certainly acts like it."

"No...Mother...He doesn't. It's all been a sham, a lie. He has only debts, property he owes on, income not substantial enough to pay for it." I sigh and look at my mother. Her tears welling in her eyes. She looks away, emotion an uncomfortable, as well as unwelcome, state for her. "I'm going to try and make the best of it. If I sell my house and slowly pay off his bills, if he does what he says he'll do, we will be all right in another five or ten years."

"Come on, you two beautiful women," Skip's voice booms from the living room. "We men are ready to beat you at cards."

Chapter 26

Today we return the Cadillac to the rental agency and fly home to California. The ensuing days find us knee-deep in negotiations, with the telephone never ceasing it's ringing.

I run back and forth on the weekends to the lake. I clean and paint.

He has been staying at his cabin on the lake most of the summer, and is lean and brown. The cabin really does look nice. I paid to have a new kitchen put in had custom curtains and bed spreads made. He has a million and one reasons why he hasn't put my name on the deed, as that had been the condition on which I would invest my money. *But* he has been busy. Not making any money, just spending mine.

His four children have emerged from the depths of humanity with their other halves and their children. They drink, smoke dope, and snort cocaine. The cabin is a virtual fly trap for his many children and grandchildren, that and news of his *wealthy new wife*. As is my very nature, I am in love with the grandchildren. His children, ranging in age from eighteen to twenty-five, *not so much*! They are loud, rude, and inconsiderate of people and things. They never offer to help or bring food for the babies. They walk on furniture that has been newly upholstered or sleep all day and party all night.

This too shall pass, I console my assaulted, obviously fragile personality.

Paige is coming this morning to stay the day, and Samantha came last night to help us paint. What a blessing for me.

One of his daughters left her six-month-old in the playpen this afternoon in the 110-degree heat, with a bottle of liquid that looked quite suspicious to me. So Paige and I took the bottle and tasted the liquid. She has given her child wine with a little sugar.

I am trying so hard to not get involved in their drama, but this is just awful. I take the baby out of the playpen, and Paige and I take her up to the house, wash her tiny hands and face in cool water. She seems so lethargic. Her diapers are dirty and soaked. As I remove them, I'm shocked to see that she is so terribly scalded she could possibly have third-degree burns.

I feel a hand on my back and turn to see Skip standing behind me. "You're such a good gramma," he says, patting my back.

"Let me tell you how good a gramma I am. I am going to call child services if you don't talk to your daughter."

"And if she doesn't, I will," Paige chimed in.

"Jesus Christ, what's the matter now?"

"Do you not see what is going on here?"

He shakes his head and looks around. "Nuthin'...we're just having a good time."

"Yes, while she is out water skiing, drinking, and snorting coke, this baby is laying in a baking oven with a bottle that is filled with wine. You have got to put a stop to this."

"Hell, Cara, there isn't anything I can do. It is their life."

"True, but they can't do it here."

"Look, this is my house—" I can feel his anger rise.

"Fine, I am going home then. And I *will* call child services."

"Ah, now, I wouldn't do that if I were you. Elaine won't like that."

"Well, I don't like this!" I stomp off. As I throw what few things I need into the small suitcase, it occurs to me that I don't have a car here, and I am four hours from home. Samantha and Paige—thank God, one of them will take me home.

It's Monday morning. I had called the Los Angeles County Department of Children and Family Services. They said they will look into it, but that their caseload is backed up almost a year. And further, they said I should be grateful the child has a home. As I hang up the telephone, I wipe the tears of anger and frustration from my cheeks. Lord, what a mess. I dress and go to work. At least I have some control there.

"Cara, Cara, where are you?" his voice booms through the house. "I have a wonderful idea that will save us money, and it's something we need."

Boy, that's an oxymoron if I ever heard one. It's been three months since we bought the properties in Washington. I have placed my house on the market, but so far no one is really interested. He says he goes to work every day, but who knows if he is making any money. He wheels and deals and trades work. No amount of pleading on my part seems to make him understand that trading for work, when you aren't going to be living here, is simply senseless. Again I hear his booming voice.

"I'm here, in the living room," I holler back, rising from the piano bench to meet him. "How was your day?"

"Good, good," he says. "Listen to this. I think we need one of those four-by-fours for up there, and I talked to a guy today, and I can trade my work van and your El Camino in on it, and we will have what we need."

"What van?" I asked, still surprised. Idiot that I am.

"You know, I have a van for work that I owe thirteen thousand on, and if I trade it and your El Camino—"

"But my El Camino is paid for," I tell him.

"Yeah, I know, that's the good part. We will have only one payment, and it will be something we can use up there."

As it was, he was driving my El Camino back and forth to work.

The very next day, we are the proud owners of a brand new four-by-four. With payments of three hundred a month. I, once more, am down one more asset. His, however continue to increase. My reason for not screaming nooo…from past experience, it had done me no good. He does what he wishes when he wishes. The El Camino was in fact paid for; however it was old and only worth three thousand dollars at best. The most compelling reason was the fact that looming out there was yet another payment, a van that I had not known of, at least this would be in my name as well as his.

Within the following two months, he does manage to sell his business and lease the property to them at very nice monthly payments.

My condo at the beach sells for a nominal amount, considering the location, but it is what I paid for it, so I accept the offer.

Each morning he rises early and leaves for work; each evening he arrives at home with flowers or a candy bar. Something nice for me. His ideas are boundless.

"With the money from the sale of his business and the money from the sale of the condo, we can make two apartments out of the house at Bass Lake," he states with great enthusiasm one evening at dinner.

"But it is nothing but a shack, other than the new kitchen and the new curtains," I tell him. "The last tax assessment was at seventeen thousand dollars. It will cost a fortune to do that."

"No, no, I'll give Glen my truck, and I can take off work and I'll do all the work. And we can rent the top one by the week, and the bottom one permanently to watch the top one. It'll work, Cara. Trust me, it'll work."

Lord, my memory of his cabin is worse than the house on Sheridan.

But…(here we go again) the big ugly red dual-wheeled pickup with its monstrous payment would be gone, and maybe he is right. The cabin could be made into apartments, and Bass

Lake was a very desirable area. It was right on the lake, with a private dock.

"I don't know. Let me think about it," I tell him. "You would have to put my name on the title if you used my money. You promised you would do that when I re-did the kitchen, and I haven't seen any paperwork yet."

"Everything I have is yours," he says as he pulls me into his arms. I lay my head against his chest, thinking not of the smell of him or the hardness of his body, but that, with the pre-nup in place, as long as I kept track of the money, the cabin would be partially mine even if he didn't keep his promise. Trust, something I no longer felt.

<hr/>

The next week brings more excitement and surprises.

"Cara! Cara!" he shouts, as his massive frame collides through the back door. "My house is sold. I sold my house. Look, I have a surprise for you." A small box, a jewelry box, gift-wrapped with a large pink bow, sits in his great open palm.

"No gifts, no spending money," I tell him. "Take it back."

"Oh, Cara, don't spoil this. I really did sell the house today, and I want you to have this. I love you."

What, I think, is there to love about me? I feel more like his mother than his wife. He is like a big kid with no common sense at all.

Take the gift and be gracious, you are getting to be a real pain. "First, tell me about the house."

"No, open the present first."

Habituation reigns supreme at this moment, and finally, I say, "All right."

The ring is a blue topaz, about twenty carats, and with an emerald cut. The gold setting is simple and elegant.

It is beautiful. "Where in the world…It is beautiful. It fits perfect. How did you know? Thank you, thank you so much." I reach up and kiss him on the lips. "Thank you." I extend my arm to gaze at the beauty of the ring.

"I bought the stone in Africa, and I had it set for you for a surprise. Do you really like it?"

"I do, Skip, I do. It is lovely. Thank you. Now tell me about the house."

"Well, I really didn't sell it. I traded it to a guy in Culver City for his house."

Lord, I cannot take any more of this. I just can't. Life is too short. I want to scream at him, to tell him to leave. Anything, just make this all stop. I cover my face with my hands and drop my head. "Tell me you really didn't do that," I said. The feel of the gold of my new ring feels cold against the heat of my face. "Please, just tell me you didn't do that."

"But, Cara, I made a good deal. He's going to take over the payments on the house and give me the one in Culver City."

"What about your equity?" I am amazed that I still have the presence of mind to ask any questions at all. I was in such a state of dismay.

"Well, you know," he looked down at the floor sheepishly, "I really didn't have any."

His size 13 tennis shoe slide in circles around the walnut burls of the hardwood floors.

"Of course you had equity. You told me you built the house yourself with trades and products you took from other jobs."

"Yeah, I did, but…well I…borrowed all they would let me to go to Africa and Tibet, and you know…"

Suddenly feeling the need to sit, I slide into the kitchen chair. I knew that Jeff had told me, but… *none at all?* He must have taken out another loan. This is a nightmare, and I *will* wake up. "Have you seen this house? Have you signed the papers?"

"Yes, yes. That's where I've been. I thought you'd be happy. I thought you'd like the ring. Isn't this what you wanted?" He drops his head and pouts.

"What I wanted!" I quell the desire to scream. "None of this is what I wanted. Not ever!"

The anger wells in me as I rise from the chair to leave the room.

———✦———

The weekend finds us gaping at a small thirty-year-old flat-roof stucco house surrounded by corrugated metal. It is in great disrepair. We scrub and paint. He rents it.

Chapter 27

"Cara," he shouts, with his hand over the phone, his voice but a whisper. "What the hell is fora and fana?" His bushy white eyebrows drawn together in perplexity.

"What?" I say in the same perplexed voice.

"She says we can't disturb the fora and the fana."

"Who is that?" I ask.

"It's the real estate agent for Eagle Point. Here, you talk to her." He shoves the telephone in my hand.

"This is Cara," I say. "Is this Sharon?"

"Yes, hello, how are you?" says the voice on the other end of the line.

"Fine," I say in reply. "What is it you were saying to Skip?"

"I was trying to explain to him that there are very stringent regulations concerning the flora and the fauna in this state, and they must be observed." I am quietly stifling a giggle. Such a funny man. "That he would have to have permission to proceed with building a home and logging and that there are very exact provisos under which you can proceed."

"I see," I say, though nearly hysterical. "Then they have accepted our offer."

"Yes," she said. "On the conditions set forth in the contract and with receipt of the down payment of fifty thousand dollars."

"And when can I expect the paperwork?"

"I'll put it in the mail in the morning," she says.

"Thank you, Sharon. I appreciate that. We will review it and return it with the down payment as soon as possible. Or I will call you and tell you we are no longer interested."

He is jumping in glee beside me. All six foot three of him. "We got it! We got it!" he is mouthing. "Tell them we will take it." As I hang up the telephone, he grabs me, swinging me around in circles. "We got it. We got it." He is exuberant beyond comprehension.

I laugh and say, "Yes, they accepted our offer."

"What the hell is fora and fana?" he says as he places me once more on the floor, his arms extended with his hands clasped firmly across my back, his myopia becoming a severe problem to his sight.

Laughing, I say, "It's flora and fauna. You know, flowers, trees, animals."

"Well, I never heard that one," he says. A perplexed look on his face, immediately reverting to his erstwhile enthusiasm. "Let's call your dad and have him start logging."

"I don't know, I think we should wait, go up, and decide which trees to log and where the road should go."

"No, no, let's call him now."

"No, we have to have the paperwork done, and they want a down payment first."

"Oh, oh, okay," he says. He is quiet now, his head lowered, tracing his big finger along the vein of gray in the marble countertop. "About the down payments," he mutters, his eyes still following the tracing motion of his finger. "I know it's stupid of me, but I don't want them to know I am not the one buying it for you."

"What do you mean?" I ask him.

"You know," he looks up at me, his eyes welling with unshed tears. "It is real important for me to take care of you, and that's a real small place up there, and everyone will know if the money comes from you. You know, I...I...just want to be the man of this family."

"Oh, I understand. That is fine with me. But where are you going to get that kind of money?"

"Well, I…I thought you can just make out the check to me, and I can deposit it and make the down payments on all of the properties. That way they won't ever know, and we do have that paper you made me sign. So nothing bad could happen."

Men and their egos, I think to myself. I'll never understand. "Who cares about that?" I say to him.

"I do. I really can't go up there with everyone thinking you are supporting me. I don't know how this happened to me. I just can't let anyone know if I have to start all over again." The tears are now spilling down his cheeks as his big weathered hand reaches up to brush them away. He turns from me.

"It's all right," I say as I reach and lay my hand on his back. "I can do that."

Chapter 28

I arrived in Seattle late last night. Skip, for once, was in agreement that he should stay and work.

The excitement in the air is palatable. The fog is a heavy mist shrouding the water, as well as the mountains, giving a white backdrop to the heavy green forest. Trucks park along the small, one-lane road leading to the end of Eagle Point, unloading Cats and backhoes.

Large grizzly-looking men pile from dirty old pick-ups, laden with great chain saws, axes, cables with giant hooks on them. Daddy stands to the side in observation and concentration. His cowboy hat set straight on his head, jeans, and boots. The look, complete. He has organized all of this with the precision of a surgeon. He can look up at a towering cedar and estimate within a few feet, the number of board feet of lumber that tree will dispense. He has executed the "deal" among the lumbermen as to what their share will be, and what mine will be. I have agreed to give him a third of my share. A bit more than is customary to be sure, but I could never do this without him, and they surely could use the money.

The loggers are a battle-scarred group of men missing an eye, a thumb, some limping badly, and still they prevail. It is the only life they or their fathers have ever known.

The property has not been logged for over seventy-five years, the timber abundant and enormous. Some of the trees, a girth of more than fifteen feet and heights of well over three hundred feet.

It is breathtakingly beautiful, the shafts of shimmering sunlight beginning to penetrate the denseness of the fog, giving the forest an ethereal quality unmatched by anything I have ever seen. The fog horns sound a woeful lowing on the shipping lanes. A distant loon calls its mournful tune, instantly pulling at my heartstrings. Tony always chided Jillian about being a 'little loon'.

The cutting of the trees and building of the roads will certainly diminish the splendor that it avails. But I cannot live in the darkness. There are two canyons on either side of each property. The plan is to cut a road through the left side of the right property, affording a gentle slope of no more than forty-five degrees to the road as it twists down to the left-hand property. The slope of the property so steep, as it meanders to the bay below, that french drains, and an expansive drainage systems, became a necessity. They have to then be left to sit, as the removal of trees and disturbance of dirt and vegetation is a real threat to the environment. Once this has been accomplished, the well and septic systems will be put in place. The septic system is the most extensive of the two, as we have to have a gravitational flow system, and a large drain field.

I stand at the road in eager anticipation as the chain saws whirr in anger and the men strap on the tools of their trade. Large grappling hooks, gaffs, and leather straps that they use to propel themselves up the mighty trees. The forest being so thick as to prohibit any and all admittance. Standing at the edge of this profoundly beautiful sight, I wonder how these loggers will execute this task.

Daddy has marked the road with orange plastic tape. The loggers have quickly perused the area in question, and with arms of steel pull the cord to start their chain saws. They are all wearing knit caps and plaid flannel shirts, with the sleeves rolled up over red or black long underwear. Suspenders hold up their pants, stiff with dirt and grime. Boots heavy with cleats, laced in orange leather to their calves.

The backhoe is off-loading, and the large logging truck takes its position. The execution, symphonic in its precision. The first man steps to the farthest side of the tree nearest him. With an exactness of long practice, he carves a large wedge in the tree. He steps to this side and proceeds, with uncanny accuracy, to cut to the center of the wedge some ten feet away.

There is a large groan as this life form acknowledges its demise, and I am at once filled with grief. I cannot bear to look. Turning my head to the forest standing behind me, the groan turns to a creaking, then a thunderous sound, as the ancient forest succumbs to my will. The earth shudders, as if by an earthquake, as the first tree plummets through the surrounding forest, taking with it smaller, weaker trees standing in its path. The resounding crash shakes the ground for acres as it lands on the ground. It bounces several times before it settles silently on the earth beneath it.

The uproarious whooping and hollering brings me from my grief. They are having fun! Men are so funny. Daddy walks over to me, and as he puts a pinch of snuff in his lip, he says, "So, Chicken, what do ya think, it's good, huh?"

I grimace and say, "Yes, I guess. But is seems a terrible waste."

"We're not gunna waste it. We build houses with it. Make paper." Wandering off to be by the other men, as they 'buck' the tree and prepare it to be cut into nine-foot lengths for the mill. They would fall two or three trees at once, then set about trimming and cutting them, the jaws of the back hoe moving in to place them on the logging truck. The Cat racing in to push the debris to one side, as the procedure repeats itself.

The soft virgin soil of the forest floor, like chocolate cake mix, beneath the tracks of the great Caterpillar, it's blade pushing and plowing all things at rest before it.

The eagles soar above, making their chirping, whistle sort of screech. It is a happy sound as they look with interest as to what is happening. They literally scream when they are disturbed, and that gives me some comfort. There are four other homes out here on this point, so they are somewhat accustomed to the guileless-ness of humans.

I feel, rather than hear, the rumbling of a truck as it tracks the road. And looking down the road see a double trailered truck loaded with rocks. These are to be put down for the base of the road; the heavy equipment will traverse this road as they work their way ever down the winding of the property to where the geologists have determined the drainage field will lie.

Mother has arrived with sandwiches and cocoa. It is exciting to think that someday soon, I will live here. The thought seems preposterous in its probability as I survey the vastness of nature, and the process involved. Mother looks at the clothes I wear—high-heeled boots, soft suede fingertip coat, with smooth elegant gloves on my hands—and at my face flushed red in the damp cold of the morning. "You need to get some decent clothing to wear here. Aren't you freezing?"

"A little."

This evening, we go to the only 'department store' here—a hardware store with clothing. And as Mother and I laugh at the preposterousness of it all, I purchase tall rubber boots, a down-filled red jacket, leather gloves lined with fur, a flannel shirt, plain Levi's, and a knit cap to wear on my head. I look like one of the loggers. We had a good time laughing at how I looked.

The logging procedure repeats itself day after day, and I must go back to my work and my home, leaving Daddy to see to its finality. The drains must be dug. The pipes laid. Gravel, in increments of sizes, laid on the heavy rock, spread to make a driveway passable to automobiles, the debris burnt or hauled away.

The ground left to settle. To heal. To learn to cope with its new experience.

To learn acceptance.

Chapter 29

The weeks fly by with papers, flights to and from Washington, and money slipping through my hands in astronomical amounts. My "mansion," as it is clouted, has still not sold. However, movie stars from Los Angeles have viewed it, and it has been advertised in the *Architectural Digest* and the *Wall Street Journal*.

On three separate occasions, Skip and I pile in his old truck—another one he neglected to inform me of, and pulling a trailer loaded with his animal heads and his work equipment, we drove up the coast. Staying in seedy motels along the way, and eating dry bologna sandwiches. On one such trip, we have just passed Medford, Oregon, Skip has been expounding on the virtues of the car carrier that now holds his baby blue Corvette. "It really follows good, don't you think?"

"It does. That's good," I say. "Where do you drop it off?"

"Oh, I bought it. It'll come in real handy up here."

"*You bought it?*" I nearly screech. "You said you rented it." I have slid to the passenger side of the cab and am glaring at him, anger mounting beyond any hope of control.

"Oh, Cara, don't be mad. It was such a good deal, and I couldn't see wasting the money to rent it."

"Pull over now. Pull over right now. I am done. I am getting out."

He looks at me, astonishment showing on his lined face. "We're in the middle of nowhere." He laughs.

"I don't care. I'll walk. I have had it! Let me out now." I am straining to open the door. "Right now. Do you hear me?"

He pulls the truck and trailer off the side of the road. I open the door and reach on the floorboard to retrieve my purse. He reaches behind him, pulls out a little tin box, and hands it to me. "Here, you may need this," he says, with a solemn grin on his face.

"What is it?" I say as I open it. It is filled with change, maybe worth two dollars.

The tears streaming down my face in utter frustration, I laugh and climb back in the truck.

"I promise I won't ever, ever, buy anything again without your permission," he intones. "You don't understand. I've been a bachelor for all these years. I'm not used to asking permission to buy things."

What can I say? People are who they are, and "they" say—whoever "they" are—that the first couple years of marriage is the hardest, and it hasn't even been a year.

Seems like a lifetime.

⁂

The "mansion" sold for a little less than listed. But it is a nice price.

The movers have packed up all my belongings, and they now rest in two large vans in front of my beautiful home. I am filled with foreboding and sadness as I embrace my daughter for, I am certain, the last time. I cannot bear this pain, this longing for her to always be a part of my life, I have never been away from her before. How shall I bear this new and painfully familiar sense of loss?

The tears stream down our faces as she says, "Go, Mother, it is a good thing." Her bravery buoys my own cowardice. We look at the large moving vans as they sit silently awaiting our departure.

The last van is towing a brand-new blue jeep with a black rag top. The tires large and deeply treaded, the chrome of the wheels glistening in the bright California sun.

"Oh my god! Samantha, look, he has bought a new jeep." I say nothing to him. Finally stunned into silence, a silence filled with loathing, and a great sense of despair. Too late. It is done. I silently acknowledge, this will be my life.

———◈———

The palm trees and the ocean gently slide from view as we cross the desert of California towards I-5. Heidi sits on my lap, a tiny ball of thick black fur. Her small, intelligent eyes look out from the delicate features of a Pomeranian. She is Jillian's dog. A quiet little thing. Obedient and comforting. The gray around her muzzle belying her years. Skip's dog, Sable, pants unendingly in the back of the SUV. Fur matted and dirty. I didn't know he had a dog. But then there are so many things I didn't know, and I can no longer bear to even ask.

The rolling desert-looking hills with their scrubby little trees, sagebrush lolling through the land and the valleys of central California give way to the tall evergreens of northern California with its bright red dirt, the crystal clear turquoise of Lake Shasta, the rising majesty of a snow-covered Mount Shasta as we wend our way among the heavily forested mountains of the Siskiyou's. The peace within me has returned; for how long, I don't know. But for this moment, I savor the splendor of God's earthly creation.

The mountainous terrain returns again to flat, open road, and we have still not spoken. We stop in Eugene for the night. I shower and dress for bed in the bathroom. I enter the bedroom and see he is resting in the bed, propped up against a mound of pillows, fingers locked behind his head. "Are you ever going to talk to me, Cara?"

"Honestly, Skip, I don't know what to say."

———◈———

We rise early and resume our journey. We are to meet the moving vans at the house on Sheridan. Tumultuous thoughts besiege my mind. I have nothing left of the world I once knew so intimately. The connections and friendships of a lifetime, once more left behind. My child, my only living child, my home, my friends, the work I loved, Tony. All gone, I have given up all of this for a man I know longer trust and obviously never knew.

We stop along the way to eat and let the dog's potty. Still, we do not speak. My anger and hurt have turned to despair and longing, for that which will never be again

For if I have learned anything at all on this life's journey, it is that you cannot go back.

Get a grip, Cara, I think to myself. But the self-talk rambles on in my head. I know that I have charted this life, and nothing happens that you cannot deal with. Ultimately, it is for your own growth and knowledge. Is it? *Lord, you ask too much.*

Finally arriving safe and sound at Mom and Daddy's, my gold Mercedes sits in front of their house. The snow piled high around it. It has always been in the garage. Silly thoughts stream through my mind.

The vans arrive, and for ten hours, they shove boxes in the tiny house, filling the basement and rooms upstairs with only small passageways to traverse the clutter. It is overwhelming. And I am colder than I have ever been in my life.

Morning after morning, I arise to empty boxes, stuffing things in the decaying cupboards and repacking most items for the "new" house.

Skip arises early each morning and doesn't return until evening, saying he is "drumming up business."

"Can't you help me?" I plead. "This is just awful."

"Yeah, sure, tomorrow, I will," he promises. But of course, tomorrow never comes.

My mother says she would like to help, but that she simply can't." She says her health is failing and simply doesn't feel up to it.

My aunt June comes. She is wonderful. Marveling at all the beautiful "things." She is organized and thorough. What would I have done without her? Our laughter rings throughout the ancient house, her proclaiming Skip to be a bigger "clothes-horse" than either her nor me, which is saying a lot. Aunt June is married to my father's youngest brother, and although we are not related by blood, we look remarkably alike. She has a perpetual smile on her face, and the eyes of merriment only found in happy, kind people. Each day she dresses, puts on her jewelry, and her makeup. Her house is meticulously clean and well organized. She has a great love of animals, her children, and her husband, Joe, my uncle, who is a far larger man than even Skip, with the same dancing eyes as June. I believe them to be among the most well-suited couples and the most outgoing people I have ever known. They moved over here when they retired, and although I think he likes it, she abhors it. So I expect them to return to Wenatchee soon. In the meantime, I thoroughly enjoy her company, and my mother hates the camaraderie we enjoy.

Weeks go by.

Long-remembered family members grace my dinner table, and Skip is filled with plans for this and that. He is still gone all day, drumming up business and setting up the shop. He seems unwilling or unable to sit with me in the evening, at the same time hating the solitude of our lives. While I am becoming more and more introverted and frightened, he has made numerous acquaintances, wanting to be out and about at every opportunity. I find it more and more difficult as everyone praises him in every respect. If I were to tell them what I know, they wouldn't believe me or they would think what a "stupid woman" I was. Sex helps him sleep, he says, as I long for loving intimacy.

He sits in the basement watching the big screen TV, drinking wine, then comes to bed to slobber on me, trying desperately to conjure up an erection.

With my mantra becoming just one more thing at the end of each day of cleaning scrubbing, shopping, painting and wallpapering, waiting sometimes three weeks for paint, as we are so isolated. A world where distance is measured in hours, not miles.

I wonder if I was kind enough to all of those that have helped me over the years.

The bookkeeping and bill paying are the most traumatic of all my duties. It is impossible to keep up with his buying, wheeling, and dealing, always using my credit. Today has not been a good day. Today I have discovered that community property in Washington state means that I am responsible for his bills, that my credit is his credit. Should I wish to get a divorce, I would have to give him half of everything I own regardless of when I purchased it. Unless I am married to him for less than five years.

Of course the same holds true of him. But what does that matter; he has disposed of all his debts, and he has no money that I know of.

Today he joined the Elks and announced to me that he had donated one thousand dollars in our name to their building fund.

I join a yoga class and go to some spiritual organizations, but alas, they are exploring things I learned years ago. I join the church and find it to be more dogmatic and darker than I have ever experienced.

And I miss my daughter.

We play cards with Mother and Daddy and Joe and June on the long winter evenings. He says he is tired of spending time with my family.

Chapter 30

They have finished logging, and the roads have been built. The french drains are finished, the detention pond is dug, the drain field lies awaiting the septic system. PVC pipes of eighteen and twenty-four inches in diameter are piled, awaiting installation.

It is difficult to conceive of that amount of water plummeting through these pipes on its way to the bay; however, having witnessed it, I am forewarned.

Stacks of debris from the logging, the sizes of a large house, dot the nearly twelve acres of property. Still, the forest is copious.

The logs have been sold, and I have given Mother and Daddy a third of the income derived from the sale of the timber. Certainly, without Daddy, I wouldn't have known how to go about that

In the frigid fall air, I have planted a dozen cottonwood trees to line the roadway to the house. They grow very tall, regal, and will blend nicely. I ordered them from a mail order house. They are about six feet and look quite healthy. This is the most difficult gardening I have ever experienced. The ground is either freezing cold and wet or hard as rocks. The shovel penetrates perhaps a full three inches of dirt before it is mired in the web of roots, some threadlike, some enormous logs. The weeds hold on tenaciously to the earth as a newborn holds to its mother's breast. There are layers of clay that harden like rock, and given water, turn to a lava-like substance. I am used to the sandy loamy soil of California and am at once equally disheartened and determined.

The hours it takes to plant these trees are endless, but alas, my efforts are rewarded and the trees stand in sentinel to the roadway. They will look wonderful by this spring, I think to myself as I smugly place my tools in the little pick up.

Arriving early in the morning on the following day to water and tend to the new trees, I am mortified to see them lying, broken and bent. Some were even pulled out by their roots.

What in the world could have done that?

"The deer," my mother informs me as she laughs at my despair. All my work. The money.

Not being one to give up, and bringing Heidi with me, I have spent several days planting daffodils—ten thousand to be exact— and Blieanna pink plum trees.

The trees line the roadway (replacing the cottonwoods so devastated by the deer), and I have fenced them to keep the deer from eating them and laying on them.

The daffodils lie in organized semicircles surrounding what will be the side yard. The directions indicated one bulb at a time, so many inches deep. *That* is hysterically funny! I opt to dig twelve-inch deep areas of approximately five hundred square feet, plump up the dirt, and set them snugly in it. I then proceed throwing the dirt over them.

Daddy thinks I should have the timber milled. I think it is simply an added expense since we can't use unseasoned timber to build with.

Mother and Daddy have brought their trailer out for us to stay in while we burn.

"We," being an interesting concept, since Skip has left me to attend to the burning of the fifty-by-fifty piles by myself.

Enthusiastically proclaiming that a football game with his new friends to be more important than tending a small fire. *"Certainly I would understand that, having spent one thousand dollars on the season tickets, it was important for him to attend."*

Burning these massive piles of debris has proven to be one of the most terrifying experiences I have had.

The object; to keep the fire contained all the while it burns, which is normally three to four days. This means keeping vigilance night and day over a raging inferno, surrounded by only a trench of dirt and garden hoses stretching approximately five hundred feet, the distance from the nearest water supply.

The blackness of the night engulfs me for the second time tonight as I cling to Sable's fur and all but crawl up the mountainous road to where the little trailer sits. The batteries of the last flashlight gone, the flames of the fire popping and leaping in the distance behind my ascent.

What would I do without Sable's eyes and ears in the pitch black night of the forest, where, just yesterday, I watched in wonder as a black mother bear came out of the woods with her tiny little cubs scurrying along behind her, their coats slick and shiny, their noses like hard black rubber.

Deer and raccoons in profusion stand unafraid as they look with intelligent interest at what is happening to their home. Eagles as big as a large man perch on stumps and cock their snowy-white heads from side to side in silent confusion of the coming devastation of their home. Their shrill whistle of protest as they spread the glossy black span of their wings and prepare for flight to soar over the acres of devastation and again return to watch in disbelief.

This morning I found a dead coyote within about five feet of the trailer. Sable will simply not leave it alone. It smells, and the flies are everywhere.

I wrap a scarf around my nose and mouth, don a hat, and an old pair of thick leather gloves Daddy has left out here, and with my old jacket, jeans, and rubber boots, I close Sable in the trailer and go out to drag away the coyote.

She is small, but dead weight, and I cannot budge her. She must weigh fifty pounds. I can't leave her here. There is Sable to think of, to say nothing of the flies and the smell. I bring the wheelbarrow over, and laying it on its side, I find I can push and pull the dead animal into the wheelbarrow.

After many bumps and blunders, I succeed in getting the wheelbarrow through the forested floor to the edge of a canyon. With exaggerated effort I manage to empty the decaying contents over the edge. The fall, soundlessly descending to the cushiony floor of the canyon.

It was not the most reverent of burials, but with few tools and fewer muscle, it was the best I could do at the time—Skip being already a day overdue.

⁂

The pump on the well broke this afternoon, so now I have no water. I drove to the small volunteer fire department today, and tomorrow they will deliver a water truck. At the cost of a small fortune to me.

Daddy is supposed to come out today, maybe he will know what to do about the well.

I haven't had a bath in three days, I smell like smoke and am so tired. Each night, setting the alarm clock for every two hours to check on the fires.

Each day I push burning debris from the edges to the white hot center of the tepee it makes of itself.

Each day I water down smoldering ash as the heap of debris diminishes in size.

Heidi lies cloistered in the center of rumpled, smoked infused bed linen, her dense fur saturated in the odor of fire. The little trailer cloistered in the dim light of the battery powered lighting. She is unwilling to descend into the darkening of the day.

———⟆●⟅———

I fix myself soup and bread and butter, and wonder where *he* is. So this is the better life. Our frustration with each other is nearly palatable.

His mind is voluminous with ideas and enthusiasm. But I seem to be the verb to his adjective. I cannot fathom what goes on in his head. He seemingly has no common sense.

In the last year he has stood on a log sprawled across a 200 foot canyon, and with a chain saw, commenced to cut it in two. Falling with the chainsaw to the forest floor below. Miraculously unscathed, only frightened. He has backed out of the closed garage door, a door so old and decayed that not only was his truck dented, but the door destroyed.

He stands raking the forest floor and pruning the ferns, rather than cutting wood and digging ditches.

Before leaving, he stood downwind while throwing diesel fuel on the fires, before lighting them. And remained there to light it. Knowing he was covered in diesel fuel. I am yelling at him to stand back, to come up wind. But the flashback came. Not enough to burn, but enough to singe.

A city mentality, my daughter calls it. He was, after all raised in the city of Los Angeles; at least that is what he told me. I am beginning to question all things that issue forth from his mouth.

However, Samantha has always been raised in a city. And when she is up here, she seems to know what to do.

I hear a truck. Thank God, it's Daddy. "Hi, Chicken, how're doin'?" He hugs me and, frowning, pushes me back. "Phew!" he says.

"A little worse for wear, and I can't remember ever being so dirty. Do you think you can fix the well?"

"I'll go take a look. Where's Skip?"

"Lord only knows."

He looks down at the ground and just shakes his head. Alas! Once again my father is triumphant. He fixed the well!

"Oh, Daddy, thank you, thank you."

"Come on, I'll show you what to do. You just had to push the reset button. Nuthin' to it. I'll stop on my way home and tell the fire guys." My relief is obvious, and with reluctance, he leaves me to deal with my own issues.

The alarm on the old wind-up clock goes off for the fourth morning. I can hear the tiny ping of the soft rain drops on the metal of the trailer as I place my bare feet on the cold of the trailer's floor and prepare for the last of my imposed fire watch. I pull the stiff and smelly clothing on. Opening the door of the trailer, the pungent smell of wood smoke thickens the air as I walk to the edge of the canyon.

I sit on the precipice of the canyon, knees drawn up and fingers laced loosely around them, the fingernails and hands, greasy and gray with the soot and smoke of the dying fires below me.

The pink of the winter dawn climbing over the western peaks of the Olympic mountains give them an iridescence and casting purple pink shadows on the waters below me.

It is over. The embers are a soft reminder of their fiery lives of yesterday.

The heavy dew glistens on the giant fronds of the sword ferns, and there is a promise of rain in the sweetness of the morning air.

I can go home.

My forest is safe.

Chapter 31

· · · · · · · · · · · · · · · · · · · ·

Spring has arrived once again, and it is the most glorious thing I have seen. The air is permeated with the scent of flowers. The lilacs are in bloom. The daffodils and tulips abound. There is lavender spirea and camellias as big as saucers with rhododendrons in a profusion of colors. The lupine fills the fields in waves of purple, with the vibrant backdrop of golden scotch broom and forsythia. All with only Mother Nature as their caretaker.

The world is a blue and green wonderland. The mountains rising to the east and to the west, snow capped and breathtaking. The flower beds are as old as the house and laid out in a lovely profusion of color, depth, and texture. With the aged gnarled trunks of lilacs that have now become trees of the most vivid purple, white and lavender.

It all just needs tender loving care. And tons of weeding.

Remembering the old woodshed in the back of the property, I decide it would make a wonderful potting shed. It has a dirt floor, but is solid from years of use as a wood shed.

"Skip, are you in here?" I shout as I go out to the building that he has all his animal heads and machinery in.

"Yeah, Cara, I'm here."

"I think I might clean out that old shed and use it for garden tools and things. What do you think?"

"I think that is a good idea. Can I help?"

"Yes, I would like that."

He helps me prune and carries all the debris away. He mows and edges the weeds that have become the lawn. With dandelions nodding their yellow heads and four-leaf clover sprouting their fluffy purple tinted white flowers.

He digs and digs to get the dandelions out. "Help me," he says in great frustration.

"Oh, let's just leave them. We aren't going to live here long anyway," I reply. Still, he digs.

His daughter has sent her two daughters to stay with us for "a couple weeks."

They are great fun, but certainly a lot of work.

Peter and Ellie come frequently during the summer. We talk and play cards. I enjoy their visits. They very rarely go to Mother and Daddy's, and I find that strange and even feel as if I should apologize to them for it.

But I do invite them all for dinner, and often we go clamming on the beach at Mom and Daddy's house.

I think we all love to clam. It is a very different thing to do, if you are into hard work and filth. Peter is as anally clean as I am. So for us, it is an even stranger avocation.

I have never ironed my jeans (and I do so religiously), without thinking of him. He is the only man I know, other than Rick, who wears starched ironed Levi's with a crease. He has his laundry done however, as Ellie isn't interested in providing such obsequious desires. A very nice girl, but hard to know. She seems happy enough, but very seldom says anything revealing about her true nature. She has a nice sense of humor and loves her children. She is beautiful, with alabaster skin, jet black hair, and a face reminiscent of Elizabeth Taylor. But as to the duties of domesticity, she seems to either not have the energy or the inclination. She can come here and simply sit for hours, perusing magazines or watching television, never once offering to help. As if she were at a bed-and-breakfast. It has never made me angry, nor does it make me unwilling to do for them. It is simply perplexing. As women, some of the best times we have is laughing and talking while cooking, and cleaning up afterwards.

She seldom, if ever, has had dinner or lunch ready and waiting when Peter comes home from work, feeding a four-year-old Karen apples for lunch at three in the afternoon. The kitchen littered with dirty dishes. Her laundry baskets filled with training pants, with various sizes of toddler clothing, some ten years after the girls have needed them. Dirty clothing and an array of unused articles clutter the entire house, with some spilling out of cardboard boxes, some simply lying on floors of closets with doors unable to close.

She is perpetually fighting a weight problem, and I wonder instinctively if all this stems from depression, as I have witnessed the same in my mother over the years.

Even before I moved up here, Peter had addressed this problem, however fleeting. Perhaps, he is the problem; he is far more interested in money and power than his family. Never able to speak in depth of any problem he was having. Because he is a man, or because he feels it makes him look inferior. Or are they the same? I don't know.

Samantha has been here for two weeks. I was so devastated this morning when she left. As she pulled out of the driveway, I couldn't even watch. I'll go down to visit her in two months, but that, today, seems an eternity away. Parents just shouldn't leave their children. It is meant that children leave their parents.

Skip's granddaughters are still here. The *month* has turned to three. I am having a great time, as they too, seem to be. After a week of timely meals, baths, and bedtimes, they have succumbed to the safety of routine and order and have blossomed. I love the laughter-filled house of children and dogs, the smell of cookies baking, the safety of a child's hand in mine as we walk along the rippling waves of the gray sand beach, spying shells coveted for their collection.

"Cara, Cara, where are you?" his voice echoes through the house. It is filled with a joy and enthusiasm I haven't heard in months. "Cara, wait till you see what I have. You'll love it."

"What?" I say as I trip over the uneven step from the hallway into the kitchen. His arms are around me and he is swinging me high in the air off the floor.

"Come see." He is grinning from ear to ear and pulling me by the hand now. "Come on, you'll love it."

Smiling, I follow. This is the first time in weeks he has been happy. My insistence that he work and not spend any money is a very large blight on our relationship. The presence of his grand-children, the only happy connection between us.

"What happened?" I laugh. I am caught up once again in his infectious enthusiasm. The screen door slams behind us as his large calloused hands come up to cover my eyes.

"Guess," he says.

"I can't imagine," I stammer. "A new puppy?" I hear the screen creak and slam, and JR laughs and jumps up and down on her squat two-year-old bare feet.

"Oh, Gamma, it's pretty." She claps her little fat hands and squeals with delight.

"What is it?" I laugh. "Let me see...."

"It's something I've always wanted, and everyone here has one," Skip says.

I immediately envision a backhoe.

They are akin here to a Corvette in California. Something every man needs. Their garages are three times the size of their homes. My fear, quickly diminished anything faintly reminiscent of joy and excitement. I reach up and pull away his hands.

On the gravel in front of the fading, mustard-colored one-hundred-year-old building we call a garage, sits a sleek new white pick-up, and attached to this large truck is a very long, very white travel trailer.

My father and my uncle stand beside the pickup. My uncle is grinning from ear to ear. My father taking one look at my face, pulls his cowboy hat down further on his forehead. He reaches for his ever-present can of snuff and takes a pinch, deposits it inside his lip, and calmly sidles to the other side of the bright shining pick up.

"Whose is it?" I ask.

"It's ours. Come and look." He grabs my hand and pulls me along behind him.

"No, Skip. It is not ours. You have to take it back."

"Oh, Cara, Cara, my darlin' wife. We will have such a good time in it. We're all goin' to the beach and to Wyoming t' see your family. Come on, Cara. You only live once. Come look at it, at least."

"But we can't afford it. Don't you understand that? You cannot just keep buying things."

"Yeah, I know, but we can. I traded the four-by-four in on it." The doors open to the truck and now the trailer as he pulls me along beside him. His joy having no limits.

I want to just sit down in the gravel and cry. This will never end. We are not living from paycheck to paycheck. We are in debt over and above any money I make, and I make six figures a year. So far, he hasn't made any at all.

JR and Tanya dance around in glee, climbing in and out of the trailer, fighting over who gets what bed.

My uncle and my dad have reappeared and are adding the joys of trailering to Skip's never-ending dialog of "how much fun we will have." All I need to do is to go to the dealership and sign the papers. With promises once again from him, "I will never ever buy another thing." I once more do what I know in my heart to be wrong.

I sign the papers.

⸎

Laying in bed that night (after my "last duty of the day" performed for his benefit only, I might add), I think I don't like me anymore. I am very tired of trying to mother this overgrown boy, of being his pawn, of yelling at him. He is using me. He is using me to create a family he never had, a security he never had, an image he would like. He doesn't love me. He covets me. He doesn't care if I work and slave all day. He doesn't care if I am happy at all. *He* is all *he* thinks about. And I do not like what and who it is turning me into.

Lord, Father in heaven, I pray in the silence of the bed I share with a man I do not love, with a man I can never love. I ask that you intervene in this, Lord, to give me a sign. Is there a lesson I am to learn from this, or have I only taken the wrong road?

It would be years before I understood the lesson. Years, before I learned that I had not listened to the beating of my own heart. The fear that caused me to make the decision is the thing I heard, that I responded to. The God within me was telling me, showing me, that this was not the right person for me. It was fear of being alone that drove me to the arms of a man unable to love, to give of himself. His charm and charisma luring me into his world. I listened only to *his* words and not to the beating of *my own heart*.

Fear may be our last enemy.

Knowing that, I still, all these years later, am uncomfortable in the presence of most people. The hurt and betrayal of those I love seared into my heart as with a branding iron. Ill equipped to make decisions concerning my own well-being.

A friend once told me, "If you take a quarter of the population of the world, and divide it in half, then take half of the half, divide that quarter into thirds, the first third of the quarter will set out to get you. The second third of the quarter will try and get you if the opportunity avails itself to them. The last third of the quarter are good, decent, trustworthy people." Considering that these *good people* are scattered throughout the world, it is a very sobering thought, to say the least.

Chapter 32

Skip's mom and dad have arrived and are here for a month. They have brought their "fifth wheel" and are free to come and go as they please.

My first shock—the profusion of thanks for the wonderful theater-size television we sent for Christmas. The very first I had heard of it. How did he accomplish that?

John, I am not sure of. But Lorraine is a joy. She is wonderful with the children, and we share many common interests. She sews proficiently and is an excellent cook. She has an unending energy and enthusiasm. With this being her second marriage, and he having done the same thing to her as Skip has to me, it isn't long before we are exchanging "war stories."

***

Lorraine's birthday comes with the early-morning hours bringing a phone call from her daughter in San Luis Obispo. The tears flood her usually contained, happy self. I enfold her in my arms, rocking and consoling her while she spills the story of John's sexual abuse to her daughter and the subsequent estrangement between this beloved daughter and herself.

She would leave him, but what then? The money she had had was gone. The house she had when she met him was sold, and she is seventy-five years old.

My shock and anger were apparent as she went on. Didn't I
know that Skip was charged with sexually abusing his daughters?
Didn't I know that he had been married numerous times? Didn't
I know that he had put his first wife in an institution? 'Didn't I
know he was looking to marry a rich woman?

Small memories of conversations flipped through my stunned
mind. Meryle had said, "Don't leave the girls alone with Dad."

His charge cards with different women's names on them, all
with his last name…found while innocently cleaning out drawers. The unlived-in house. The leased trucks and cars. The buffed
and suntanned man I first met. The stooped and aging man he
is now.

I feel the nausea as it rises in my throat, the sweat as it forms
on my upper lip and down the center of my back. Revulsion now
has a taste. I pull away from her.

"Oh, Cara, I am so sorry, I never intended to say those things
to you. Please don't say anything, please, John will kill me. You
can make a fresh start. You're strong. You can make him behave."

"I don't think anyone can make him 'behave,' as you say. He
will tell you what you want to hear and do what he wants to do."

"What are you going to do?" she asks, wiping tears from her
face and sliding her tiny body from the kitchen stool.

"I am going to make coffee now, and then we will get dressed.
Then, I am making your birthday cake. What I'm going to do
about Skip? I don't know, Lorraine. I really don't know."

⟞●⟝

The next Monday morning finds us piling into the truck. We are
all going to caravan to the beach. Ocean Shores is our destination,
with Mother and Daddy in the lead—the 'Wagon Master' he
would soon be called. Skip and I and the girls are next, Lorraine
and John third, with Joe and June pulling up the rear. All in our
trucks and trailers, motor homes, and fifth wheels.

We careen down the small scenic two-lane Highway One. Through the Olympic Mountains, with the sheer rock faces shrouded in heavy wire to keep the rocks in place. Through the tiny towns of Lilliput and Duckabush. Along the four hundred-foot depths of the Hood Canal with its vast oyster beds and salmon farms.

We are all equipped with short wave radios, and there is a constant din of chatter between the men.

Mother decides we need to stop at Potlatch to sample the oysters from the beach. The girls are delighted, as are the dogs.

We arrive at Ocean Shores in the evening light of the Pacific Northwest. The darkness falling lightly on the ocean, the sun dips and sizzles, sending out an aura of the brightest pinkish orange, as it seems to strike the water in some distant land.

My mother and I are in awe. No one else seems to care.

Skip cannot, for the life of him, park the trailer. So finally Daddy climbs in and shows him for the fourth time, climbs back out, and shouts explicit instructions. At last they have success.

We have a succession of days that find us flying kites, clamming for razor back clams, and playing in the frigid waters of the northern pacific. We let the girl's surf fish, and they catch tiny crabs, with bags of sand and shells to "keep forever."

We play cards at night and roast marshmallows by firelight. Skip's laughter and enthusiasm are akin to Joe and June's.

A memorable time to be sure... *if you have no other memories.*

We all saddle up on our fourth day. It is evening, and the plan is to go around the Peninsula, stop at the Ho River to have dinner, and then go on home.

As we are entering a small town, Skip radios ahead to tell them he is going to stop at this drive-in we can see at a distance and get ice cream cones for the girls.

"Sounds like a good idea," comes back the cacophony of voices.

As we all pull up, it is apparent that it is a drive-through, not a drive-in. "Just pull over to the side and park. We can just walk in," I tell him as I am assessing the parking situation. Remembering vividly his problem in this department. I watch as the rest of our caravan pull up along the curb.

"No," Skip says. "I am just gonna pull her on through."

"You can't get around that corner," I say. Certain he would see the logic in my statement.

After all, everyone was watching.

"Yeah, I can. It follows good."

We are now at the talk box, and he is telling the girl on the other end what we all want.

"Skip," I whisper to him. "Look, you can back up and go down there and park, we will just walk up."

Ignoring me, he puts the truck in drive and pulls ever so slowly around the corner, looking at me with an I-told-you-so look. Then I hear a horrendous crash. I look in the side mirror to see the trailer pulling an enormous dumpster along behind it. "Skip! Stop! Look!"

He stops, looks, and puts the truck in reverse. He turns the wheel too hard to the left and backs into the speaker, bending it awkwardly to the rear of us. Forward again. Aiming straight for the six-foot wood fencing that surrounds the drive thru area. A loud pop, and several boards snap back to reveal a canyon below. "Skip! Stop!"

"Shut up!" he says as he rams it into reverse, and the clanking of metal-to-metal reverberates throughout the truck. He pulls up close to the far left side. He is determined to drive through! Forward we go, dragging the now-battered dumpster behind us.

Ah, but the corner is too sharp as we now plow over the side of the curb, truck pummeling any and all fencing in the path. Our newfound friend, the dumpster, rips out all fencing as it hangs on to our trailer with all its might.

Not to be outwitted in the least, he will try again and again. We are, at last, around the corner where our ice creams await. However the fence is gone, the speaker lies resting at half mast. All but one small corner of the fence is gone. The dumpster is permanently attached to the trailer as we sit precariously perched above a small canyon. High centered on the twelve-inch high curbing that surrounds the driveway. Our ice creams only twenty feet from us.

The tears stream down my face from laughter. I can't remember when I have laughed so hard. Oh yes, Paris!

I look out at the devastation of this poor business. The owner stands with arms folded across his chest. Joe and Daddy stand beside him. Joe laughs and slaps his leg. Daddy just shakes his head.

The whole caravan has witnessed this, as well as other customers.

JR is climbing into my arms, tears streaming down her face, "Gamma, Gamma, are we going to get our ice cream? Grampa, you was bad!"

"Shush…come, let's go find Great Gramma.," I seem to have found some semblance of control at this point, as I take the girls out of the truck. The door creaks, as I discover it has rippled. I look over at Skip, his wrists dangle over the steering wheel. His head is slumped to let his chin rest on his chest. "I'm taking the girls, and we are going to get the ice cream. Maybe you can get this straightened out."

Strange as it may seem, the tow truck arrived within about half an hour, and Skip and the owner of this small-town drive-in came to an agreement within the same amount of time.

One thousand dollars is all he wanted, and he wouldn't turn it in to his insurance. Our truck and trailer, on the other hand, were a little worse for wear, but surprisingly, we drove it home.

At home, alone, in our bedroom, I said no to the nightly ritual of fumbling and groping. He threatens. He mouths words of anger. He begs. He pleads.

I don't care. "No," I tell him. "You are irresponsible. You are thoughtless."

At last, he simply turns to his side of the bed and, like a child, cries himself to sleep.

On any other night, I would have tossed and turned, felt unending guilt and remorse. After all, people are who they are and for the most part cannot rise from their deep-rooted emotional conditioning. But I am tired, bone-tired. The stress, the company, the children. The work.

I crawl into bed and sleep.

<hr />

August draws to a close, and I take the girls to the airport and send them back to their mother.

It's the night before Lorraine and John are to leave, and I had fixed a big dinner. Joe and June, Peter and Ellie, Mom and Daddy, Skip and I have a delicious dinner of fried halibut dipped in milk and bread crumbs, milk again, then fried to perfection, with salad and clam chowder, and baked russet potatoes, accompanied by freshly shelled peas out of the garden.

The card game is on, with great laughter and happy camaraderie.

Uncle Joe suggests we all caravan to Wyoming in June next year. We have relatives that own a guest ranch there. A primitive one. After much back-slapping and jubilant praises of his excellent idea, it was settled. We would leave in June. Samantha would come, along with other relatives who might be interested.

Lorraine and John leave.

Skip's friends come for a week.

Paige and her girls come for a week.

As all the company dissipates, life resumes its normality.

Chapter 33

Heidi died this morning. She screamed and dropped at my feet. I couldn't get hold of Skip, so I called Daddy. He came and took us to the vet. I simply couldn't believe it as I held her soft body in my arms. This quiet, unassuming little dog had given me so much comfort. Jillian's dog. Now she too was gone. Eighteen years is old for a dog. But, Lord, I will miss her. Tears of grief slide down my cheeks. Grief, an emotion I am on intimate terms with…funny, is it not obvious to the common observer that I might possibly rest dangerously close to insanity?

Skip built a metal box for me, and Daddy and I buried her at Eagle Point.

Our lives once again resume the mundane cycle of rising and sleeping as the long winter nights set in.

I have a small social gathering of women I have met and find that I really do not fit in. For the most part, they are wives and mothers without any experience in the outside world. They are dubious of me. My manner, my dress, my looks. Even my household furnishings. These people go to the store in their sweats, sleep in their sweats. Make-up and high heels, a laughable, nearly embarrassing condition of a wicked city woman. Many of them have not been outside this small historic town and are quite happy in these circumstances, with its ever-increasing number of homeless and indigent and drug use so rampant as to be epidemic. "Shed boys," a term used for the people who literally live in sheds. Their value lies in the very essence of their lack of materialism.

They exist, and that is their only aspiration. They are consumers, at the very highest level. They use, destroy, once more consuming again.

The upkeep of homes, automobiles, land and even such minor things as clothing, unheard of, such things allowed to disintegrate, in their quest for an unfettered life.

They work when the notion or necessity avails itself. And the cycle of their life repeats itself.

There are, of course, exceptions to this mind-set. People who have moved here from other areas try to fight this apathy concerning life. But in the end, you are at the mercy of the remoteness of the area.

In years to come, I would understand this to some extent. The weather is harsh and unrelenting. Without the extremes of other lands, it remains Mother Nature rules. Wind, rain, and the elements undo any and all work and order you try to create. Moss grows on roofs and in yards. Water erodes driveways and creates mudslides you have to witness to believe, and in its wake, buildings topple. Mold and moss covers all in its path as the majestic trees shroud the world in darkness. Wind plummets the land with unrelenting devastation. Trees come crashing down on your homes; limbs burrow their way into the earth as the force of the wind drives them from the trees. Litter is everywhere, Mother Nature's litter to be sure. But litter and disorder nonetheless. Pipes freeze and break.

Automobiles suffer from the sand and salt used to keep the main roads passable. To say nothing of the salt of the sea water as it washes over your vehicle as it traverses the many floating bridges.

To be vigilant in caring for 'things' in this country is daunting to be sure. And in no small measure, it is futile. As it is never-ending.

With this information gleaned over the years, I can now more thoroughly understand the near-despondency of the populace, 'on this side' as all who reside in western Washington refer to it.

Having freshly arrived from a 'land of milk and honey', I am accustomed to access to all things material, as well as spiritual and intellectual. Services abound. Everything your heart or mind desires is available. Instant gratification. The sunshine being the only thing there nature has made available, to rot and destroy, taking its sweet time to do so.

Lawns are manicured. Neighborhoods are beautifully maintained. Ordinances prohibit the piling up of debris, of garbage and old cars from scarring the neighborhoods. With the land lying outside the city limits, structured and verdant in their straight rows of produce.

Beyond that, cattle dot the golden rolling hills as they graze on the stubby grass and sagebrush. Ancient oak trees stand in sentinel as six-lane freeways wend gracefully from city to city. A place to go daily, as well as peer pressure, provided me with all the reason I needed to dress in the latest fashion. To have a beautiful wardrobe. These things are not always gotten at great expense, but often sewn by myself. Copied from magazines and from items I found in Neiman's or Saks Fifth Avenue.

Hair and make-up artists are always consulted when necessary. I practiced yoga daily, and I closely watch my diet. A throwback from the days of New York, to be sure. But also expected and practiced by most women in California.

I stand out here, certainly. But not necessarily in a good way.

It is an enigma to my brother and his family, as well as my other relatives, who are many and varied. They find me unsettling, garish sometimes, even embarrassing. I am outspoken and have very new-age views on life, as well as the world we live in. I have traveled and married more than once. I own 'things'. I am considered suspect and dangerous in my views and behavior. The kindnesses, enthusiasm, outgoing nature, and my work ethic only cause them further confusion as to my true personality.

In an attempt at fitting in, I peel off my false eyelashes and cut off my hair. But my ideals and idioms are of a more complex nature, and they are ingrained in *who* I am.

I say what I think, have the occasional cigarette, and alcoholic beverage. I whip out a gourmet meal along with the crystal, china, and impeccably ironed white linen. For my birthday, I received crystal candle stick holders, and a chainsaw. I needed both.

My interests are wide and varied. And I pursue them with diligent abandon. I am alone, not lonely, but certainly alone. There is a difference…

I am becoming more and more introverted; I seek my own interests and entertainment. I miss only my children…and my Heidi.

Chapter 34

She has jumped up on the armrest of the truck that sits between Skip and me, stretching her tiny little body up to its full length, which might be twelve inches. Standing with her tiny little paws against the back of the seat, she peers with her jet-black eyes into the darkness of the home she has so recently left behind.

A sense of excitement envelopes us as we take this little puppy home, leaving behind a sense of well-being and a warm fuzzy household of minuscule puppies that smelled of warm milk, laughing children, and yipping frolicking dogs.

"Her name is Daisie," said the little girl. "And this one is Violet, and this one is Rose, and this one is Petunia." A smile spreads across my face as I stoop to pick up the nearest ball of fluff. What funny little names for dogs, I think to myself as I nuzzle the tiniest of the litter. The cacophony of yips and barks is nearly deafening as they jump around my feet and scratch at my legs. "How will I know which one? They are all so cute," I tell the little girl, whose name is Carmen.

"Oh they pick you," she says with certainty. The parents of this very much in-charge little girl stand back, allowing her to orchestrate the entire proceedings.

I soon find myself on the floor with the rest of the puppies as they play and scamper around, chasing their tails and chewing on each other's ears.

Not even aware I was looking, I spied the ad in the newspaper last night and, on a whim, called to see if in fact they "had any little Shih Tzu's left." Samantha's 'Fritzi' is a Shih Tzu, and the most adorable of dogs. I can just look.

"We still have six of them," the lady on the other end of the telephone line tells me. "You're welcome to come and see them." With excitement I haven't felt for some time, I went to the basement to ask Skip if he wanted to go with me.

"Sure, why not."

Shih Tzu's are small and furry, with flat little faces and big round intelligent eyes. Their tails curl up over their backs, and their bodies are generally rather stocky with soft coloring of gold, white and grey.

But Daisie is long legged and black and white, shy yet at the same time curious. She comes and plops her little body next to me. It is love at first sight. This is the one.

It has been a year since Heidi died, at the ripe old age of eighteen, and I miss a little dog around. Skip has Sable, and she is a nice dog, but she is his dog, and she is an outside dog. I need joy, I need a baby; there was Dainty and Inga and Heidi, over the last few years of my life. I thought I loved each of them more than the last.

I turn and scoop the baby fuzzball up into my arms; she's not pudgy like the rest of the puppies, but long and lean.

"She's the runt," Carmen calls out. "She likes you. She's the one. And she is Daisie because of the white flower on the top of her head. See?" She points to the spray of white fur sprouting from the center of the little angel's head. Her nose holes are as small as common dressmakers pins, and I wonder how she can breathe.

"Daisie it is then," I tell Carmen. "Is that all right with you?" Carmen looks sad and somewhat uncertain, but Mom and Dad are delighted.

"Yeah," Carmen says. "I think you'll love her, and she'll be happy."

"I will love her and take good care of her," I assure the motherly little Carmen.

As we travel the road towards home, Daisie is all eyes and ears. Leaping from the armrest onto my lap to stand and look out the passenger window with her paw placed on the door just below the window, looking up to me with questioning, excited, enormous black eyes. "You are the most curious, darling little thing I have ever seen," I tell her as I nuzzle her little furry neck. To me, puppies smell as good as babies. "Let's take her and show her to Mom and Daddy," I tell Skip.

"Okay," he says, laughing at the antics of this new member of our little family.

Autumn has disappeared with the chirping of eagles as they swoop and glide amid the flutter of falling leaves burnished with copper and gold. Of crisp fall mornings and the smell of wood smoke in the evening air. By November, Washington is shrouded in darkness at four o'clock, damp and cold as we arrive at Mom and Dad's.

I have Daisie tucked in my jacket. I hold her tightly to keep her warm as we rap at the door to let Mom and Daddy know we are coming in.

The minute the door opens, this wiggly little thing jumps from my arms and goes bounding up the two steps to the living room. The steps being three times the size of this new furry child of mine.

My parents both turn from the television and gaze with laughter as this miniature, highly animated little fuzz ball comes bounding to them. "Oh my gosh," my mother chuckles. "Where in the world did you come from?"

"I'll be damned," says Daddy, laughing as he reaches for an excited happy, tiny puppy.

She's run to Mother (who, by the way, has absolutely no use for animals of any description), and now stands at the side of her chair. Lo and behold, Mother reaches down and tentatively pets her. Well, she touched her.

Now to Daddy. He gingerly scoops her up in his arms and nuzzles her. She leaps from his arms onto the floor.

"Oh," I say. "She's going to hurt herself jumping so far." Undaunted by my concern, she runs from one to the other, joy filling the whole world by the energy and enthusiasm of this minute entity.

Life for us has changed forever as the mighty heart and curiosity of a lion is packed into the soul of one of God's smallest creatures.

In the ensuing months she will learn to play with the feral cats in the old desolate neighborhood we live in, learn to arch her back and hiss like a cat, bringing peals of laughter to anyone that happens to witnesses such insanity. It is nothing to see her perched on the limb of the giant old lilac tree in the backyard, some ten feet off the ground with her friends the feral cats peering out from the branches above, seeing no harm comes to what they think of as one of their own.

She is into everything. Weighing in at about two pounds, two ounces, and approximately six inches tall, she is a dynamite and quick as lightning. I am reminded of the story of the prince whose little Tibetan dog has turned to a lion, and they ride to safety.

To open a base cabinet is inviting problems; she can have the SOS and scrubbing things off the shelf and in the living room before you can say, "Oh."

The aspirin bottle has the same fate. With the only cabinet in the bathroom on the floor, that is where I have always kept the aspirin, but alas, no more, as she grabs the bottle with her teeth and shakes it, aspirin flying in all directions, as I scurry hither and yon, trying to pick them up before she eats them. Laughing all the while at this newest love of my life.

She sits in the windowsill in the living room, having jumped from the floor to the sofa, from the sofa back to the windowsill.

Embroidery not being her thing and certainly taking more of my attention than she thinks necessary, she pulls at the cloth with her teeth, clawing at the thread until it is a mass of tangles. So we play ball and run through the house like small children, my days of embroidering clearly over for the next few years.

Soon, she is bringing the ball back to me. She will lie quietly on her stomach, paws stretched out in front of her, her head and ears pitched forward in alert anticipation, scoot back on the floor, and wait for me to roll the ball to her, yipping softly if I was not as quick as she would like, then with her nose push it back to me. At two months old, she has to be the smartest little puppy in the world. Well, at least we all think so, and with the agility of a cat, I might add.

The first snow was the most exciting since I had small children. Daisie sniffed it. She lifts her tiny little legs high and plummets down through the cold white fluffy stuff, yipped in delight. But no way is she going to go potty in that white stuff.

Of course, I shoveled out a green grassy area every few hours for our Princess Daisie.

Joy prevails.

The bridge between Skip and I is flailing in our inability to find a common ground. The rising debt causes further complications to our lives as winter sits firmly on our doorstep, and he is unable to work. He sits in the damp cold of the basement surrounded by boxes, watching his theater-size television and drinking.

I sit upstairs in the warmth of the living room crocheting and playing with my little Daisie.

Spring comes softly, the ice and snow slowly turning to the dirty slush of sanded roads. The shattered landscape rejuvenating as if by a miracle, and Daisie has something she wants me to see. She has run up to me half a dozen times, barking, jumping up on my legs, running ten feet away, coming back, and seems to be saying, "Come, Mom, come!"

"Okay, okay, I'm coming,"

She runs to the window well of the basement around the side of the old house, and lo and behold, there is a whole pile of newborn kittens, "Oh Daisie, they are so cute," I tell her. She lies down and looks at me as if to say, "See, I've been trying to tell you."

I reach in to pick one up, and the little monster bites my thumb, its little teeth like needles clinging to my skin. Now all the little kittens are whining, and Daisie is yipping and running around in circles.

Finally disengaging the critter from my thumb, a major ordeal to be sure, I return to the house to retrieve some gloves. If she wants kittens, we can put them in the shed until they get more hospitable. With Daisie in tow, we make a bed, placing them ever so carefully, one by one in the potting shed with milk and water. She lays on guard outside the door the remainder of the day, and asks to go check them in the evening. A little mother to cats.

The next morning at the break of daylight she wants to check on her new babies. Opening the door to the old shed, we find they are gone. How, I will never figure out, but Daisie is sad for the remainder of the day.

Chapter 35

The trees burst with a pinkish red color of new growth. The skies clear from heavy gray to crystal clear blue. Large puffy cumulous clouds dance jubilantly.

My daffodils bloom, and they are spectacular. The blossoms the size of my fist, a profusion of color and fragrance I had never imagined.

The house plans are ready and waiting. But there is no money to build a new home. It is little enough to provide for this ancient building we reside in.

Skip's properties haven't paid rent in two months, and I finally call, only to hear that in fact they have paid, that the checks had been cashed. Going out to the old shed he calls an office, I find he is not there. I look over the items piled on the desk. Receipts for new equipment and a brochure for an Alaskan hunt, along with a confirmation for a fishing trip on the Campbell River, all litter the desk.

Anger swells in my throat as I pull open the desk drawer. There would be no reason for him to hide things as I rarely venture into his realm of work.

Lying in the drawer is a checkbook. Opened January of this year. With a balance of $577,000. My knees are weak as I drop to the chair. Opening the small file drawer in the desk, I search through the many meticulously filed papers, not really knowing what I am looking for, intuition pushes me to pull each folder in turn. The Bass Lake folder held in my sweating palms, my premonition of doom is profound. My hands tremble as I peruse the papers within. Dated February of this year is a loan application, with my credit references and my signature. Attached to this is an appraisal for the cabin at the lake.

The appraisal for $740,000 generated by my investment. He has never put my name on the property.

Deeds of trust marked paid. The house in Culver City, his properties in Lompoc—paid for, while I continue to wallow in the reams of billings for equipment for his work, charge cards that were maxed out on our trip to Europe, and on items for the store, never reimbursed. It goes on and on…

All this time I am paying for our living expenses, his bills, the improvements at Eagle Point.

I can't believe this is happening.

How is he making these payments? The payments have to be $7,500 a month. Where was the money I had sent to pay on those loans all this time?

The post office box. The realization of what lengths he had gone to deceive me is implausible. His insistence on getting a post office box. That is the reason I don't know of any of this. He picks up the mail daily, and I see what he wants me to see.

I just want to get in the car and go. Run, run from this insanity that is my life. Where, it doesn't even matter. I just want to be away from him. But I am stuck here. No taxis. My car sits in the garage with the rats having eaten all the wiring. I have to get it to Seattle to have it repaired. There are no Mercedes dealers except for Seattle. There is no one here to trailer the car over there. And I can't afford the repair bills now at any rate. His jeep and Corvette sit locked in an abandoned warehouse that came with the property. The new truck attached to the trailer. The only one I have keys to. He has his work truck.

As if a light bulb went off in my mind, I see the futility of it all. The foolish trust, the rationalizations I had been immersing myself in. The tolerance of the intolerable. I am not sad. I am embarrassed. Stupidity has no boundaries.

I start to gather up paperwork and see the copy machine setting silently in the corner—when did he get that?

I decide it best to copy everything and leave it as it is. This done, I scoop Daisie up into my arms, murmuring soft words about love and betrayal to her. I carry her and the mound of evidence into the house.

What to do? I have no money; I can't just up and leave. Where would I go?

Another divorce. Another failure. Another loss, the loss of a dream, certainly, but a profound loss, nonetheless. This realization is more devastating than I would have ever imagined. This is the last time, I understand that instinctively, the last time I will ever be married, ever trust another man, ever trust my ability to make a decision concerning another individual.

I will always be alone.

My heart breaks in silent acknowledgment, and I feel it harden and am further saddened.

Should I talk to him about it? But why, he has obviously never been truthful with me and would only lie. I have told Samantha most of it. But I can't burden her now. She will just worry, and there is nothing she can do. Not now, later. I could call Mother, but they think he is wonderful as do most of the people I know. It is all impossible to believe. The fear sits firmly on my heart. I have failed yet again.

The soft furry puppy stirs in my arms. "Let me down," she seems to say as we approach the sagging screen door. Bending to set her down in the grassy lawn, the fragrance of the daffodils and lilacs envelop my senses. The tulips with their vibrant colors bob their radiant heads. The old garden restored, it is resplendent in its beauty, and I am rewarded for my efforts. The large Italian fountain I insisted on bringing here gurgles as it spouts its lovely spray of water.

Daisie sits on the limb of the old lilac tree, ten feet off the ground, as if she were a cat. "Come, sweetheart, Mommy will fix you dinner," I say to my furry child. "We'll think about this tomorrow." Again I am reminded of Scarlett O'Hara.

The kitchen counter is a mass of preparations for Easter dinner. Cabbage leaves covered in chocolate, waiting to become leaves for a centerpiece. Pies are cooling on the counter. The soft pink of apple blossoms, cut for table decorations, await my attention.

***

I nearly forgot that I was having dinner Sunday.

Samantha and her boyfriend are coming. I am to pick them up at the small international airport here today. Peter and Ellie. Their oldest daughter and her boyfriend, Judith and Dick, Mom and Daddy. Peter and Ellie's youngest daughter, Karen and her friend. Joe and June. And some new friends. This might be a troubled Easter, as Karen is bringing her new boyfriend.

When she called to ask if it was all right, I said, "Most certainly."

"But…" she stammered, "he is black."

"Well, my dear, as far as I am concerned, it is fine, I personally think you need to have the courage of your convictions."

Yes, this 'other' problem would have to wait. There were other more pressing concerns right now, and after all, this has been going on forever. My refusal to believe it, to see the truth, had not made it disappear. Sad but true.

***

Samantha is returning home on Wednesday, and although I have vowed not to burden her with my problems, I need someone to talk to, someone that has some understanding of me, and some knowledge of him.

As we walk on the gray sand of North Beach, the waves crash on the littered shore, my story spills out, interrupted only by the screeching of gulls as they swoop in to retrieve the small tidbits on the driftwood amassed on the beach and the barking of tiny little dogs dragging their leashes in their wakes as they scamper along the ripple of the water's edge. Daisie, certain she can catch a seagull, Fritzi, afraid she might.

"Mother, I am so sorry," she says, tears cresting on her eyelids. "Are you all right?"

"Yes, I am all right. I am just *so disappointed.* Disappointed in him, but most of all, I am disappointed in me. I thought I had it all figured out. I thought he was a good guy. Disappointed that I can *never, ever* do this again. That I obviously don't know how to do this. I know I have to leave him. But quite honestly, I don't even know where to begin. And I have no money. It is all gone."

"Oh, Mother, I am so very sorry. Mother, we both thought he was a good guy, lots of people do. It isn't just you. What can I do to help you?" Her arms are around me, tenderly holding me as I sob into her shoulder. The cold breeze off the Straits whipping the golden red of her curls around my face and shoulders. The fragrance of her hair; as soothing as her embrace.

<hr />

As one sleepless night follows another, the silence between Skip and me becomes more deafening. I retreat more and more to the peaceful tranquility of Eagle Point. To weed, to plan, to clear away dead and dying trees, evergreen berries growing rampant and untamed in the newly cleared land as the sun beats down on them and they are driven from the earth. Digitalis rebound in profusion, stalks of slipper-like flowers grow in a sea of white, pink, and lavender, some growing to a height of eight and nine feet. There is bracken and sword ferns. And elderberry trees sporting red berries.

The masked faces of raccoons peer down from the trunks of the evergreen cedar, fir, and hemlock trees. Their young, small and inviting, taunt Daisie with their squeals. The chirping of squirrels, as they scamper to freedom from Daisie. Small field mice succumb to her never-yielding chase as this tiny lap dog behaves as if she were a bloodhound.

I feel peaceful, digging in the dirt and clearing the land, surprised at how physically strong I have become. Unbridled passion surges through my very being, as I discover a new flower, or a bud near to bursting, or stand in the shadow of a majestic cedar.

A reverence for God and all his creation envelops my shattered heart, and I feel the peacefulness of His grace.

Evenings at home are spent playing with Daisie as she is not going to let me embroider or knit. She pulls on the threads, running with them, and her exuberant play holds me captive. She jumps on the sofa, and off the bed, sits on the edge of the tub while I bathe in the evening. Without a doubt the most agile little dog I have ever seen.

It is nearing the end of April as I decide what must be done.

He has resumed work and is gone during the day. I go through all the files, making copies of all his "handiwork." I discover divorce papers from several other women and testimonies to the same things that are happening now.

Determined to go forward, I acknowledge them, putting them aside. I gather all my personal property and files, the large bronze lions as well as other large objects I have been saving for our new home, call a storage company, and have them transferred to a storage unit. I call Seattle to have the Mercedes dealer there come and get the car to repair it.

He doesn't appear to notice anything has been removed. Strange.

In the soft quiet of the night, I sit and write a letter to Skip telling him that I will not be paying for any more of his bills, and further, I expect him to pay all household expenses from the first of June forward. I will pay no bills at all until the properties that I paid for are put in my name as well as reimbursement for all I have spent on his credit card debts as well as the addition to his financial worth. Will this work, Lord only knows, but I really must do something.

The next evening, after dinner, I hand him the letter. "What's this?" he says.

"I want you to read it," I tell him. Unfolding the paper, reaches in his pocket for his glasses, I watch as his hands begin to shake, and his face becomes swollen with rage.

A small tremor erupts near my heart, but my resolve beats it back. This all has to stop.

"So you want a divorce," he says, his voice a silent threat. He stands so suddenly, causing the chair to fall backward to the floor.

"No, I don't necessarily want a divorce, but this has to stop. I found the papers for the loan. I saw that you have forged my signature. You have been literally stealing from me for over two years. I am done. I won't tolerate it anymore. That is all I am saying."

I sit quietly at the kitchen table. As he paces the floor, the paper flapping in his hand as he becomes more angry by the minute.

It is peculiar how the written word has such an immediate impact. "You can't do this. You won't get away with this!" He rushes to the back door. It slams shut, and he is gone.

Taking a deep breath, I pick up Daisie, hug her, and go to call Samantha. I need someone to talk to. As always, she is encouraging. "You did the right thing, Mother, the only thing you could do. I'm so proud of you, I know how hard this must be." Her voice, mellifluous, soothing my mind as she talks.

I clean up the kitchen and make his lunch for the next day. Through the kitchen window, I can see the light in his little hovel of an office, the outline of his head and shoulders as he sits bent over his desk.

The hours go by as I wait, *for what?* I know not.

I draw my bath and immersed in the hot cleansing water, surrounded by bubbles of ivory liquid, with Daisie perched at the edge of the tub. I slide down further, surrendering to the calming effects of the warmth as it flows through my body.

I hear the slam of the screen door and am jolted from my too short repose.

He stands looming above me. "Have you paid for the trip to Wyoming?" His voice softer than usual, his presence more calm than usual.

"Yes," I said as I scoot up in the tub

"Good, I'll get the paperwork ready to transfer all the properties into your name." He turned and went to the basement.

He did transfer Eagle Point to my name and said, "The paperwork for the other properties are on their way."

April turned to May, and my hopes were borne on the wings of fantasy. For I thought he understood.

June arrives in all its glory. The weather warm, the days long, with the sun rising at four o'clock and not setting until nearly ten o'clock in the evening. Tiny green nubbins of fruit laden the apple and pear trees, and the oriental poppies dance in the breezes of warm summer evenings.

And I do not pay his bills.

I hand him all the household bills, and the bill for the repair of my car. He is incensed, nearly trembling in rage, as he takes the pile of bills from my hands, saying nothing.

Two days go by, and my father pulls up in his pick up. I am happy to see him, and think nothing of it as he often stops by when in town. Mother however never stops by, explaining, "I forget you are here."

Lord!

Pushing open the screen door, Daisie and I go out to greet him. "What a pleasant surprise. Come on in, and I'll fix you some lunch."

"Okay," he says.

Over tuna sandwiches and coffee, he tells me Skip has come by to see him and has told him of my letter to him. "Did he tell you why?" I ask.

"No, I want to hear your side of the story. But first let me tell you, I told him what I thought, that is; *what a man does* is provide for a wife, that after all didn't you cook and clean and take care of his grandchildren, care for the house, garden, him, his clothing, do the shopping, the ironing, all of those things? He said yeah, ya did, but you had your own money, and he wasn't going to pay for you. I just thought you should know what to expect."

I sit at the little kitchen table, shocked. Stupidly, insanely, shocked. I thought he understood, I thought he had agreed. I look up, Daddy is just looking at me. "Cara...?" He reaches over to touch my hand. "Are you all right?"

I shake my head. "Yes, yes, I guess...I mean, no...I thought he understood. I thought it was settled. I mean...he knows I know the things he has done..."

"Cara, he doesn't care. Men like him don't care. Where do you find these men..." My father lays his hand on mine, patting it as if I were a child.

"Oh, Daddy, what am I going to do?" The story spilling from me in gulping sobs and anguish.

"I figured that's what was goin' on, but your mother didn't think we should interfere. If you want to know what I think, I'm gonna tell ya. I think you should stick to your guns. Ya said ya weren't gonna pay his bills, don't pay his bills. Ya said ya weren't gonna pay the household bills, don't. They really are his responsibility as a man. How would it look if I didn't take care of you kids and your mother? What kind of man is that?"

"I know, Daddy, but what will happen? I have no more money. I am as broke as when I married Tony."

"You have the hospitals still, don't you? Those aren't his too, are they?"

"No," I stammer. "Thank God I didn't sell all of them. He wanted me to."

"So it might take you ten, maybe fifteen years, but you'll get back on your feet. The girls are all grown up, and this little thing here"—he looks down at Daisie lying at his feet—"doesn't eat much. Just do what you told him you were gonna do. I'd stick to it, by God I would." He paused and was quiet for a moment. "I gotta git home. Your mother will be wunderin' where I went to."

Standing, he gives me a hug and vigorously pounds me on the back. "You'll do all right."

"What about Wyoming? I've already paid and everything."

"Ah hell, go. It's only a couple a weeks away. You're sleepin' with him, aren't you?"

"Well, yeah, but that doesn't work either." I smile at him, knowingly.

"That doesn't surprise me. It takes an honest man to do an honest night's work." Chuckling, he leaves.

Somehow bolstered by finally revealing my stupidity, I feel much better. My resolve renewed, I am determined to stand my ground, and I have a growing support system.

Chapter 36

The Wyoming trip is an interesting disaster. Why is it that people find it necessary to get away from home, security, and familiarity, only to find they have those things?

Traveling with Skip is a disaster. He will not shift the gears to climb the Rocky Mountains. The transmission grinding, the engine smoking, he says he is shifting with his feet…Parking it was again, a nightmare.

We drive down the road with the awning flapping, ripping from its housing, or the steps down, skidding along the pavement as we make a turn too sharp for the trailer to follow. Left to his own devices, he would travel at thirty-five miles an hour, on open freeways, or winding mountainous roads. He has but one speed.

Joe and Daddy chide him each evening as we stop for the night, and by nightfall, he was laughing and saying, "Yeah, I will tomorrow."

But of course "tomorrow" never came as he really did not know what he was doing. Furthermore, he would listen to no one.

The scenery is resplendent. "Big Sky," Montana has taken on new meaning, firsthand and personal. I will forever wonder at people who say we are running out of places for people to live. Such vast, open spaces. We would travel all day and never see signs of habitation.

Our arrival in Jackson Hole was momentous. We had made it. We were all in one piece, and other than being the butt of all jokes, Skip too had survived.

We did a brief but thorough tour of the sleepy little town and were off to the desolate spaces coveted by city slickers.

Pretty mountainous roads quickly turned to unpaved graveled roads. Finally, thirty-five miles an hour was good! Then to dusty dirt roads, where, again, thirty-five was a grinding, trailer-shattering speed. As the hours slowly crawled by, the dirt road turned to a wagon road, and then a cattle trail.

But alas, we have arrived at the Double J Dude Ranch. A two-story log house, sits in the distance, corrals and grazing land as far as the eye could see. With the backdrop of the Grand Tetons surrounding us. Everywhere I look, small and large structures are scattered in disrepair. A real covered wagon stands to the side of the house. Just beyond the house is a pristine lake, two or three small row boats resting at its edge. There is no lawn or landscaping. Just small tufts of green, sparsely dotting the somewhat reddish soil.

As the rumble of the trucks and trailer ascend the slight hill, I can see the door fly open, dogs, and people emerging in profusion. Molly and Jeff, ranch hands, and cooks come out to greet us.

As we all pile out of the truck, I am pleased I brought some warmer clothing. It is nippy to say the least. After much conversation, I find that all but five of us will have to leave and go to Yvonne's to stay as Jeff will not let them park their trailers unless they are willing to pay a fee.

Some hospitality from relatives; considering that five of us have each paid fifteen hundred dollars apiece for five days. But the ones concerned took it in their stride. And our ordeal commenced.

We were fed a hearty meal and shown to our cabins. Charming, rustic affairs with large iron bedsteads, a rocking chair, with animal heads mounted on each and every wall. The bathroom sported toilets with pull chains to flush, and instructions to flush only between the hours of 8:00 a.m. and 7:00 p.m. Showers are every other day between 10:00 a.m. and noon. Why? Well, those were the only hours the generator ran. This was not good for me! Or Samantha! What was I thinking? Molly had said it was primitive. We were to be at breakfast at five a.m. each morning. In the saddle by seven. After being introduced to the cabin and our surroundings, we were led to the corral to pick our horses.

"Has anyone here ridden ever?" Jeff shouts as he stands in front of a gallery of horses.

No one raised their hand, so I, being the idiot that I am, say, "I have ridden a little bit." Thinking of Goliath.

"Okay, git yur ass over here," he says, pointing to a spot not three feet from where he stands with a very large sorrel gelding. Perhaps eighteen hands.

Pushing my cowboy hat down a little firmer on my head, I saunter over to where the king of the palace stands. "Jis git on up there. This here is my best cuttin' horse." Holding the reigns of the horse, he pivots him around so I can mount. For some reason, my hands are now sweating and my knees feel far too weak to mount this creature standing before me. But up I go, boot in stirrup, swinging my long leg over the saddle. By God's grace, I am on, but my hands are trembling as I grasp the saddle horn.

I know the horse knows I'm frightened. It doesn't seem to help. We are each in turn assigned a mount that we are to ride for the duration of our stay. We will be doing the duties of the ranch hands—currying our horses, feeding them. They are to be our responsibility.

Peter has been assigned a dapple-gray nag, hysterically funny. Samantha; a very pretty, well-muscled roan. Skip, a small horse, his long legs dangling from the sides of the horse, giving the comical appearance that he was larger than the horse. Ellie; a large gentle mare.

Jeff mounts a large gelding, and in his tough cowboy words, says, "Arite ya green-horns, weel' jis see wha' ya ken do."

Having arrived less than three hours ago, I am a bit dazzled by the transition. The gate is opened by a young ranch hand, and we are off.

My horse takes off like a shot out of a cannon. Not three hundred feet from the corral, I find myself hurling through the air. Holding tight to my hat. Not to the reins.

"Ass over teakettle" was the term.

As it turned out, I was by far the worst rider, terrified of the horse itself. I suffered daily bouts of near tears and virtual nonstop whining. But morning after morning I was up and in the saddle with the intimate knowledge that this is a new experience but *not one I will ever repeat.*

The rest of them did very nicely. Ellie and Samantha, calm and straight-backed in their saddles. Skip, a very good horseman. Peter, defiantly making profound progress. He acted as reticent as I initially, getting off and walking at a snail's pace with back bowed, and legs equally bowed, laughingly saying, "I am running." We all just guffawed.

Some mornings, we moved cattle from one pasture to another, only to move them back in the afternoon. We herded them from ranch to ranch, through rivers and wooded mountainous area. We herded the cattle through wind and snow during the first week of July.

We ate starch and grease and wonderful biscuits and delicious pancakes.

Molly did all of this. She looked older than my mother but was in fact several years younger than me. If I thought my life was difficult now, it was most apparent hers made mine look like a piece of cake.

We all survived, and as always, nostalgia remembers only the wonderful things in life. The snow-covered Cascades loom before us as we approach our sleepy little town.

Samantha goes home tomorrow, and once more, I am devastated. Fighting to cover the despair that envelops me.

Chapter 37

Sitting quietly on the sofa the next evening, I am astonished to see Skip come in and sit on the loveseat opposite me and Daisie. "Just thought we could talk," he says.

"That's nice. Can I get you some tea or something cool to drink? It has been so hot today."

"No, thanks." He is sitting on the edge of the loveseat, his elbows leaning on his thighs, fingers laced in front of him.

"Is something the matter?" My antennae picks up sadness, or was it resolve?

His voice unusually soft, his diction more clear than usual. "I found the bills on my desk this evening and your note asking for grocery money. *Is there anything else you want?*" The softness has turned to coldness—hard, brittle sarcasm.

"No," I reply as softly. "Not unless you can give me some gas money or you have extra money to begin to pay me back."

"You know, Cara, I can't pay these bills."

"Of course you can, you did it last month. You can do it."

"No, I didn't do it last month. I didn't pay the bills you gave me last month. I can't. I don't have any money. You're the one with all the goddamn money!" His anger escalates and his voice resumes its booming quality. He is nearly venomous now as his bent and aging body rises to its full stature, hands clenched as he collides into the coffee table.

Daisie has risen to the occasion, all four-and-a-half pounds of her. She stands next to me, looking at Skip and barking.

"Shut that stupid dog up, or I'll wring her little neck."

"I don't think so. I think you need to calm down. This is all fixable, Skip. I saw the loan documents. I know you forged my signature. I know you have all of that money you borrowed on the cabin." My voice is a match for his own, my resolution firm. I am done.

His shock instantaneous as it washes across the carved crevices of his face.

I too am at once shocked and relieved. He doesn't know what I have done. Daisie sits down hard on the sofa beside me. The threat, no longer immediate.

"You lied to me. You said you would pay your own way!" His words are clouded with anger and betrayal.

I wonder how he does that? *Manipulation at its finest-a Master at deceit.* Daddy was right…*where did I find these men…. In truth they found me,* I had never looked.

"I lied to you? That's a good one! You agreed to give me, at the very least, four thousand dollars a month. Not only have I never seen that, you haven't given me enough to pay *your* monthly bills, and you keep spending. You are the one who has lied, cheated, and conned me into doing your bidding. You say I have more money than you do. Well, there is a good reason for that. I don't spend it like water. If you had been willing to listen to me, you would have more money too."

Standing near the kitchen doorway, he turns to me, hands hanging at his sides. Standing straighter than I have seen him stand in a year. "Are you going to pay these bills?"

"No, I told you I wouldn't." My heart fluttering in my chest as I look at him, just a little frightened by my own courage and the tenacity with which I feel to see this thing through. "So it's over then." He turns, and walks away. The screen slams. I can tell by the clanging noise, it has once more come off its hinges.

What does that mean? I wonder to myself as I go to see about the screen door.

It is hot and muggy out. I can nearly see the air. The mosqui-toes are thick. The evening is long, and the heat is stifling. My bare feet pad softly across the kitchen floor, and I retrieve the screwdriver and proceed to repair the hinge.

I watch him as he hurries toward the trailer, keys jingling in hand. Again, I watch as he goes to the shop, comes out with something shiny in his hand. Bending down, he proceeds to put a new handle on his office door.

Well, I think to myself, at least I got most everything out of there before he did that. Funny, he can't fix the damn screen door, but it didn't take him long to change the locks on his office.

He stayed in the trailer that night.

Strange, I never got used to him in my bed, but the lack of his presence was somehow disconcerting.

Over the next few days, things more or less returned to normal.

He left for work every day while I fixed meals, did laundry, and went about the daily routine of living. He returned to our bed. We made small talk and had people in to play cards. The utilities were still on, so I assumed he had paid the bills and was going to do the right thing.

I have always liked to cook, but he ate with such lustful aban-don, complimenting my efforts as to taste, texture, presentation, and variety that I have become a wonderful cook. Interest, prac-tice, and gratitude being the primary ingredient for success.

I tried out new recipes, having both time and interest in per-fecting them.

Even though the day was hot and the heat was oppressive, I had made the lasagna in the morning and tiramisu for dessert.

The delphiniums and gladiolas arranged beautifully on the dining room table set for two. While chopping vegetables, pep-peroncini, salami and olives for an Italian salad, I hear the door-bell ring.

No one ever comes to the front door. It is inconveniently located in the back of the house as that is the original dwelling.

Wiping my hands on the dishtowel, I go to answer the door. "Are you Cara Borhen?" the man in the suit asks.

"Yes."

"Here, you have been served." He thrusts a paper to me and backs down the steps.

"Served? Served, what does that mean?" I stammer after him.

"Just read it, ma'am." He was gone.

Envelope in my hand, I turn to see Skip standing in the kitchen as I tear into the envelope. It is divorce papers. I look up at him and back down to the papers, "You son of a bitch, you could have at least had the decency to tell me you were going to do this. What were you thinking?" Anger rises at an alarming rate as I stalk toward him.

"Does this mean we aren't having dinner?" He backs slowly out of the kitchen.

I would have thrown the lasagna at him, but I knew I would have to clean it up.

The marriage had lasted two and a half years. The divorce would take three years of my life. One grueling battle after another. And it would cost me one million dollars.

I learned a number of things during that three years. Sometimes, you can't even quit if you want to. I thought it took two people to fight. It doesn't. All it takes is one with a vengeance to win at all costs.

I discovered that my pre-nuptial was not valid in the state of Washington. Although this is a community property state, that means what you have is his, and vice versa. Unless of course, it hadn't changed hands during the time of your marriage.

That means I only have one asset. The hospitals. The wonderful, life-giving hospitals, my car, and my furniture.

Certainly, my income, but having been remanded to pay any and all outstanding bills, his or mine. I was to pay him alimony, and if that wasn't enough, I had to let him live in the house. He couldn't live anyplace else. He had no money. And was so "distraught" that he couldn't work. He wanted the Kramer Lions, he wanted the lots and house in Port Townsend, and he wanted the twelve acres at Eagle Point.

His properties were all still in his name, but he had heavily mortgaged them; therefore, he could not provide for himself. Of course, these were his to keep without question. The mortgages, however, were my responsibility as I, and I alone, had the funds to pay for them.

Trying to prove that it was my money that purchased all the properties here was difficult. It would be two years of going to court, two different attorneys, and accountants. The first attorney, mortified beyond belief, was simply not up to the deceit and conniving of such a person as we were dealing with. The second, a quite realistic woman, stated, "The bigger the bastard, the more it's going to cost you, and I think this is going to cost you a bundle." Suzzanne Paul set about immediately to have him vacated from the house. The alimony payments would stop after a period of six months. A very long time. However, something to look forward to.

Not having to share my living space with him granted me a reprieve from the bitterness and with it a resolve to forgive.

I could at last show the courts the trail of events, regaining some semblance of respect for the slanderous attitude in which they viewed me. The long paper trail of the money I had given him to pay for these properties, so as not to *"belittle his manhood,"* was by far the most interesting. With this information, the courts more readily could fathom the extreme duplicity of his "charismatic personality." Even I was shocked by his innovative skills.

He first deposited my checks into his own bank account immediately upon receiving them, making arrangements with the real estate person here to delay payment for forty-five days "as his CD would not mature until then." He transferred the money into his company in California. Five days later, the same amount was transferred to another bank in the same city in a personal checking account for his rentals. Three days later, it was transferred into a CD in a bank in Los Angeles. As agreed, the money was then sent by him, via a cashier's check, to escrow here.

Nearly three hundred thousand dollars that by now was irrefutably his.

Was I shocked? Beyond measure.

I certainly had never experienced this kind of elaborate, premeditated deception in my existence. Certainly, I never imagined it would involve me. Then again, that is what I had thought about Rick, who beat and battered me and my children; Tony, who in his grief stricken mind resorted to Russian roulette to relieve us both, then of course... Philippe.

Skips previous marriages and divorces also helped identify his proclivity toward deception as he never entered them on the application for the marriage license. These things I could prove only because of my daughter's prodding to see to it that I copied papers of interest in order to protect myself.

When faced with these documents and questioned about his sexual abuse charges, he immediately thought we had evidence supporting such accusations and confessed. My immediate thoughts, as I heard him confess to this most grievous crime, sickened me with disgust and loathing.

For a period of nearly three years, I had done, what seemed now to be despicable, filthy things with a man who was not only a liar and a thief, but a confessed pedophile. I had defended him to the public, even praised him for his charm. Certainly, I had not defended these grievous crimes' as I knew nothing of them. I had defended him as a wife ought to do, for minor transgression of personality.

It was over.

Was I the worse for wear? Certainly. My life had changed dramatically. The word *trust* erased forever from my vocabulary. As was the word *marriage* or *relationship*.

However, the trust issues were with myself, more than with anyone else. My judgment was faulty, to be sure. My ego was more than a little bruised. I was embarrassed, wracked with guilt, as I had known. I did it for all the wrong reasons. I was as guilty of preying on the innocent as he was. I had married him out of fear. Fear of being alone, fear of societal considerations, fear of arriving at dinner parties unescorted, fear of people talking about me, fear of being different.

We were complicit in our subterfuge.

The town was small, a tiny village really, all that I feared came to roost. They all knew all my secrets, or I thought they did, and a person's imagination is far worse than the truth itself.

I had to start over. *Again.*

Chapter 38

I think I am suffering from exhaustion or hysteria. I am so tired of the constant emergencies of my life, of my parents' lives. For the first time in years, I have sought out a doctor for medication to help me to sleep, and I am contemplating calling a counselor.

The divorce is certainly over. But Mother has had one battle after another with her health, and Daddy is undergoing radiation and chemotherapy for prostate cancer. Daily treks to Seattle, only to come home to care for Mother.

On top of all of that, my sister Denise has brought her daughter, Michelle, and Michelle's five-year-old daughter, Morgan, as well as Denise's friend Lynn to stay with me. As she is on a kill list from her ex-husband. She was married at the age of fourteen to a member of the Mexican Mafia. She and her daughter have had a very difficult time.

"Who said you could do this? I have my hands full," I chastise Denise on the first day of her arrival.

"Mom said you would be happy to help. I am so sorry, I should have called." Denise is extremely apologetic, explaining that she really didn't know what to do. She didn't want anyone to know she was helping Michelle, so she brought her to Mom and Daddy's, and Mom said to come here. "I really am sorry, but I don't know what else to do." She is at a loss, certainly. What can you do but try to help. The history is horrific and vile.

Denise and her friend, Lynn stay for a week, with Michelle leaving to go find work, leaving Morgan with me.

Once again, I have a small child in my care. I know full well that her mother will snatch her back to the level of existence of her previous life, once *she* has sufficiently rested. But in the meantime, Morgan needed me.

Mother and Daddy's health is deteriorating rapidly. They need so much help.

Morgan is a frightened four-year-old. One of the most beautiful children I have yet to see. Her skin is a soft honey color. Her hair is the largest mass of soft black curls springing from her near-perfect features. Large round eyes, the color of almonds, are surrounded by luxurious thick black lashes, the soft pink of a rosebud mouth. The button of her small nose. She is tall for her age and stocky. She is not accustomed to eating at regular intervals or going to bed on a regular basis. Her level of understanding and socializing skills is less than that of my little dog. Within two weeks, I am in love, yet again. This time I know I will lose her, but she is delightful. I build her a swing and hang it in the old apple tree. Once again, I walk on the beach, her tiny brown hand in mine. We watch movies. She is so smart. She knows all the words to her favorite movies and has a wonderful sense of humor. With the most infectious laugh. Her voice, one of an angel, singing all the time, a high soprano, with near-perfect pitch. Not unlike my own Samantha Jeanne. One of the most joyous experiences I have ever had was to hear Samantha sing "Ava Maria" in her third grade Christmas pageant. Her high soprano voice pierced our hearts, and lifted our souls, as the tears streaked my cheeks, the joy near bursting in my heart.

Driving to Eagle Point and surveying it all with wonder, I decide it is simply too big an undertaking for a woman alone. I have decided to put it up for sale. I tell the Lord that if indeed He wished for me to live there, it would not sell. After six months I had my answer, or at least felt I did. No one even looked at it.

I began looking for money and at contractors in the area. I put the final touches on the house plans and once again resume my gardening. A very gentle word for such a terse undertaking. Rather than the customary tools, such as a small hand shovel and rake, I am armed with a spade, an axe, a chainsaw and a .22 caliber Ruger revolver strapped at my waist. Digging giant logs from the earth and heaving them to the canyon below. My tiny little wheelbarrow has been replaced with a masonry one.

***

Today I have packed us a lunch, and we are off to garden. I am in deep meditation as to the manner in which I should proceed, with Daisie lying at my feet, and Morgan filling the small wheelbarrow with little rocks, as she "don't like to weed. Auntie"

I hear Daisie whine and look to see four of the scraggliest, brindle-colored dogs I have ever seen. Daisie proceeds to run toward them, barking. I am hollering at the top of my lungs for her to stop. When all of a sudden, they turn and begin the chase, she pauses but for a fracture of a second and turns, running toward me. They are gaining on her rapidly as I shout, "Hurry, Daisie, hurry!" She is full-grown and very swift for a small lap dog. But they are rapidly gaining on her.

They are perhaps twenty-five feet from her, when I shout, *"Morgan, stay where you are. Do not move!"*

Cocking the pistol, I shoot approximately five paces in front of the nearest one. The bullet sprays dust and small rocks in the face of our predators. They halt so suddenly, I am shocked as I bend to pick up Daisie. She is shaking and whimpering, smelling of fear, as we go to sit with Morgan. My heart is still racing, my breath coming haltingly. Both my babies are safe, and after a short period of time, it became an exciting adventure.

"We could go to Gramma and Poppa's and tell 'em all 'bout it, can we, Auntie, can we?" Morgan says, still quiet and hesitant.

"We can. They will be so excited." The trembling for me has just now begun. They must have been coyotes.

The contractors here are inexperienced and unfamiliar in building the sort of home I sought. They were inept in their abilities to even give me a bid.

They ask 'Why did I need a house like that...No one on 'this side' lived like that, and they suggest...perhaps I had better go someplace else to live."

Marble to them was something they played with as children.

"I never worked for a woman 'afore. How are ya' expectin' to pay for this?"

The banks are equally unaccommodating. Each in turn saying, my business is out of state....How did they know I would not leave?

"Exactly what kind of business is that?" they queried. "We don't normally lend such large amounts of money to women by themselves."

It is exhausting and emotionally debilitating.

But knowing the laws of the universal mind, I persevere. I pray for guidance, once more asking that if this was a sign, I would give up. Bank after bank, mortgage company after mortgage company, I set up appointments and took my house plans, as well as what I thought the cost would be, my financials, and my bank records, only to be dismissed.

"Perhaps it would be best if you returned to California." (*Californians* being a bad word in this ultra-conservative state.) It is suggested numerous times. "They are more accustomed to things of this nature."

Things of this nature, I understood to be the fact that I was female, and alone.

Lying in bed at night I think, perhaps I should go back to California. I truly miss my friends and my work, the way of life.

And Samantha…the thought of her causes my heart to actually ache. I take Daisie in my arms and tell her all my sad stories as she listens with rapt attention. Never dismissing, never ubiquitous, but with great sympathy and understanding.

But I could not, in good conscience, leave my failing parents. I simply could not. Even as much as I missed Samantha. I could not bring myself to leave them. Perhaps in three or four years, they will be fine.

But I know in my heart that it was not to be.

I cannot explain the dilemma of my emotions. They are at once ecstatic and complexly hesitant in experiencing the joy and peacefulness I feel at this moment.

Samantha has called and said that the real estate market is very good down there, and she thinks she will sell her house and move up here. She asks if that would be all right and if I would like that.

Oh Lord God in heaven, thank you, I say a prayerful praise of thanks.

"Are you sure? This is a whole different world. It wouldn't be like you were moving to Seattle." Seattle is a place we always visited when she visited. The city, small and compact, newly rising from its diminished past. Its obscurity is one of interest for its unbridled beauty and that of the surrounding area, to countless young people looking for a more simplistic life and the chance to change their financial fortunes as certainly the cost of living was considerably less here than that of New York, Los Angeles, or San Francisco.

Seattle offered the ambiance afforded those cities, if only in small measure. However, Samantha and I found it to be a city steeped in the mires of political correctness to the loss of the individual. It is apparent in their manner of dress; dark, bland colors, even in midsummer, in their carriage, in their automobiles, and their homes. Due, in some small part, to the climate.

The ostentation and the frivolity of Southern Californians is offensive to them. And threatening. It is an expression of who you are, not something anyone is willing to participate in as it would possibly upset their sensibilities. Religion as a whole treated as some pagan ritual held for only those of lesser intelligence.

The University owns much of the land, the rest owned in part by the persons made millionaires by Microsoft, academics reign supreme.

These same institutions have imbued this lovely Emerald City with new life. Creating jobs, and a need for services. Still, in my opinion, degrees, intelligence, power, and money are what drives them in their quest for acceptance. I reminded her of these things as we spoke, not wishing for her to give up a life she was accustomed too for the life she would live here, even if it meant her not coming.

"I know, Mother, at least I think I understand. Who truly understands that has not walked that path?" My ever-pragmatic daughter, yet willing to risk safety and comfort for an adventure and the chance to live close to me.

"Are you certain you are not doing this for me? I will be all right, you know. I simply can't leave them now. And really, I can't tell at this point what the future holds, as you know the problems facing me with the property and the loan. You can stay here with me as long as you wish."

"I'd like that. I was hoping you would say that. No, I have thought about it, and other than Daddy, there is no one here I would rather be with than you. I've talked to my boss, and he said they need brokers everywhere, and I could transfer up there."

Lord, let this be what the divine design her life dictates and not out of one of obligation to me, I silently issue up a prayer.

The following day, I have an appointment with a loan officer in Bremerton, leaving Morgan and Daisie with Mother and Daddy. I proceed with the long one-hour drive, knowing that it would more than likely come to naught.

Behind the desk sits a small stocky man dressed nicely in suit and tie, not something that is prevalent in this area. He is polite and to the point as he looks at the house plans, my financials, and requests.

I sit with my hands folded neatly in my lap my back straight. I am prepared for the outcome. However, I intend to persevere to the end.

He looks up at me, a smile lighting his face. "My mother was in your facility. I remember you. You and your staff were so nice to her and took such good care of her."

"Oh my gosh, are you from California?"

"I am," he said. "Didn't you marry Skip Borhen?"

"Yes, I did, but as you can see, we are now divorced."

"Thank goodness," he says, leaning back in his chair, removing his eyeglasses, and smiling at me. "I was working at the bank there, and I tried to tell them they were crazy to give him all that money, that he was nothing more than a con man. So you were taken in by all his charm and good looks." A statement, not a question.

"Much to my embarrassment, I was." And I briefly told him the story of what had transpired over the past five years.

"Let me see what I can do for you. The property you intend to build the house on is free and clear, correct?" He again sits close to his desk and replaces his glasses. He was once more, all business.

"Yes, the roads are in, as well as the drain field, and I own the house I live in."

"What about utilities, do you have them in?"

"Yes, I do. With the help of my father, I have that accomplished too."

"That's quite an undertaking. This is harsh country compared to California. I am amazed you were able to do that. Do you really think you can build a house up here without a man?"

"Well, I do intend on doing that. I do have my father, but he is not well right now. I am a determined woman, and even though that is something they are unaccustomed to here, I think I can do it. I just need a loan."

"Yes, well, it's been a pleasure meeting you, and I am so sorry about your misfortune. Men like that should have to wear a sign around their neck."

I laugh. We shake hands, and I go home to tell my parents that possibly, just possibly, I will get the loan. The following day he called and said, "I have your loan papers ready to sign." I was ecstatic. It was beyond belief.

When I went to sign the papers, he was not there. I signed them. Later on that month, I went to tell him thank you. No one knew who I was speaking of.

The Lord was waiting for Samantha to come. Otherwise, I would go there. Again, the thread of my life revealed itself. The threads seem to be only of silver, not of gold, but I'll take them anyway. Let go and let the Lord....Be still and know that He is God.

I call Samantha to tell her the wonderful news, and lo and behold, her house has sold. I was ecstatic with joy! She decides to have a moving company take the furniture and put it in storage in a nearby city up here. Daddy insists she can rent a truck, and he can get the rest of it up here. It was the trip from hell.

Chapter 39

Samantha rented a thirty-five-foot moving van. With friends and family, we packed and loaded all of her things into that truck.

With Daddy at the helm, Samantha and I are there to do his bidding. We are bringing our two small dogs, her Fritzi and my Daisie. We are off. There is power steering of a sort, but manual transmission with twice the number of gears as on a car.

"Not to worry. Poppa will tell us how to do it," Samantha says knowingly.

"We'll drive in three-hour shifts. We'll do fine." His confidence, as always, inspires us with at the very least, determination. If Daddy thinks we can do it, so be it.

It is September, and the weather is stifling as we lumber up Interstate Five with no air conditioning—sweat trickling down our faces, dogs panting as if they will die, the plastic on the straight bench seat one of constant stickiness.

Daddy is visibly tired. He stops at the rest stop and says, "Okay, your turn, Chicken."

As I grind the gears of the enormous truck, we pull out into open traffic, finding that it takes innumerable minutes for the damn thing to rise to the snail's pace of fifty miles an hour. "Just stay in this lane," he says, undaunted by my frustrations. "It's loaded." He stuffs his lip with snuff.

We lumber on into the early evening with dusk upon us, deciding it best not to try the 'Pass' until early morning. The chances of hitting a deer are less, and with the early morning, it should be much cooler. We will stop at a motel for the night.

"There is a place not too far up the road. We can go into Redding and stay there," Daddy says. "Right here, turn here," he says.

I quickly gear down the massive truck, taking the first right hand turn. It looks to me as if we are going onto a long lonely two-lane road. One without a line in the middle.

"Not here," he says. For Daddy, he is agitated.

"You said to turn here," I reply. "What do you want me to do?"

"I meant, at the next intersection."

"But that isn't what you said."

"Okay, okay." He is somewhat calmer, but extremely frustrated with me.

"So what do you want me to do?" I ask, as I am limping along at a scant five miles per hour, the width of the road quickly diminishing.

"Well, ya gotta do somethin'. Yur gonna git rear-ended. You got us here, you git us out."

My Lord. Men, I think to myself. I decide to make a right hand turn. It seemed the easiest thing to do given the circumstances.

"Why are ya goin' this way?" he asks.

"I'm going to go down here and turn around."

"How are ya gunna turn this truck around on this little road?" Oh, dear, he is really upset.

"Well, I don't know, but I guess now I have no choice."

More snuff goes into his lip. As for me, I'd love a cigarette right now...

The whole truck is rocking sideways. The road is very narrow and very bumpy. Large old oak trees line this small little lane, the darkness has fallen, and I can't see ten feet in front of me. The limbs are scraping the sides of the truck as the road turns into a gravel lane.

Samantha and I are starting to laugh out of sheer exhaustion, for how in the world am I going to do this? Knowing my father,

I *will* do it. Finally, we see a small recess in the trees that looks as if it would allow me to turn around.

I make a left-hand turn, just as the headlights flash on a ditch in front of me. "Ah, fudge!" my father says.

So Daddy sits quietly fuming. In increments of not more than three feet at a time. I turned the truck around, the sweat pouring off me, and I am weak from laughter.

It took us four days of agonizing driving. A ton of gasoline and the frayed nerves of everyone. But we arrived safe and sound.

Unpacking all her boxes, standing beside mine in the basement of the old house.

Chapter 40

I have an appointment with three different contractors today, and Samantha is going to go with me. One is in Port Angeles, and the other two in Bremerton. Hopefully we can get this done before any more time goes by.

Our plan is to build two houses now. One for her, and one for me. We have entertained the idea of contracting it ourselves; however, here, I think we would have numerous problems.

We have decided on the contractor from Port Angeles. He is typical of the area, but he says he built homes in the San Francisco area. Hopefully he is telling the truth. We have spoken with him twice now and had gone to see two of the homes in the area he built. He seems to have done a very nice job, saying he "understands" what we want.

I am upset by his demeanor and his dress as I have seen him in nothing but sweats, thin old orange sweats, with apparently nothing underneath them. Everything he has is visible, at least in outline.

But as Samantha so poignantly points out, "Mother, we are not going to sleep with him. We just need him to build us houses." True, my ever-practical daughter.

In the years since the inception of planning for my home, many things have changed. The very first problem was that the county did not want me to build the house on the pad without a geological survey. After hiring an engineer and receiving documentation of what, in his opinion, needed to be done, this small exercise in opinions would cost nearly twenty thousand dollars and prove to be incorrect. The amount of money, overwhelming.

I'm trying to explain to Daddy what was necessary. He said, "You can do that yourself. Just rent a Cat." When I was twenty, he made me change the oil in my car. I hated it. I was no more pleased with this.

"I can't drive a Cat," I tell him.

"Sure you can. I'll show you. I can't drive it long, but I can show you and Samantha what to do."

"If Daddy thinks we can do it—" I tell Samantha.

"Mother, he thinks you should be able to do anything." So in the car we all pile to go to "a place he knows" some three hours from here that has good, well-maintained Cats. We rent a D8. They deliver it the following Tuesday morning. And lo and behold, we could run it.

We were unable to walk after we got off. And Samantha laughed so hard all the time she was driving it, I could hear her above the drum of the engine.

Alas, we have permission from the county to build the house. Without having spent but two thousand dollars plus gas.

As always, the framing went quickly, and I was in awe of the size and dimension of the rooms. It had now been years I had lived in the little old house with the sloping floors and the inappropriately placed rooms. From a near mansion to that.

This is palatial in comparison to what I had learned to expect. The front porch has four large Corinthian columns with stacked molding, the interior of the foyer boasting twenty-two-foot foot ceilings. The rest of the rooms have ten foot ceilings with stacked crown molding, deep, eight-inch baseboards.

The house is very formal. I thought I still needed that. I have always entertained. The dining room is to the left of the foyer as you enter the house. The living room is to the right, with a large spacious area for my concert grand piano. Would I ever play again? It seems a frivolous pursuit in light of the daily problems in my life.

There are three bedrooms. The smaller one is downstairs with a small sitting area. Hopefully it will be adequate for my parents, should that be necessary. The two bedrooms are upstairs. My bedroom and bathroom are lavish to be sure. The other bedroom and bathroom will very nice guest accommodations. Each room has a fireplace of marble, a sensible decision to be sure as it is cold here.

The library is situated at the top of the stairs to the left. I am as excited about that as anything. I so very much miss my books. I have numerous new ones, 'how to' build, plumb, prune; the Western Garden book, a book on birds, bears, the list goes on.

The kitchen is wonderful. Small in comparison to my mansion, but adequate, with two ovens, which is a must to cook for all I cook for. All the cabinets have a soft ornamental raised depiction of fruits or vegetables that I applied to them prior to their painting in a light butter color, the ceiling a vibrant persimmon red.

The family room, breakfast area, and laundry area ablaze in walls of windows, the view spectacular as they look out on the bay and up the cut. With the Olympic mountain range across the bay and the exposure west, the sunsets will be spectacular.

The production of the house fraught with ongoing problems, problems I had never associated with building a home—like lack or delay of materials because we are "on the other side." The same held true for workers as they would not cross the bridge.

Garbage is everywhere, very little of it being biodegradable. There is no garbage disposal company that comes to this area, and the contractor states he is not responsible for that. Daily, we go to the dump—the most exciting place we venture nowadays. The smell is atrocious, and the large black deer flies sting with more ferocity than that of the mosquito. Samantha and I step in filth at every conceivable turn. We laugh as we do so because what is the alternative? Morgan, Daisie, and Fritzi peer from inside the cab of the truck where they have been instructed to stay.

As the building of my home progresses, other areas of my life decline. Michelle will come to get Morgan as I knew she would. The parting will be difficult for us both. Even little Daisie will miss her.

Samantha is happy at her new job, but she must drive through winding, snow-covered roads to arrive there in the dark, only to return in the darkness. Winter once more cloaking us in cold darkness.

Mother has had numerous strokes of varying intensity, leaving her unable to carry on a sensible conversation or to perform the most simplistic of household duties. As I daily run between the building of my house, caring for Samantha's and my home, Morgan, Daisie and Fritzi, to cook and clean for my parents.

My father sits in his chair, the afghan wrapped tightly around his shoulders, his chin resting on his chest, and sleeps. He complains of being "so cold" all of the time, and the house is a veritable oven.

On the two occasions he has ventured to the garage to work, he passed out. He was rushed to the emergency room. The diagnoses—"old and fragile."

The draining fatigue of caring for Mother, and her 'craziness', leaving him lifeless. As she continues to berate him for having "burnt her toast," or not bringing her food in a "presentable" fashion.

She is angry at him for his slow departure from their marriage, angry at their aging bodies and the loss of their youth. For in fact, they are but *one person*.

My heart breaks for them as I pick up the pieces of their shattered lives, watching their ever-so-slow exit from this world.

I am not certain I can carry on one more day, not certain I can deal with their loss.

It took over a year for them to finish my house. It is spectacularly wonderful, at least in my eyes. It is homey and warm, with a formal air of sophistication. It is many-gabled, with the roof being twelve on twelve. The siding is painted white, with black-green shutters at the windows. It stands magnificent in God's majestic garden.

My finances have dwindled yet again; however, I have a home and a place to garden. For out of the trials and tribulations endured, I have found a peacefulness I had not known, gardening in this wilderness. It has been necessary to let go and let God. As I have *no control*.

Chapter 41

The moving van is here with all our things. The telephone rings. "Cara, you must come now. I think Daddy is having a heart attack." Mother's emotions are turbulent as she sobs into the telephone.

"Call the aid car. I will be right there. He'll be fine. I'm sure, Mother. I'll be right there."

It is a forty-minute drive.

I arrived at their home. Mother sits in her chair, sobbing. Tissues everywhere. Her hair is not combed, and she can't seem to speak or at least not intelligently. Her face and mouth, drooping to one side.

"Mother. Mother. Look at me." She stares up at me with blank eyes. I go to get a washcloth to clean her face as the spittle has run down from her hanging mouth.

As I return, she turns in the chair, and says, "You're here."

"Mother, are you all right?" I try to explain what I just saw as she proclaims adamantly that my *imagination is far too vivid.*

"Are you in any pain?" I ask as trying to argue with her will only delay in getting to the hospital.

"No, of course not. Why do you ask that? It is your father who is sick." She is indignant.

"Do you want to come with me?"

"Of course, you know I don't drive." She is obdurate in that fact, convinced it to be true. This woman who drove a logging truck for my father, now proclaims she has never driven. I can only look at her in astonishment.

There would be many more such strokes I would witness, only to have the symptoms disappear as rapidly as the onset. And she never remembers that they had happened.

She is consistent in claiming there is no pain associated with these episodes. That was the one thing I clung to most fervently over the years to come.

Daddy indeed has had a very bad heart attack, and they air-lifted him to Seattle, where he would undergo a four-way bypass.

He has been on the heart-lung machine for four agonizing days. As he lay in the hospital bed, bloated and indistinguish-able, I again drive to Seattle every day, coming home to care for Mother at her home as she will not come to mine. Probably very sensible of her. As mine is filled with boxes half unpacked, lit-tered with packing paper, and the like.

Samantha works daily.

Mother would go no more. She adamantly states, "No." I no longer ask her why, but I feel the fear in her reserve. Daddy is confused, and doesn't seem to know anyone but Peter. And he is extremely agitated over the cost of the surgery, unable to under-stand that he was at the VA hospital, and there would be no fee. Bless the VA.

He is not unlike the patients at my hospital. The men are always concerned with their work and their finances; the women with their children and their husbands; and some, though not many, with their appearance.

Finally he is able to come home. It has been three weeks. He seems alert and physically better. Getting him home was an exercise in determination because in the midst of summer, the bridge is closed, and the car was hotter than hell, so I decided to drive around the canal. As did countless others. It took five hours to drive a distance of approximately sixty miles. We arrive safe at last.

He cannot sit in the chair, and if he can, he can't get up. "You'll have to build me a platform to put the chair on," he says, his voice a soft 'old man' whisper, but with all the acclivity of someone who knew I could do that.

"Sure you can, Chicken. All the tools you need are in the garage."

So I built him a platform for the chair to sit upon. It wasn't too difficult, all things considered. My mother pouted for days and refused to fix him anything to eat or to help him in any way. Daily, I went and spent the day, and daily, she refused to do the smallest of things. Never did I think her condition could possibly be one of lost abilities. I saw it only as mean, spitefulness. Exhausted, I hired help. She fired them. Again, I would return.

After six weeks, I told Daddy, "I can't do it any longer. She is driving me crazy. You will not die from dirt. You will have to fix the meals I bring." So I went every other day, bringing food for them to eat, cleaning and doing laundry while I was there. Leaving them to their banter.

Early one morning, as I was changing their bed, the telephone rings. Mother, after answering the phone, comes running in the bedroom. "The roof's on fire!" She is in a state of panic.

"What!" I say, aghast.

"That was Mabel, across the street, and she says the roof is on fire." Running outside, we look to the roof. No fire, but out of the chimney leapt tall, brightly colored flames of orange, blue, and red. "What'll we do?" she sobs.

"I don't know. We'll ask Daddy, and then if he doesn't know, we'll have to call the fire department."

"What does he know? Look at him. He might as well be dead."

"Mother, he knows what to do. He's sick, he isn't stupid."

So...I think to myself, she is mad at him for 'leaving' her all alone. And terrified.

Daddy said, "Call the fire department, and douse the flames on the fireplace."

Hugging her, I softly say, "See, Mother, he does know what to do. He'll get better, and he'll be better than he has been in years, the doctors say so."

"I hope so." She sobs great heaving sobs of relief against my chest. "I don't know how you live all alone. It frightens me so."

"Shush, shush, Mother. You won't be alone. He's going to be all right."

<hr/>

As they slowly reemerge into thinking adults once again, I get on with the unpacking and decorating, and gardening.

I build a brick walkway to the house, serpentine, four feet wide, and edged with soldier bricks. I laid brick on the front porch. Tiring of pushing the wheelbarrow around the house and down the road, I decided to build bridges that would span the french drains, allowing access to the entire property.

Because there were no street lamps in the forest, I decided I needed outdoor lighting for the walkways and pathways. I installed landscape lighting. I must admit I tried to hire someone first. But alas, as always, they didn't "cross the bridge" and the people here "don't do that." Certainly it added to the loveliness of the house, but the first concern was one of convenience and necessity.

I planted a lovely rose garden of hybrid tea roses, forty in all. The deer ate them as fast as I could plant them.

When asked what I wanted for my birthday, my request was for fifteen twelve-foot four-by-fours, and twelve two-by-twos, treated. They laughed and laughed, but friends and family arrived at my home with the requested wood. Peter, always amazed at what I thought was necessary, said, "Why? Why would you need those?"

"Because I am going to fence my roses, and if I have to have a fence, I am going to make a pretty one."

"Why have roses if it's so much trouble?" was his retort.

"Because I love them."

I have hired Nancy. She is the hardest worker I have known, and she can do anything.

When she comes. She is *terribly unreliable*, often coming out and not working. But when she works, she is a godsend.

I have painted all the wood white and made eighteen-inch square lattice for the corners, which are to be six feet wide. Nancy digs the holes to place the posts in the designated spot. We stand the posts in the hole, and lo and behold, they are enormous, nearly dwarfing the house. We laughed so hard and cut the post down to eight feet.

Daffodils, which are deadly to the animals, grow in profusion, along with the native foxglove. All day, I plant plants, pansies, violets, snapdragons, and petunias, only to wake in the morning and find them pulled up and lying about.

Early one morning I arise to find the culprit—the raccoons sit pulling up each plant, looking at the label as if they can read, discarding it as they move on to yet another.

The bright spring sunshine is an aphrodisiac to my senses as I scurry around doing laundry, the morning dishes, and other minor details of daily living. I pull the left side of the French door open, and pull the screen closed, a bit nippy out, but what a glorious morning.

Having gone upstairs to dress, I hear the distress in Daisie's voice as her barking reverberates through our home. As I enter the family room off the kitchen, I see my darling standing on the arm of the chair, her front paws braced precariously against the pane of the window. They slide with each mortified bark.

The wood pile is stacked beneath those windows, and the prettiest little cat is peering back at her inquisitively. At the edge of the lawn, stands a very strange-looking deer. Perhaps it has been injured, or it is just deformed. I have seen some that are surely diseased or malformed. This one is short for a deer but with a massive body, long and lean and muscular. Its legs are thick and stocky, and its neck is turned to view the water.

The little cat and Daisie continue their conversation at alarming notes.

"Daisie, Daisie, shush, it's all right." I go towards her.

The cat sees my pink and white form through the glass of the window. Alarmed, it bounds down from the wood pile. Oh my gosh, it's not a cat; it's a baby cougar. It stops and peers in at us as it scratches at the screen on the french doors.

Daisie leaps from my arms in her excitement and claws at the door. The kitten claws back. There have been a lot of cougars lately, and it is mildly frightening.

Hearing the ruckus, the deer raises its head and tail. Oh my god, what I thought to be a "deer" is a *cougar*, obviously the baby cougar's mother, and she is now coming to get her baby.

I am not certain what to do, only that that cougar cannot take up residence so near my home. I slowly back up to the closet door. Opening it, I reach in for the rifle. It is only a .22, but it will scare her.

Whispering for Daisie to stay in my most authoritative voice, I slowly walk to the back door of the kitchen, ever keeping watch through the glass of the house facing the water. The cat is massive, weighing perhaps 220 pounds. Her sleek buckskin hide rippling as she slinks ever closer to the house. Her stride is graceful and purposeful. As with each step of the enormous paws, the distance between us diminishes.

She has seen me now and heard the creak of the opening door. My skin is slick with sweat under my pink and white bathrobe as I raise the rifle to my shoulder and pull the hammer back. My hands sweat so profusely that I am not certain I can maintain a grip on the trigger.

The plunge of her weight will break the windows, and the screen of the door is nothing but a gauze-like structure to her, why didn't I think to close it? Visions fill my head of being mauled by a cougar as they are relentless, their jaws and teeth can pull a person apart. At a scant 120 pounds, I haven't a chance in hell.

She is approximately thirty feet from me as I aim, and with sweat running behind my ears, I pull the hammer all the way back. She is twenty-five feet now, when suddenly it flashes through my mind that she can leap twenty-two feet—I read that somewhere. If I miss, or worse if I only wound her, she will eat me, *while I am alive*. And Daisie, my Daisie.

A low, guttural noise issues forth from her still-closed jaws, her ears laid back Abruptly, she bares her large fangs, fangs nearly four inches in length.

Do it now, I think. Do it now. My body shakes as if in an earthquake. She pauses and seems to survey the situation, all the while looking at her cub. There are usually two cubs, where is the other one?

Instantly, I pull the rifle up at an angle and pull the trigger, successfully blowing a large branch out of a 250 foot fir tree. I see two small cubs race towards her, and in a flash they are gone.

So much for my safari for today.

Now my gardening is delayed further as I must shower and lay down. And maybe throw up.

Chapter 42

· · · · · · · · · · · · · · · · · · · ·

The sky is as blue as Big Sky, Montana. The sun is shimmering on the glazing of the skyscrapers of this beautiful Emerald City. I look into the rearview mirror—my Lord, my hair is carrot orange. Sticking up and carrot orange. It is the style today—"bed head," "finger comb"—whatever they choose to call it. But I look like some kind of rock star wannabe. I glance at my sister in the backseat as she gazes out the car window at the buildings, the buzz, and bustle of the city. Both intrigued and intimidated, Denise huddles in the corner of the car. She has never ventured into the city, with its many hills, stoplights gracing each one, frightened she will roll back down the hill. She is clean and dressed up in khakis and a white knit top with white tennis shoes. The gray is predominant in her thinning hair. Her round intelligent eyes cast down in her fine-boned face, lined with the wrinkles of a lifetime, old and frail beyond her years. She too has ventured into this unknown territory at Daddy's request.

How quickly this adventure called life has flown by. I can still see her as a baby learning to walk, so small she would walk under the chrome of the kitchen table. Black eyes dancing, mother holding out her arms to receive her. The rest of us, clapping and cheering.

Lynne called yesterday—funny that as much as we care for each other, we seldom talk. Once started, we go on for hours. Perhaps that's why we seldom talk. She's as busy as I, with her mother, her family, and Kyle. She brought up Tony, asking if I would ever think of going back to him. She said that he had called and talked to her for hours, sometimes sobbing, she was sure, saying he "was all fucked up." I didn't respond at all except, "I am so sorry." I was shocked and frankly didn't believe he would do that.

I told Samantha about it, and she said, "Yes, Mother, I think he would."

The blaring of a horn honking brings me back to the present, where once again uncharted territory lies before me. With the car sitting at a nearly a sixty-degree angle, I sit perched atop the pavement, awaiting the change of the light.

Daddy has been mumbling since we left this morning. "If this is what he wants…If this is what he wants…I'm only doing this for him."

I have whined to anyone that will listen, mainly Jenny and Samantha. I don't want to do this. It feels wrong. Paul said I didn't have to go in, but of course, I am far too curious for that. I can't drive Daddy all the way over here, park the car, take him to the office, and let it go at that. But I have a bad feeling.

Peter said he didn't know where the attorney was. So I have Denise in the backseat looking up the address.

<hr />

We are to meet Peter for lunch at the Union St. Grill. Our appointment is not until one thirty. I push through the revolving door to the restaurant. I love this restaurant. Like so many in the city, it is reminiscent of San Francisco. Dark wood paneling, gleaming wood floors with high-backed plush leather booths of rich hunter green leather. White tablecloths clothe the crystal-covered tables, and even at midday, it cast a warm rich ambiance throughout the room. The back wall is mirrored, ensconced with brass fixtures and little black shades.

Oh, thank God, they made it. I had left Denise and Daddy to meet Peter on the street while I parked the car and wondered if they would be all right.

I glance at the image in front of me and see that, in fact, I look quite nice. The suit I have on is the rich color of eggplant, and being tall and thin, it looks elegant. Thank God, my hair looks normal in this lighting. *What is this all about?* I think to myself as I cross the immense expanse of the room. *Why would anyone leave the side of a critically ill wife to keep an appointment with an attorney for help with a will?*

I don't believe he doesn't know where "she" (she, being the attorney he has made an appointment with) is, and I have a sneaking suspicion he is lying to me. But about what, I don't have a clue.

He stands as I arrive at the table. Elegant as always. His shirt, the softest of Egyptian cotton. Starched, pressed, and finished, with beautiful gold cuff links. His navy blazer and tan slacks, impeccably tailored. With expensive Gucci loafers to add a finished touch.

"How are you?" I say as he hugs me, extracting butterfly kisses from one another. His hand, small for a man's hand, clean, uncalloused, and perfectly manicured, rests at the small of my back as he gently guides me into the booth.

"How is Ellie?" I ask.

"Not good," he says, the emotion and tiredness evident in his voice. "She is delusional, confused, and in pain, and can't seem to tell anyone where the pain is. However, she had the presence of mind to call me, so I went down at midnight and stayed with her all night."

"Oh, Peter, then let's not do this. Cancel the appointment. We will just go visit her for a moment and go back home."

"No, this needs to be taken care of." His voice bristles, as if on the verge of anger.

Denise and Daddy are perusing the menu, each looking as if the prices will swallow them up. I wonder what they will decide to order.

Ah, soup it is.

Peter gives us a brief description of Ellie's adventures in the world of the ill and infirm, and we end our lunch with a sense of morbid fascination.

Arriving at the attorney's office, I again have the feeling he is withholding something. It was obvious to all of us that he was well aware of the location of the office and was treating us as Hansel and Gretel on a quest for bread crumbs.

As he often does, he is looking at me with an aloof curiosity, his hands clasped in front of him as he watches the numbers on the elevator fly by. What is he thinking?…More importantly, what is he doing? "This is gonna cost you, Pops," he says to our father.

We are early for the appointment, and as we enter the prestigious office, facing the magnificent view of Puget Sound and the Olympic mountains, I lean toward him and whisper, "And what might you think this is costing her a month—"

"Everything she makes today," is his reply.

Peter hands me a real estate paper and tells me I should subscribe to it. "No, I just go by my intuition," I tell him. Again, that look of disgust.

I was shocked when he said that his attorney was female. I am mortified when I see her enter the room. She is young, about 35, of medium height, and stocky, with mousy brown hair that is shoulder length and of no particular style. She is wearing a white cotton plain T-shirt. Her arms are large and tanned as are her hands. She is somewhat plain-looking, but with a nice complexion, large masculine features and, before the waxing, possibly a single eyebrow. She is sporting un-ironed khakis and—good grief—socks and Birkenstocks. Peter is making introductions, and as she grasps my hand in a manly handshake, she exclaims, "I apologize, I left my blazer in the car."

Like that would help, I think to myself. If this city gets any more politically correct, it will self-destruct. Surely they know that is over. Lenin and communism, I mean.

There is no receptionist, and there are files and books stacked all over. Possibly he is telling the truth. It does appear as if she just moved in here.

We gather to the conference room. The small one. Pleasantries are expressed, and we all proclaim the beauty of the view. It is, to be sure, breathtaking.

The conference table is small and circular. Daddy proceeds to the far left, and I follow, then Denise. Ms. Knoph slides to the opposite side of the table across from Daddy, and Peter positions his chair next to hers. She leans forward toward Daddy. Peter leans back in his chair with his arms folded across his chest.

The hair on the back of my neck rises. I can feel the perspiration as it forms on my chest preparing to trickle down the cleavage of my breasts. Every sense I have is heightened, and I am not certain why. Only that I am vulnerable, unprepared, frightened, and angry. The emotions are immediate, and I can't justify them. After all, is this not the family I have always trusted and loved?

Where is the businesswoman, the sharp, fearless woman who managed an empire? Alas, only my father's daughter sits in this seat. Only responding to stimulus, a Neanderthal stimulus at that. I retrieve my tablet and pen from my purse as I try to compose myself.

"Ah, you came prepared," says the predator.

No! I want to scream. But I hear my voice as it responds. "Hopefully, yes."

She leans into my father and says, "So you wish to change your will. We can do that today."

"Well, no. I just want to know about probate and some other things, and then, I'll be honest with you..." Daddy is visibly upset and stammering. "I...I want to go to the VA and talk to them. They have always been good to me, and I used them for some other stuff, and my son here has been after me to do this for the last few months, and that's why I'm here."

I'm looking at my paper, writing *probate*.

"Probate is not necessary in this state, but I strongly suggest you do it. It is a means to speed up the process."

That is a lot of crap, I think, and I no longer can hear her voice.

"I understand you have a house in Cape George." She looks at my father.

How did she know that? I wonder. The sweat now trickles down my back and cleavage.

I look at my sister, and she looks at me. I look at my brother, arms still folded across his chest, he's leaning back in the chair and watching the predator and Daddy. His face exposes a satisfied smirk.

"So tell me again about the probate," I ask her.

"Just a minute." She silences me with a raise of her hand. Still leaning into my father's face with elbows and forearms on the table, wrists and hands raised and splayed. She says, "So, Mr. McDonald, how much to you think your house is worth?"

"Well...I've been told that, well...you see I have this real estate person coming around ever since the wife died, and she says—"

"Mr. McDonald, do you know how much your house is worth?"

"Well...Linda, the lady I was telling you about...well, and then there are some houses...down around...where I am. Remember..." he gestures with his hand to Peter, "when you came over the other day and you wanted to go look at all the real estate for sale—"

"Mr. McDonald, do...you...know how much your house is worth? Just give me an idea." The questions are rapid-fire, no chance for thought or explanations. Her speech, clipped and intimidating.

Daddy turns to me. I raise my eyebrows, as a disclaimer, and shrug my shoulders in ignorance.

The predator looks to me, questioningly. Leaning further across the table. "Well?"

"I *have* been handling their finances for the past couple of years and have been asked to not divulge any information. My standard reply is, 'I only do their bookkeeping.'"

The predator is quite upset by this statement and decides to hone in on Daddy. "Mr. McDonald. What do you think the house is worth?" Her demeanor is menacing, intimidating, unrelenting.

He drops his head. His hands are resting on the table, and they are shaking. His color, a ghostly gray. "Maybe...I've been told...I think I can get $400,000."

"What do you think the house is worth?" She looks at me.

"I really don't know," I tell her.

"You must have some idea. Tell me. I am interested," she says, leaning ever closer to breech the distance that exists between us.

"Maybe three fifty, I don't know."

"And you, what do you think it is worth?" She looks to Denise. Denise shrugs her shoulders and answers, "Three seventy-five."

Still, her questions come in rapid-fire as she leans further into the space I occupy.

"Do you want the house?"

"No!" I vehemently reply.

She swivels her head to Denise. "Do you want the house?"

"No, I...I...I couldn't afford it even if I wanted it," she stammers.

Again she leans toward me, "Does your brother in California want the house?"

"I don't think I can speak for him."

"Try," she says, with sarcasm dripping and exuding all the vehemence a human being is capable of, all the while leaning in toward me with the questions coming more rapidly than in the beginning.

"I doubt it. They live in California..."

She leans back in her chair, hands clasped on the table, pen held between her thumbs, and glances at Peter and back at us. "My client does."

I am so taken aback and angry that I have lost all control. *"Absolutely not! My father is still living in it,"* I say in clipped, concise whispered words, as I too, lean into her

"Why, I don't see what the difference is between me wanting the house and you asking for Mom's wedding ring," my brother interjects, even as his attorney is glaring at him.

"The difference is, I *asked Daddy* for Mother's rings *after* she had died, in the privacy of his home, only he and I were there, and I might add, he said no. He wasn't ready to give them up. I understand that completely."

The predator, standing from her chair, fingers splayed out to hold her better-than-average weight, leans within inches of my face, and says very quietly, "We are not here to discuss that." She is incensed that I would speak, interrupting her line of intimidation.

The die is cast; there is no going back. I feel as if I were in a surreal world of bizarre unreality. Surely this cannot be happening. "Peter, Mother just died. I think we could do this after Daddy is gone," I say through the fog that is my mind.

All the little signs now have meaning and structure. All the silly disconnected things he has said and done over the last few months, now coming into focus. My family is split. Greed has won and could not wait a moment longer. The greed of a man already a multi-millionaire.

He wants his father's home, and he wants it now, so he needn't worry about that in conjunction with his many other concerns. He is eight and not willing to let you play with his toys, or allow you to have any control. Frightened of his own shadow, angry if you show him you are aware of his fears, his vulnerability.

I no longer can hear as this pandemonium of voices continues, berating my father and dissolving all I have held sacrosanct.

Stand up, do something, my mind reverberates with instructions to put an end to this cacophony that goes on without reverence to our father. What good does it do to be evolved enough to sense danger if I do not listen and am unable to protect, if I can't decipher the message? It seems I have no survival instincts for myself, except in relation to those I love.

And what of Peter, I would have never thought him to be so un-evolved as to stoop so low. The soliloquy continues, and I am brought to the present by the sound of my father's shaking voice. Daddy has regained some semblance of control again. The trembling has subsided as he stands up from the chair. "I think this meeting is over."

Daddy rides to the hospital with Peter to visit Ellie, and during the course of that ride, Peter would encourage him to consider what the attorney had to say, that perhaps our cousin Tom could be the executor.

We visit Ellie for perhaps half an hour.

On the ride home, Daddy, Denise, and I discuss in detail what had just transpired.

Daddy says, "I knew he was up to something. That's why I wanted you to come. You're not afraid, and I knew you would do something."

I cannot *ever* remember being so mad at him. "How dare you do that to me?" I ask him, tears welling in my eyes. "I am so mad at you, Daddy. You had no right to do that. How would I *ever* know he would do something like that to you?"

"Ah, Chicken. You know what I mean. I thought you would know what to do."

"How could I possibly know what to do? I would have never thought that possible...that Peter would treat you as if you were already dead. Doesn't it upset you that he did this?" I asked, knowing full well that in fact Daddy was devastated.

One month later, the bill came. I returned it to her (with Daddy's permission) with a nice little note, telling her to send it to "her client."

I sent a copy of the same to Peter.

It was the right thing to do. The only thing to do.

Betrayal, lies, treachery...all things I am acquainted with intimately.

You would think I would expect it of everyone.

Chapter 43

· · · · · · · · · · · · · · · · · · · ·

The theatre is opulent in its resplendent appointments. Lush ruby red draperies adorn the entrances to the theatre, as well as the massive stage. They are arranged in a profusion of velvet fabric that is at once flowing freely and still tied elegantly with golden cording and long graceful tassels.

The carpets are the same rich red, with gold fleur-de-lis successfully cushioning the footfalls of the masses. There is gilt overleaf applied to the beautiful carvings and relief that cover the walls and ceiling. The building is old by this country's standards and is reminiscent of something you would find in an ancient European city.

The orchestra is just starting the overture, and the crowd is starting to disperse.

Where is she? I think, always pushing time, always thinking she has more of it. Or at least wishing she did. "Fashionably late" is the polite term, I believe. I don't want to miss the first act. I look to the top of the gracefully curved stairway, and against all the splendor of this lovely theatre stands the most elegantly beautiful woman, tall, curvaceously slender, draped in the most lovely of emerald green gowns. Her slender hand rests on the golden banister, she descends the stairs with all the grace and poise of royalty.

Her hair a shining mass of curls the color of strawberry gold, her azure blue eyes filled with laughter. Her facial features unflawed, with beautiful high cheekbones, a perfect patrician nose, her mouth perfection, smiling, showing perfect white teeth. Her porcelain skin burnished by the sun she loves so much.

She waves to me.

What must men think, whom she graces with her smile, when she can cause the heart of her mother to flutter. This child, this beautiful woman, is the child to whom I gave birth when I was but a child myself, who has been the reason for my very survival. Because she exists, because she has insisted I do survive. She, who has survived the sins of the fathers in so many ways. She was born to care for me, it has seemed so often. Never able to be the child, the little girl. As I, her mother, was always having some dramatic event in my life, she always there to say, "Mama, it will be all right."

And now, here we are. This magnificent woman who is my only surviving child. And I feel so very, very blessed.

Enough!

She's here. I reach up to give her a kiss. "You look devastatingly beautiful," I say to her. "Come, they are about to start. You came by yourself. Where is that dashing man you are seeing?"

"Oh, Mother, I knew you would be worried. We have lots of time. You look beautiful too. As for the man, well, they are all the same. He didn't wish to see the opera."

I laugh. We are the same in so many ways. Independent to a fault. I hug her close to me as we walk to our seats and prepare to be transformed by the beauty of the music.

I take out my handkerchief as I always weep at the opera.

There will be time after to catch up on her life.

The music begins.

God made my Cathedral
Under the Stars
He gave my Cathedral
Trees for its Spires
And I felt as I knelt

On the velvet like sod
I had supped of the Spirit
In the Temple of God

—author unknown

Domestic Violence
The Psyche Anatomy of Abuse
· · · · · · · · · · · · · · · · · · · ·

Abuse begins in the Psyche, the mind if you will. It is not confined to a socioeconomic group. In fact, I would not be surprised to find that the higher up on this scale of socioeconomics you climb, the more inclined you are to be an abuser of your family as you find you have tremendous power in the world around you and power is an aphrodisiac to most persons.

The most primal reason that drives abusers is fear. Fear of a loss of control of your own world, your surroundings, ego (What will other people think of me, if I cannot control those within my very family?), anger—but then is not anger a feeling of frustration, frustration at a lack of control?

But behind it all is a lack of reverence. Reverence for humanity, for nature, for infinite intelligence. Most who are abusers started out by abusing small animals and were in other ways destructive. A lack of understanding, i.e.; as all metaphysicians know, "When we know better, we do better."

Certainly they realize it is not socially acceptable, or they would perform these violations of humanity in public, but the ramifications of the exacting consequences to their soul, they are not evolved enough to understand.

Abuse starts at a psychic level within a person—small innuendoes of disapproval, leaving the victim willing to do anything to return to that previous level of comfort within their relationship, a feeling of trust that that other person has your back and will always love and protect you. Abusers are most usually men. For they control both physical and financial power. However, women play a very solid role in this game of control as well. They often are abusers of their children and, at times, of men. Adults seek comfort and security within the confines of how they found that same comfort zone within their childhood structure.

Victimology notwithstanding, again, we cannot have abusers without victims. Domestic abuse starts at a very indiscernible level and escalates with rapidity due to the power the abuser recognizes as his. If in fact that abuse was nipped in the bud, you would find a mutual respect and a certain level of reverence for the parties involved.

In reality, the structure of a family leaves that without option as there is always some person who holds that power, either for food, money, shelter. And most desirably love, comfort, and security.

Women who find themselves in an abusive relationship stay because of their children. Ironically, that is the very same reason they leave that relationship, to protect their children.

A person can beat, maim, or kill a stranger and receive more punishment by the legal system, than having committed that same act toward someone who was entrusted to you for care, nurture, and love, someone that you have promised to love and cherish. Yet it happens at a minimum of *every 9 seconds*. The laws providing for domestic violence are as yet not even written in ink on the books of the legislature, but they only *suggest* as to how to proceed to add safety to the victims involved. "We suggest," and "we will try" are terms used in the police departments around the few states who have laws at all. Most frequently, it is understood by all law enforcement officials that they will not get involved in a domestic dispute. The victim, or most often, *victims* are left relying on friends for relief and deliverance, for their families wish not to get involved as well.

Our very nation is at risk to try to understand and appre-hend this criminal that lurks beneath the surfaces of our famil-ial structure.

Men are the primary cause of great physical harm as they are physically stronger and more capable of performing acts of vio-lence. Laws must be more damaging to persons who perpetrate injuries against those who love and trusted them or those who are entrusted to them than for perfect strangers. Our foster children's program is another example of this great sin against humanity. But then, there would be fewer foster children should we be more cognizant in our family structure.

Women who accomplish the act of killing their abuser should not be prosecuted; self-defense is not a crime. Perhaps that alone would have some deterrent to the abuser, should they know that.

Family structure, as well as parenting, needs to be taught in the home as well as in schools; it would make a profound differ-ence in our world as a ripple effect throughout society if we would teach our children early on the meaning of reverence, a reverence for life and the brevity of it. Surely, people with any sensibilities at all understand that the accumulation of wealth and power, in a world that you exist for but a brief period of time, is insignificant in the big picture. How we treat one another in the here and now is the only difference that we can make as individuals.

In my work I have found that the very best competitive skills I had were ones that sought excellence in the care of the persons I was entrusted with, to share those skills with my competitors, to provide my employees with a structure of trust and continuity, and very high expectations.

My desire now is that you who read this learn from these experiences, that by bringing this ugliness into the light, someone will help our declining familial structure.

The following are "early warning signs" taken from Gavin De Becker's book, *The Gift of Fear*, chapter 4;

- FORCED TEAMING—*We are both in the same boat*
- CHARM AND NICENESS—Think of charm as a *verb*, it has *motive* to compel, to control by allure or attraction. (Not all charm is sinister) Niceness is a *decision;* a strategy of social interaction-not a character trait.
- TOO MANY DETAILS—Every type of *con* relies upon distracting us with details.
- TYPECASTING—"You're probably to snobbish to talk to someone like me…" hoping to engage the woman, to cause her to defend herself.
- LOAN SHARKING—Generously offering his *assistance* but always calculating the *debt.*
- UNSOLICITED PROMISE—When a man says *I promise* he holds a mirror for you to see…*you do not believe anything* he says and he needs to *promise.*
- NO, NO—is a word that must never be negotiated because the person who chooses not to hear it is trying to control you. Refusal to hear *no* can be an important survival signal, as with a suitor, a friend, a boyfriend even a husband, declining to hear *no* is a signal that someone is either seeking control or refusing to relinquish it. For you to let someone ever, even a friend, talk you out of the word *no* you might as well wear a sign that reads '*you are in contro*l'.

Remember, the nicest guy, the guy with no self-serving agenda, will not approach you at all.

There are shelters now, help lines, information on the internet.

CAREFUL…*Every 9 seconds. A woman dies at the hands of a husband or lover, even a brother.*

Whatever doesn't kill you will not make you stronger. You can be strong *now.*

also by Carroll Silvera: *every 9 seconds*